Wild in the Country

Ian Marsh, the gamekeeper, lifted me effortlessly and slung me across his shoulder, my naked bottom high and vulnerable. He carried me, unhurried and so easily, as if I weighed nothing at all, past the enclosures and up the track, back to his cottage. There, he opened the door with a kick and dumped me in the hall. I went sprawling on my back, legs up, everything open to him. I was filthy, my clothes soiled, my hair full of mud and leaves and bits of twig, my bottom caked with the same mess. I didn't care, and nor did he.

His hands went straight to his belt, and for one horrible moment I thought he was going to whip me with it. That was not what he had in mind. The belt came open, then his trousers, to let him pull out his cock. I'd felt it. Now I saw it – a monstrous thing, thick and brown and heavy, at once grotesque and magnificent, still glossy with my juices, and his own. I had waited so long, and now I was finally going to get my rough sex in the woods.

Other books by Monica Belle:

Noble Vices
Valentina's Rules

Wild in the Country
Monica Belle

BLACK LACE

Black Lace books contain sexual fantasies.
In real life, always practise safe sex.

First published in 2003 by
Black Lace
Thames Wharf Studios
Rainville Road
London W6 9HA

Design by Smith & Gilmour, London
Printed and bound by Mackays of Chatham PLC

ISBN 0 352 33824 5

1

Never argue with Gabriel Blane.

It had been a sort of catchphrase at catering college, used as a joke, like saying 'I'll be back' or 'Play it again, Sam.' I'd heard it on my first day at The Seasons, only it hadn't been a joke any more. It had been serious advice, good advice too.

He's the best, and he knows it. He knows everybody – at least, everybody who matters in the restaurant trade. His good opinion is worth ten years' experience. Having worked for him looks better on a CV than any official qualification.

Oh, and he's a vindictive little shit.

If I crossed him, the only job I'd be able to get after that would be peeling spuds eight decks below the water-line of a cruise ship. I was about to cross him.

It had come as a major shock to the ego to realise that I'd not got the job on my own merits, or at least, not the ones I'd like to have been considered for. At the interview I'd explained my dedication to real English cooking and the regional and seasonal approach he favoured. And if his eyes had spent more time on my chest than my face, then that was nothing new to me. He was a man, after all. I'd still thought he'd be far too professional to take a girl on because he wanted to get into her knickers, though.

I'd been wrong. OK, so I can't have been completely crap, but there was no question that he expected some payback for the privilege of working for him. It had started with little things, like pushing up close when he wanted to show me how he liked carrots to be chopped, or putting his arm around my shoulder if he was pleased with my work. I'd taken that, trying to play it cool and be neutral, neither rejecting nor accepting.

It hadn't put him off. The compliments had started, never direct, but always to compare me with other people, praising both my work and my figure, and usually in front of them. It was sneaky, trying to isolate me as well as flatter me, so that I'd turn to him. Still I forced myself to be diplomatic, and to hold my temper down, contenting myself with minor rebellions, like turning up in a pair of jeans after he had remarked on how much more feminine women looked in skirts. It had been a mistake, as his eyes had been riveted to my bottom from the moment I walked in the door. I'd put my kitchen coat on as fast as I could, and the next day turned up in a knee-length woollen skirt.

I'd known where it was leading from the start. So I'd tried to wriggle out of it, by asking to go to one of the three new restaurants he'd bought instead. I was refused, and told I was 'pretty to have about the place'.

Next came privileges, small at first, like letting me join the tastings to choose new wines. I'd accepted them, politely, knowing full well what he wanted, but hoping he wouldn't actually make a move. I'd been wrong. Just a month after I'd started work, he offered me the chance to put a dish of my own on the menu, with a clear hint that something would be expected in return – something sexual. A 'special favour', he'd said, and winked at me.

It was not going to happen.

Even if a man with the body of a Greek god had approached me the way Gabriel had I'd have turned him down. As it was, there was no chance.

He was short, and thin. It's not that I've got anything

against weasely little pipsqueaks, I just don't want to have sex with them. I like my men tall, and powerful.

He was oily; the sort of man who thinks women need to be tricked into sex. In his case, it was probably true.

He wore a toupee. Thank you, but no thank you.

It was not going to happen, but I simply could not bring myself to turn down the chance of presenting my own dish. I could worry about the consequences later.

I'd gone for Magdalen Venison; seasonal, traditional, and, as we were under half-an-hour's drive from Oxford, at least fairly regional. It is probably illegal too.

Like most things really worth eating, just reading the recipe would be enough to give a health inspector a fit. You take a good cut of venison, from a fallow deer and preferably not too young. This is then marinated in an open dish of red wine from the same district as that with which it is to be served, and herbs, cool, but not cold, for two weeks. Brush it off, roast very slowly, and serve with good bread, perhaps roast parsnips, field mushrooms, no sauce. Simple and delicious. Only a true fanatic would strain the marinade and boil it down to make a gravy.

Not that I'd given Gabriel the full details. It was a bit too 'real' for him, for all his pretensions of wanting to rediscover traditional English cooking.

Tonight was the night.

I'd done it in style, the proper way. I'd even completed the last few details in the boiler room, nearly been caught, and had to abandon the bowl of strainings behind the console for the air conditioning. I'd got away with it, though, and now it was ready.

I was seriously nervous, both because of my dish and because I knew I was going to have to wriggle out of the 'special favour' Gabriel thought he was getting. The venison, I was suddenly sure, would be far too rich for our customers, while what Gabriel expected of me simply didn't bear thinking about. So I stuck close to my fellow trainee, Teo, a big, easy-going black guy who was usually the butt of Gabriel's anger and sarcasm. There was a chemistry between Teo and I, and I was hoping Gabriel might take the hint from our intimacy. It didn't work.

We were preparing one of the other dishes on offer, quail breasts in a sauce of ceps, when Gabriel came over. He was even more tense than usual, and immediately snatched Teo's knife away as he launched into a tirade I was sure was rehearsed.

'What do you think you're doing? Look at the amount of meat you're wasting. Watch, like this.'

He took a quail and, with two deft cuts, excised the breast, leaving it perfectly in shape and with as little wastage as possible. Teo reached for the knife, but Gabriel hadn't finished with him.

'I haven't time for your incompetence now, Teo. Go and prepare the parsnips, peel potatoes, scrub the floor ... anything, just get out of my sight.'

Teo left without a word, leaving Gabriel with me, still talking as he excised another quail breast.

'Useless oaf! God only knows why I took him on. God knows why I take trainees on full stop, I just haven't the time. Except for you, of course, Juliet. You're good, and you brighten the place up. Now is that dish of yours ready?'

'Yes.'

'Well let's hope to God nobody important orders it. No offence, but God knows I'm cutting you a hell of a lot of slack.'

'Thank you.'

'You will, later.'

I just went pink and my mouth came open in an angry remonstrance that I only just managed to choke back. He went on, without pause, as if it was perfectly reasonable to demand sexual favours from his staff.

'Tonight is important. Signor di Gavi, the tenor, is coming in. That means press. I want perfection, and I mean to get it. And we're staying open late.'

I hid a sigh. Dedication was one thing, but when it came to celebrities he was a complete brown-nose. More than once we'd kept everything going until the early hours just because some big cheese wanted to sit drinking with a bunch of his cronies, just on the off chance that they might want more food. I'd accepted it as part of the deal, but overtime would have been nice.

He paused to scoop the pile of quail carcasses into a pot, then spoke again as he took a fresh bird.

'Plump-breasted little darling, aren't you?'

The blood rushed to my face again, hot and angry, but once more I bit back the words that rose with it. What he wanted me to do was giggle and simper a bit at his supposed compliment, like the sort of brainless moppet that exists only in men's imaginations would have done. Just knowing that he thought I might act that way had my teeth gritted, but I could say nothing. I knew that if I complained he would just pretend he'd been referring to the quail, trying to make me look silly, or a bitch. For the thousandth time I swallowed my feelings.

He was going to speak again, but I was rescued by the wine waiter, Charles, making frantic signals to him from across the kitchens. I was left to my quail, and my thoughts. As I went on with the delicate process of filleting out the breasts, my mind was running over the excuses I could make. It was pointless to claim I had a boyfriend. If he didn't care about his wife, he was hardly going to worry about any partner of mine. I couldn't see him being impressed by claims of lesbianism or celibacy either. To him, sex was a currency, and I was a body, my feelings and opinions irrelevant. The thought of pretending I had some highly infectious STD even flashed through my mind, only to be dismissed as just too gross. Besides, I was pretty sure he'd just demand something kinky, like rubbing his cock between my breasts.

Just the thought put a shiver right through me, and not the right kind. I'd put the image in my head though, and it wouldn't go away. He was sure to have a little wrinkly one, and it was just too easy to imagine the shiny tip bobbing up and down in my cleavage as he fucked my breasts . . .

I forced myself to think of Teo instead. He was gorgeous, six foot of smooth muscle under skin like dark chocolate. He wouldn't be small and wrinkly. He would have a great, fat python of a thing, thick and long and hard, a delight to caress and lick and suck and hold between the smooth, soft pillows of my chest.

That was the answer. I could ask Teo to come home with me. That way he would stick close once we'd finished work instead of hurrying away as he usually did. I'd been wanting to do it anyway, but I prefer to keep my private life separate from work. As it was, it was Teo or a confrontation with Gabriel, and there was really no choice.

It might work, but it would only delay things, and there was a choking feeling in my throat as I finished the last quail. What Gabriel was doing to me was just so utterly unfair: to try and force me to accept sex as a prerequisite of a career I wanted so, so badly. He had me on a hook too, because whatever I did, whichever way I turned, the choice was the same. Even if I blew up in his face and accused him of harassment it would be the end of my career. They'd take his word over mine, I was sure. He was the media's darling, seen as tough but fair – a personality. He'd just say I hadn't been able to handle the pressure, slick and condescending as he made me look like a stupid little girl. Even if I was believed, nobody else worthwhile would want to employ me. I'd be seen as a troublemaker, a loose cannon. I'd end up serving truckers and sales reps in a Happy Chef on the A1.

I passed my quail breasts to Anna, Gabriel's number two. She bustled off, busy as ever, destroying my half-hearted intention of asking her advice. I didn't want to tell her anyway. She was the only other woman there, but she was constantly irritable, maybe bitter because she was working for a man ten years younger than her. She did most of the actual work, took the brunt of his temper and got none of the praise, so I could understand. I couldn't really talk, not when so much of her bad feeling got passed down the line to me.

A glance through the doors showed Gabriel talking to an enormously fat man in a black suit. It had to be Signor di Gavi, not just because he looked the part for an Italian tenor, but because Gabriel had his most sycophantic smile on his face and was twisting his fingers together. The fingers were a sure sign that he was brown-nosing.

I thought again of his little cock-head poking up from between my breasts, which for no sensible reason was what I had decided he would expect to do to me. He'd be smiling, only it would be a big, smug grin. That was until he started to get really excited. He'd probably call me dirty names, and grunt and wheeze as he got near to his climax, then do it, all over . . .

I was going to Teo. It was that or walk straight out of the door. He was still preparing vegetables, and I knew I had only a moment before Gabriel came back or Anna assigned me a new task. I went over, my heart hammering at the prospect of rejection, and of acceptance. He turned as I approached, his full mouth immediately moving into his wry, good-humoured smile, then opening in abrupt surprise as my hand closed on his crotch.

He wasn't the only one surprised. My own mouth had come open as I discovered what a big boy he was, the mass of his cock and balls more than I could take in one hand, far more. The cheeky remark I'd been planning died on my lips and a single word came out.

'Later.'

Teo smiled. I'd done it. No question. I'd made my offer and he'd accepted and if he didn't stick to me like glue the moment we'd finished I would be very surprised indeed. Gabriel wouldn't push me in front of him, or anyone else, and I'd be free, free to become better acquainted with the impressive handful of manflesh I'd just felt through several layers of cloth.

Just thinking about it made me dizzy with need, and drove Gabriel Blane from my mind, at least for the ten seconds or so until he pushed through the door. His face had gone red, a sure sign that he was in one of his tempers. I made a quick move towards safety, but too late as he snapped out my name.

'Juliet!'

'Yes?'

'What are you doing? It's ready, yes, this venison of yours? Signor de Gavi wants it, and half the other people on his table. God, why tonight, of all nights?'

'That's fine. I'll be ready in five minutes.'

'No, it is not fine, Juliet. He has come here to enjoy my cooking, my gift, and he's going to end up eating some tossed-together scrag from a trainee. By tomorrow my name will be mud across half of Europe!'

'It'll be good, it will.'

'It had better be, Juliet, that's all. Hell! And what do you think you're doing just standing there? Get it ready, three covers.'

I moved, with my heart very much back in my mouth. Suddenly the venison seemed a big mistake. It just wasn't designed for modern tastes. It was supposed to be eaten by ripe old dons: eighteenth-century dons, people whose palates were attuned to well-hung meat, old Burgundy, vintage port, big cigars. People who came into The Seasons thought they liked real food, but a great many were just kidding themselves. If Signor di Gavi was one of them, I was going to be in disgrace big time.

Extracting the venison from the oven made my misgivings worse. It smelt glorious, rich and meaty to the very edge of decay, exactly as it should – or it stank to high heaven, depending on viewpoint. It was too late to go back anyway, and I made quick work of preparing the covers. Signor di Gavi looked as if he weighed a good twenty stone, so I piled it high, reasoning that I might as well be hung for a sheep as a lamb, or in this case, a deer. I even added the evil gravy.

Gabriel himself took the plates, throwing me an angry look that turned to horror as he smelt the venison. He was going to speak, but didn't, perhaps unable to find words. I tried to look confident, but followed, as he wheeled through the doors, to peer into the restaurant. Signor di Gavi was in full view, laughing, with his triple chin quivering and his wine glass held close to his mouth. I could see the bottle, and recognised the gold on black label of a Magnien burgundy. Which it was I couldn't be sure, but Magnien's style is pretty earthy, and it had to be a good sign. Di Gavi turned as Gabriel approached, his good-natured face beaming as his eyes lit on the food. One sniff and I'd know . . .

'Juliet!'

I turned at my name. It was Anna, as harassed as ever as she proceeded to bite my head off.

'What do you think you're doing? You're in a dream

this evening. There are things to be done. We need two covers of quail to table six, quickly.'

I snatched a last glance, but Gabriel was blocking my view. Telling myself to be more professional, I hurried to prepare the quail, my back to the door, expecting Gabriel's angry accusation at any instant.

It never came. I finished the quail and was immediately told to take over the mushroom sauce from Anna. When Gabriel did come back he said nothing, busying himself with a rapid-fire criticism of Teo's abilities before disappearing into the storeroom. He came out quickly, holding a pepper mill, and hurried back into the restaurant without so much as a glance for me. I breathed a sigh of relief, but it was tinged with disappointment. For the first time a paying customer was eating something not just prepared by me, but to a recipe of my choice, and I had no feedback.

Not just any old customer either. I had to at least look. The instant I'd handed the sauce on I took a peep through the doors. Gabriel was by Signor di Gavi's table, twisting his fingers in an ecstasy of fawning satisfaction. The great tenor looked well pleased, and not a single morsel remained on his plate.

I wasn't supposed to go out, but I just had to. Not to accept my due praise would have been unbearable. Slipping quickly through the doors, I approached the table, catching Signor Gavi's words as I approached.

'– truly divine. I confess that I had not expected to find such quality here, or in England at all.'

I hovered, trying to fight down my blushes as I waited to be introduced. Gabriel hadn't seen me, and went on.

'I don't expect you would find it elsewhere in England, Signor, true English cooking is almost a lost art, and one I am struggling to revive.'

'This then is a traditional English dish? I had thought French.'

'Not at all. It was originally the speciality of one of the Oxford colleges, Magdalen, for which it is named, and which has a famous deer park. Even there it hasn't been served in years, but I had the recipe from an elderly don who could remember it being served in the fifties. As you say, it is in a style seldom found today, and that is because I have been absolutely faithful to the original. I never compromise, Signor, even at the risk of offending those whose palates are insufficiently sophisticated to appreciate what I am doing.'

'I commend you, Mr Blane, but I think somebody is trying to draw your attention.'

Gabriel turned abruptly, his face showing irritation for just an instant before he spoke.

'Is there some problem, Juliet?'

For a moment I just couldn't speak. What I'd heard him say was just so outrageous, yet to accuse him of stealing my credit in front of a customer was a quicker route to the door than refusing to go along with his dirty little 'special favour'. Finally, I mumbled something about wanting his opinion and beat a hasty retreat back to the kitchen, close to tears.

He followed after a brief but obsequious apology to Signor di Gavi. No sooner had the door closed behind him than he had caught me by the arm and pulled me out of earshot of the others, speaking a low hiss.

'What the hell did you think you were doing, embarrassing me like that? And in front of the Signor!'

'I'm sorry, Gabriel, but ... but it was my dish!'

'What? It was The Seasons' dish, Juliet, and to the public, and to our customers, I am The Seasons.'

'Yes, but –'

'I'm going to say this just once. This is my restaurant. That is how the customers want it, and that is how celebrity works, Juliet. Don't you realise that? Don't you think that every well-known person has a team behind them?'

'Well, yes, but –'

'No buts, Juliet. I pay you to stay in the background and do as you are told. Is that clear?'

'Yes, Gabriel.'

'It had better be. You do not come out to the front, not ever. That means never, Juliet. Do you understand?'

'Yes, Gabriel.'

'And you wouldn't want me to have to get rid of you, would you?'

'No, Gabriel.'

'Then you'll be a good girl in future?'

'Yes, Gabriel.'

'Good. In fact, I rather like the way you said that, very meek. Perhaps I should have you call me "sir", later, just before you take my cock in that pretty mouth of yours, eh?'

He walked away, leaving me staring after him in fury and disgust. I was seething, so angry I could hardly breathe, and my eyes felt hot with tears. It took all my will power to choke my feelings back, but I managed.

I went back to work; it was all I could do. We were busy, with a string of customers from the operatic society at which Signor di Gavi had been lecturing. I was running around like a mad thing, trying to follow both Gabriel's and Anna's instructions at the same time, which was not easy. Even that didn't stop me thinking of what Gabriel had said, of how he had told me what was going to happen, what he was going to make me do. It wasn't going between my breasts. It was going in my mouth. Only it wasn't – not if I had to set fire to the place first.

No man had ever treated me with such arrogance. I'm no innocent, I wasn't shocked, but I was furious. I can be asked anything and I'll keep my cool, saying yes or no according to what I want, how I feel. Nobody tells me what I should or shouldn't do with my own body, either way, to restrict me, or to make me do something I don't want to.

So I was going to be sacked and, as the evening went on, I grew more and more angry at the sheer injustice of it. Again and again I tried to steel myself to just walk out and avoid the angry scene I knew was coming. I couldn't do it, not for anything, clinging onto the faint hope that my arrangement with Teo would save me, or anything.

We were late, as Gabriel had said we would be, but only by half an hour. Signor di Gavi stayed almost to the end, drinking grappa and talking to his companions in Italian. When he finally did leave he insisted on thanking Gabriel again, with a bearlike hug and kisses on both cheeks. I watched, praying di Gavi would slip and flatten the bastard. He didn't, and I had to watch the Italian party go, leaving one last group who were lingering over their coffee.

We began to clear up, with my tension soaring until I could barely speak for the lump in my throat. Teo began to be attentive, just as I'd hoped, and I found myself growing more and more grateful as time and again he managed to be just within earshot when Gabriel was close to me.

Not that it bothered Gabriel. He really thought he had me, and was even amusing himself by giving me the worst jobs. With the amount of money he was making, you'd have thought he'd have employed somebody to do the shitty jobs. Not Gabriel. He liked to remind us of our place.

Maybe he hadn't realised that there was something

between Teo and I. Maybe he was just too arrogant to care, or wanted to show off his power over me. In any case, he sent us out to do the bins. Big mistake.

There was too much going on in my head for me to want to make a move. Not Teo.

I had stepped out from the little enclosure around the big bins, to take a breath of night air and try and calm my nerves. It was warm for this time of night in September, the air filled with autumnal scents – wet leaves, ripeness, a hint of bonfire smoke. The only sounds were the faint hum of the air-conditioning units and the ubiquitous background throb of distant traffic.

'Hey.'

It was Teo, behind me, and as he spoke he reached out his hand to me, just a faint touch on the nape of my neck, right below the hairline. A shiver went down my spine. This time it was the right sort, and it went all the way to my pussy. He touched again, stroking my neck ever so gently. I bit my lip as a second shudder went through my bottom. My body was responding, and I wanted to, only my anger at Gabriel's behaviour making it hard to give in to my instincts. That realisation brought new anger at the idea of him in any way influencing what I did, or with whom.

I was opening my arms for Teo as I turned, and then we were together, his body hard against mine, tall and strong, a real man. He bent a little, his lips touching my forehead, my nose, my lips, and we were kissing. Our mouths came open, our tongues touched. He pulled me in closer, his arms tight around my back, then lower, holding me by my bottom. I returned the favour, feeling the hard muscle of one buttock in my hand as my head filled with his taste and scent.

It felt glorious, and I wanted him then and there. It was daring too. I love daring sex: in a car parked somewhere not so very safe; at a party with others just beyond an unlocked door; on the beach with only a windbreak to hide me from a hundred eyes. It makes me feel so naughty, so alive.

Now it was going to be sex at the back of The Seasons, with Gabriel Blane just metres away, just one door away. I'd have been happy for Teo to pick me up and slip me onto his cock right there by the back door. More cautious, or sensible, he began to steer me into the shade of a tree, but I wasn't having it. I wanted to see him properly, with every detail of his gorgeous cock on show in the bright glare of the security light, which would stay on just as long as we kept moving.

I intended to. I was going to suck his cock. If he wanted to take it further, then that was just fine by me, but first I wanted to give him what Gabriel had wanted. I wanted Gabriel to know too, or at least suspect, to see me flushed, or a bit dishevelled. As I took a firm grip on Teo's belt and began to sink down, I pulled my hairnet free. I shook my hair out around my shoulders as I squatted down, at cock level.

Teo gave a pleased sigh as he realised what I was going to do. I tugged his kitchen coat open, fumbling the buttons in my eagerness to get to him. Beneath, he was in jeans – heavy, soft denim with a big plastic zip that made a wonderfully familiar noise as I tugged it down over the impressive bulge of his penis. He had boxers on underneath, making it difficult to get him out, with my fingers shaking so hard I could hardly grip. He laughed at my eagerness and I returned a grin, just as I finally managed to get a hold on the waistband. Down came the front of his shorts, in went my hand, and out came his cock.

Just the man smell as he came free was enough to put an urgent tingling in my pussy. He was everything I had hoped for, long and thick and beautiful, his cock smooth and straight, his balls heavy and big. I took him in hand, admiring my prize as I stroked and he began to swell. He was very dark, a deeper shade than his face, the flesh of his foreskin so dark it was close to true black.

I desperately wanted to take him in my mouth, but I forced myself to hold the moment back. It was too good to rush, a rare chance to play with a really lovely cock, and in such deliciously rude and daring circumstances. I was stroking the silky smooth skin, squeezing his shaft as it stiffened, feeling the weight of his balls, just revelling in his masculinity, until at last I could hold back no more.

My mouth came open and I took him in, just as the tip of his cock-head had begun to peep from his foreskin. He said nothing, no dirty remarks, no crude jokes, no empty declarations of love – just a long sigh of pleasure. I pursed my lips to roll his foreskin back and take the head into my mouth. He sighed again, more urgently. Then I was sucking, easing my head down to slide his shaft between my lips and as well into my throat as he would go. I got about half in, with his cock-head nudging against the side of my mouth to bring me that rich, musky man taste that just goes straight to my head and makes me want to go on sucking and sucking and sucking...

I had to come while I was doing it. Whatever else happened, I had to come. He was swelling rapidly, already close to full erection, and he had begun to stroke my hair and pull gently on my head as I sucked. I steadied myself, squatting low as my hands went to my kitchen coat, to tug the buttons wide.

For once I was glad I was in a skirt. A couple of tugs and it was up around my hips, letting the fresh, cool air to my knickers. I took hold of Teo's cock again, tugging on it as I sucked, with him now in full, glorious erection, so long and so thick I had to gape. My other hand went to my panties, to stroke myself through the silky material for a moment before I slipped my fingers in around the gusset. I was soaking wet, warm, and very, very ready.

My finger went straight to my clitoris, my need too strong to want to tease myself lightly. I started to rub as he began to moan softly and push his cock forwards into my mouth. It was going to happen, all the possibilities of what we might have done forgotten in the ecstasy of the moment. He was rock solid in my mouth and hand, perfect for my pussy, which felt open and eager to be filled, only I was already too close to orgasm to make him do it.

He was going to come, his legs bowed out as he thrust into my mouth, his head thrown back, his eyes closed in bliss. I was too, and I was determined we should do it together, tugging faster and faster, rubbing faster and faster, my two hands working to the same eager rhythm.

It happened all at once. My thighs went tight, my bottom cheeks, my belly, my pussy, all contracting as I went into orgasm. So did he, at the perfect moment, right in my mouth and across my face as he snatched at his cock. I kept rubbing, so high, my body bouncing to the motion of my fingers as he milked himself onto me and I lapped and kissed at his cock, finishing by taking him back in my mouth and swallowing.

I was left shaking and weak, so that I had to hold onto him to stop myself falling over. He held onto me too, until I finally let his cock slip from my mouth, then lifted me under my arms to hold me to his chest. I was still trembling as I came slowly back down to earth. Teo held on, cuddling me until I dissolved in giggles for the sheer naughtiness of what we'd done. His response was a big, happy grin, at which point the security light went out.

We tidied up quickly, sure that we would be missed.

Nobody came, and when went back inside there was only my loose hair to indicate that anything had happened. Gabriel was nowhere to be seen. Nor was Anna, which made it the perfect time to dispose of what I'd strained from the marinade for the Magdalen Venison. I nipped quickly round to the boiler room. The bowl was where I'd left it, to my immense relief, but as I reached for it I heard a noise behind me. I pulled back quickly, pretending to adjust the air conditioning as the door swung open.

It was Gabriel. I froze. He spoke.

'As good a place as any, I suppose. Nice and quiet.'

He closed the door, slowly, purposefully, the catch clicking into place with a horrible finality. I found myself biting my lip then smiling stupidly, my face working with my emotions. He took a step forwards, smiling. I took a step back, struggling for a way of refusing him that wouldn't mean the end of my cherished career. His eyes flicked over my body, my legs, my hips, my waist, my breasts (he lingered there), and my hair. His expression turned from lust and amusement to curiosity, to anger.

'What have you been doing?'

'Nothing.'

'Outside, with Teo?'

'Emptying the bins.'

'Oh really? Just emptying the bins?'

'Yes.'

'Then why have you got come in your hair?'

My hand went to my hair in an instinctive, guilty reaction and that was it – I was caught. There was no point in trying to deny it, and I found myself looking at my shoes as a mixture of anger and embarrassment welled up inside me. There was a long silence, then Gabriel began to speak, his voice now harsh and aggressive.

'I've been fucking good to you, and this is how you reward me, is it, you dirty little bitch? Well, that's it, no more Mr Nice Guy. From now on, if you want to keep your job you do as you're told, and don't give me any bullshit, because I know what you're like. Now, on your knees, tits out and get sucking.'

My temper just snapped.

'No. Go and suck yourself, you slimy little creep. I wouldn't touch you if threatened to kill me. Look at yourself, you're short, you're bald, you're ugly, and you're old enough to be my father! Now fuck off!'

2

I got the sack.

They say bad luck comes in threes, which is crap. My bad luck comes in clusters. The first blow was being kicked out of The Seasons with no references and a 'you'll never work in this town again' speech straight out of a B-movie. I didn't even try to protest, let alone apologise, but stormed out.

That was that, and for all the injustice of what had happened, there was absolutely nothing I could do. He was Gabriel Blane. I was nothing, not even a trainee any more.

I'd expected Teo to get the same treatment but, for whatever reason, he hadn't. That struck me as pretty unfair, but it did mean Teo had no reason to be against me, and plenty of reason to be sympathetic. He was, giving me a cuddle and a few reassuring words in the road outside the restaurant. I needed the cuddle, and asked if he'd like to come back with me, more than happy to have sex if it meant I also had someone to hold me. He declined, sensing the ambiguity of my feelings, or so I thought.

So I had to content myself with Grumpy. Grumpy is not a man, or even a toy dwarf, but a huge teddy bear. He is also slightly worn, as I've had him since I was six. He'd been in a shop for rejects, because something had gone wrong with the sewing for his mouth, giving him a sulky look instead of the normal fatuous stare. He had appealed to something deep in me, but not to my parents.

I'd stood in the middle of the shop and howled my head off until they'd given in. He'd been my favourite for the rest of my childhood. Even in adolescence I'd held long 'conversations' with him, something I only really gave up when I went to college. I still slept with him.

The morning was one of those awful ones when all the bad memories of the day before come slowly back as you wake up. It didn't get any better. Being a Friday, all four of my housemates were off to work. We'd always got on well, five young women, all full of drive and energy, all professional, or on their way there. Sarah and Maggie were in law, Chloe was a theatre technician, Heather was in PR. I'd fitted in well, with my cooking very much appreciated by the others. Now I was unemployed, highly unlikely to find a worthwhile job anytime in the near future and unable to pay my share of the rent.

So I stayed in bed until they'd all gone, pretending to be ill, and spent the rest of the morning sipping black coffee and feeling sorry for myself. The thought of going through the whole hideous and demeaning rigmarole of claiming benefits was more than I could stand, at least until I'd tried to find something else. So I spent the afternoon looking for worthwhile vacancies on the net. There were one or two really good ones, and my optimism rose slowly, along with the thought that Gabriel might just possibly have the decency not to slander my name to all his trade friends. After all, what he'd done was pretty unspeakable, and if I was going to be out of a job anyway it didn't matter what I said. By the evening, I had made four applications and had plucked up the courage to give the others an edited version of what had happened.

I took Saturday off completely, taking a train down to the North Downs so that I could walk in the beech woods and just be alone. Maybe it was the ten years spent at school in the countryside, maybe it's just part of my character, but I can never feel completely at ease in a town or city. I like space and solitude and all the sounds and scents of open places, most of all woodland. There is nothing quite so therapeutic for me as walking for hours among trees, preferably without another person.

The day left me feeling refreshed, strong, ready to get on with my life and determined to succeed. In fact, the remainder of the following week was hell.

Sunday I decided it was about time I saw Teo again. He had my mobile number, but he hadn't rung, and I didn't have his. So I swallowed my pride and went down to The Seasons so that I could meet him after work. Not wanting to risk running into Gabriel, I snatched a couple of fortifying drinks in a nearby pub, then came out into the street so that I could lurk in the shadows. Just as I was settling into what I thought was a convenient dark niche, a girl came by. She was impressive: tall, black and full of attitude, in a short top worn tight over big breasts and a pair of jeans so low slung the rear of a white satin thong showed behind. As she reached me, she threw me an odd look, then walked past and straight to The Seasons and into Teo's arms as he stepped from the door. So much for my wonderful new boyfriend.

Monday was my first interview at a new outfit based on a river cruiser. It was nowhere near as useful as The Seasons career-wise, but it appealed to me and was the best of those I'd applied for. The owner was Ralph Brookman, a big bearded man, who was perfectly friendly and full of enthusiasm until he discovered which of the various people he was interviewing I actually was. At that, his manner changed abruptly, to something not far from outright hostility. I left knowing something had been said and wondering what. Evidently it wasn't the truth.

In the evening, Maggie announced that she'd been accepted by a firm in Croydon and was leaving the house. I tried to feel happy for her.

Tuesday was the second interview, west of Oxford. It was too far to commute, and was going to mean moving, but the restaurant was great, just a year old and very much the place to be. Their style wasn't ideal for me, being largely focused on fusion cooking, but I was prepared to compromise. Unfortunately, they weren't and, while I did actually get a fair interview, I left feeling very sure they would not be picking me. Because I'd been out, I'd missed my chance to help interview the new girl in the house. The others had chosen anyway, by majority vote, someone called Roberta.

Wednesday was blank, boring and wet. I spent it in my room staring out of the window and thinking black thoughts about Gabriel Blane, men in general and life in particular. There was a party for Maggie in the evening, and I did my best to join in and not be the skeleton at the feast. I didn't succeed.

Thursday was the third interview, at a chic city restaurant that was hoping to exploit the demand for organic, free-range food. The owner was a brisk, middle-aged woman, very businesslike, who asked me a lot of questions about reliability and accepted my answers with little clicks of her tongue. I knew I wasn't going to get the job long before the interview was over. That evening I met the new girl, Roberta. She was very kind and thoughtful, pointedly so, as if it was her duty. She was also a committed Christian and a vegetarian, but live and let live.

Friday started with a long note pushed under my door asking me not to keep pigeons in the fridge because it was 'personally offensive and inappropriate in a caring, aware community'. I could tell Roberta and I were heading for a confrontation. That put me in a bad mood for my last interview. It was in the King's Road, and popular with minor celebrities and so forth, but definitely down-market from what I had been hoping for. The advantage was that the owners were some anonymous US company, and weren't going to be influenced by Gabriel Blane. Unfortunately, the manager was, and told me to my face that if he'd realised who I was he would never have considered me for an instant. I left feeling miserable, furious, and wondering even more what had been said about me. To judge by the man's reaction, I had to have peed in the soup at the very least.

Saturday my Mum called to say that Granny had died.

That really put the seal on things. I hadn't even known her all that well, only when I was a child, and I hadn't seen her at all since going to college, but that left me feeling guilty as well as sad. I spent most of the day in my room, repeatedly in tears, fed up with everything and wondering why life seemed to have turned completely against me. That evening I found myself talking to my teddy bear for the first time in four years.

The following week was just plain miserable, six rainy days in a row. I didn't make any more job applications and I didn't sign on either. The funeral was awful, a cold church with a vicar who hadn't even known her talking on and on about God; a dank graveyard with a mixture of rain and tears dripping from the end of my nose, a church hall with my cousins and aunts speculating about the will in excited undertones. When I finally got back to the flat it was to find Roberta explaining in vivid detail about the problems caused by undigested meat building up in the lower colon.

When a fat brown envelope postmarked Newbury arrived I realised that it was from the firm of solicitors handling Granny's will, which I confidently expected to leave me in a blacker mood than ever. My grandfather had died before I was born, and with the children grown up, she had immediately retired to the cottage in Berkshire I had so often visited as a little girl. I had always pictured her as living on bread and dripping while scraping together the pennies so that she could treat me to strawberries and cream or chocolate-chip biscuits. I had no idea she had actually owned the cottage.

She had, and she'd left it to me, despite having three children and eight grandchildren to choose from, along with nearly three hundred thousand pounds. I couldn't take it in at first, and sat reading the letter over and over to try and find the catch. There wasn't one, unless you counted the amount of tax I was going to have to pay. I ended up feeling very unworthy, also guilty, both for neglecting her over the last few years and for the rest of my family. I felt gratitude too, but something else: an unexpected sense of security.

Until that moment I had never realised I felt so ... not insecure, but rootless. Suddenly I had a house and enough money, if not to keep me in style, then at least to ensure I never starved or went without a roof over my head. It turned my whole life upside down, with all my priorities changed.

The determination which had seen me come out of college at the head of my year, into The Seasons and still had me searching for trainee jobs in the best restaurants when it had been hopeless was gone. It no longer seemed to matter, or no more so than a setback in some hobby or casual interest would. Instead, I found myself focused on something I had always hoped for but never expected to be able to do until I'd been working for years, more likely decades. That was to be in the country, independent, with nobody to answer to and nobody to tell me what to do.

I had to do it. Where I was, everything was wrong. My

friends were all right, but they, and others, exerted a constant social pressure to fit in, to dress the right way, to look the right way, to date the right men, to see the right films. I couldn't even eat the way I wanted to without drawing rude notes.

In the country it would be different. I could slob out in dungarees and an old T-shirt, or dress up in a 1920s cocktail dress just to eat dinner, or wander around stark naked if I felt like it. I could grow my hair down to my bottom, or put it in plaits, or shave my head. I could invite some over-muscled farm boy in for a good, hard fucking. I could watch *The Blues Brothers* and *The Rocky Horror Picture Show*. Better, I could watch them in the nude while I ate well-hung pheasant with my fingers while the equally well-hung farm boy attended to my sexual needs.

That was maybe a bit hopeful, but the rest was perfectly realistic. With interest rates so low I wouldn't have much money if I tried to live on just the interest, but then I wouldn't need much. The garden was big, and there was a half-acre of wild ground as well. I could be close to self-sufficient, and my training would come in handy for making preserves, even smoking meat. Not only that, but I had the contacts to sell produce at full price, perhaps to the people wanting real quality without having to worry about regulations.

That really appealed, the idea of running high-quality meat products to the back doors of restaurants run by my fellow free-range fanatics, of whom there were plenty. It was illegal, but only in the sense of breaking idiotic EC regulations, such as the one on hanging meat. It was not immoral, far from it. I could do hams, bacon, exotic pâtés, game preserves. The possibilities were endless.

With luck, whatever Gabriel Blane had done to damage my reputation wouldn't matter. He was likely to have said I was a thief or something, but that wasn't going to put people off if I offered them black-market food; not when they found out how good it was.

It took two days for my bad feelings to fade, leaving just a touch of sorrow for my granny and a dull antipathy for Gabriel Blane. Mum had been supportive, which helped, but it wasn't until the weekend that I decided to go down to Berkshire.

Newbury was as wet and uninviting as it had been the week before, but my feelings were very different. Once the train was past Reading, I found myself staring out of the window at the low, wooded hills to the north, beyond which what was to be my new home lay. I'd already burnt my bridges by announcing that I was leaving the flat, and by telling Roberta exactly where she could stick her Bible and her tofu cutlets. All I had to do was collect my things.

By the time I came out of the solicitor's office, the weather had begun to clear, with the clouds breaking up in the west and sunlight striking in to paint the wet surfaces silver and gold. The key to the cottage was in my pocket, and I was feeling increasingly excited, and also free, as my cab drove north and east.

It was just as I remembered it – little valleys separated by hills bulking slowly towards the downs, a patchwork of fields and woods, and clusters of red-brick houses. Only an occasional modern barn or piece of brightly coloured plastic showed that I was in the twenty-first century rather than the 1930s. There was even a ford, deep enough after the recent rain to make my driver think twice about crossing it, and stop. It was no more than a half-mile to the cottage anyway, so I told him I'd walk.

I remembered the ford, splashing across it on my bicycle and catching minnows in the stream below. The memory brought a new pang of melancholy, but that faded as I crossed the narrow footbridge to one side and began to walk up the lane, my bag humped up on my shoulder. It had been over ten years since I'd been there, but so far as I could see, nothing had changed. The woods were the same, now richly coloured in the foliage of early autumn and alive with birds: rooks, wood pigeons, and the sudden blue flash of a jay's wing. The sounds were the same – the low babble of water in the stream, the occasional strident call from a pheasant or distant bark of a dog. There was also the constant faint hum of the M4 from where it cut through the hills, but what I had thought would clash only seemed nostalgic. Even the smells were the same – the autumnal tang strong in the nose, along with newly turned earth and a faint hint of something richer.

There was no difficulty at all in remembering where to go. The lane split, and I took the right-hand fork up a rough track so little used that a thick belt of grass and weeds had grown up along the centre. I now had a wood to one side and a tall hedge on the other, locking me into an aisle of rich golden light and making my sense of timelessness stronger still.

A memory came to me, of playing in the same wood at around the age of ten or eleven, and being shouted at by a keeper for picking bluebells. He hadn't caught me, but I'd told Granny. She had given me a lecture on respect for other people's property I could still remember, then marched me to a big house a good mile away. It had been on the far side of the motorway and I'd been made to apologise to a red-faced, mustachioed old man in tweeds. We had met him in the driveway, and he had been holding a shotgun, to my utter terror. Now I laughed.

I could even remember his name: Paxham-Jennings, which had seemed like something out of a fairy tale to me. There had been a boy too, very smartly dressed and very stuck-up, looking down on me as I stammered my way through my apology. He'd been around fourteen, which made him now twenty-four or so, and I wondered if I would run into him, or his father.

That assumed the same family still ran the estate, but if it had changed hands, then the new owners hadn't removed the big, white PRIVATE signs nailed to every gate and the occasional tree. I smiled as I passed one, remembering how I had always taken the signs as a dare, even as a personal affront in a way. There was still a hint of the same emotion, resentment that somebody owning so much beautiful land should deny it to others, or, to be really honest, that they should deny it to me.

There are two sides to that argument, as I learnt the moment the cottage came into view. It was exactly as I remembered it, a squat, irregular building of red brick and flint with a high roof of brown tiles and disproportionately tall chimneys, all surrounded by a thick hedge. What I could see of the garden was much the same too, neat and tidy, with lawn, pathways, box hedges and a herb garden, all in miniature. Beyond was the wild patch, also the same, except for one thing. A section of the scrub birch and hazel had been cut back, and on it was a caravan with smoke issuing from a crooked stack. Somebody was living on my land!

I felt an immediate flush of irritation and walked forwards more quickly, determined to make it absolutely clear to whoever it was that the cottage and garden were now my property, and that they were not welcome. It was easy to imagine what might have happened. Whoever it was would have moved in, ostensibly to keep an eye on her, and gradually taken over. She, or he, even, would probably have been hoping to be left the cottage.

That was not good, and it also broke the bittersweet mood that had been growing slowly stronger all day. I pushed through the garden gate, determined to be polite but firm and to get rid of the invader, whatever it took. There was a well-beaten path to the caravan, and I took it. The curtains were closed, but one twitched briefly aside as I approached. The door swung open, to reveal the occupant – a girl, no older than me, small, slightly plump, with a round face looking out from among abundant gold curls, smiling. She spoke first.

'Hi, Juliet! Oh, I'm so sorry about Jean. I know how you must feel. My own gran died last year. Everything's as it should be. The post's all junk and bills, but I've put it all on the hall table anyway. I've cancelled the paper, but Bob's going to call round Thursday to see if you want delivery or what. Cherry's fine, and I've milked Harriet and Hilary. There were six eggs this morning, but I'm afraid I pinched one. I've got a fire laid for you, and I'll be out this afternoon, once Dad has finished in Plain Simon's Lot and I can have the tractor. I'm Emma, by the way. Do you want some tea?'

It was so friendly, so sympathetic, and so apparently inexhaustible that the little stern speech I'd been building up as I approached never came. All I could manage was two words.

'Yes. Thanks.'

She bounced back into the caravan and I followed, feeling somewhat dazed by the flood of information she had given me. She hadn't finished either.

'Sugar? Milk? I've got lemon if you like. Biccies? I've got chocolate digestives. Oh, there's a stock dove's nest in the bedroom chimney. Jean couldn't bear to move it. There's a heater though, and the loft was only lagged the year before last. Don't mind a mug, do you?'

'No, that's fine. Milk but no sugar please. That's fresh goat's milk?'

'Sure. Harriet's up, but Hilary hasn't been doing so well. The vet's number is in Jean's book if you need him.'

I nodded, somewhat overwhelmed by my dreams of having livestock suddenly having become real, and immediate. Give me a pail of goat's milk and I'll do all sorts of wonderful things, or give me a goat for that matter, so long as it's dead. With a live one I really had no idea where to start. Then there were the chickens, which I could remember, although I felt I could handle them, just about. Cherry had been the name of Granny's ginger kitten, presumably now a large and middle-aged cat. He, at least, I could manage.

Emma had shut up for a moment as she did something to a cylinder of Calor gas popped in one corner. It came to life with an alarming hiss, and she busied herself about making tea. I moved a pile of clothes on the tiny and messy bed and sat down as she went on.

'Sorry about the mess. That's just me. So what are you going to do? I hope you're not selling up.'

'No, I, er . . . I was thinking of moving in.'

'Great! We'll be neighbours. You must have passed our place on the way, Bourne Farm, with the new barn, down by the river?'

'Yes, I saw . . .'

I stopped. A memory had come to me, of a little girl with blonde curls and a face stained purple around the mouth, scowling at me. I'd been picking blackberries in the lane. She'd said they were hers. When I'd refused to stop she had thrown mud at me. I'd retaliated, and had been getting the better of her when three bigger boys had turned up, her brothers. I'd beaten a hasty retreat, but after that there had been a long-running childhood feud between them and I, my cousins too. We'd had a horrible nickname for her, the invention of my eldest boy cousin – The Pudding. She was still talking, but I broke into the flow of her conversation.

'You're . . . I mean, you remember me, don't you, from when we were little?'

'Yes, of course . . . Snooty.'

She giggled.

'Snooty?'

'Yeah, sorry, it's just what we used to call you. You always looked so superior.'

'Me? Superior! Well, we used to call you The Pudding –'

I stopped abruptly, suddenly sure that it was a really stupid thing to say. She wasn't fat exactly, but definitely plump. I'd been remembering her as a solid little girl, and her figure had rather run away with itself. To my relief she just smiled.

'I know, Jean told me. Kids are like that. After all, we used to throw sticks and stuff at you.'

'I remember. We used to take it so seriously, the boys especially. They used to do commando raids on your farm, and pinch maize and apples and things. Until John had a fight with . . .'

'Mark. Boy, did Jean tell him off!'

'He had made John's nose bleed, badly. Still, that was then.'

'Yeah, we grow up, but not everyone. Do you remember Toby Paxham-Jennings?'

'Vaguely, the name anyway. The guy who owns the Alderhouse Estate, or his son?'

'His son, the old man is called Donald. He's bad enough, but Toby's an arsehole. They're trying to make the estate into a place for rich sods to come and shoot and stuff, and they expect Dad to pay half for all the hedge work and fencing on the boundaries between us. They've threatened to take us to court too, 'cause their pheasants get onto our land and we take them. That's our right, but no ... Anyway, it's all bullshit. The old man's never forgiven us for pinching his quinces when we were kids, and Toby used to be scared of the boys. Bogus Tobus they used to call him, still do. Look, balls to the tea, let's have a bottle of wine. I'll do us some lunch if you like? Or do you want to check the cottage over?'

'Not yet, I ... suddenly I don't feel ready. Let me make something for you. I trained as a chef. I was one until I got sacked ...'

Suddenly I was telling her my life story, backwards: The Seasons, college, school. I gave her the full details too, even about Teo, which set her giggling. She was just so easy to talk to, completely non-judgemental, and almost as eager to listen as she was to talk herself, especially when it came to the rude bits.

By the time I'd finished she had a bottle open, a cheap Piesporter. She poured generously, into the mugs she'd put out for the tea. I took mine, swirling and sniffing by instinct, then sipping and trying not to look too unhappy at the thin, sugary taste. She laughed and shook her head.

'What's the matter?'

'You haven't changed. I remember that expression, from when I got some mud in your hair. Snooty.'

'Pudding.'

We both began to laugh, then chinked our mugs together and drank. I'd found a friend, and if we seemed very different on the surface, perhaps underneath we were much the same. Certainly she wasn't going to start criticising me for eating meat or not following the latest fashion.

She was considerate too, and not a scrounger at all. I didn't like to ask directly, but from what she'd been saying it seemed as if she'd been looking after Granny for nothing, and sleeping in the ramshackle old caravan just to be on hand. Meanwhile, I'd been doing my career-woman bit, which suddenly seemed completely self-centred.

Not only that, but as she clearly had the keys she could perfectly well have moved into the cottage.

I swallowed my mug full of German mouthwash and let her fill me up.

'So what's to eat?'

She pulled a cupboard open.

'Eggs.'

'Eggs it is. Stay here.'

She didn't, but came to stand in the door of the caravan as I looked for ingredients. I could remember Granny growing her own vegetables. Their richness of taste had done a lot to mould my attitudes to food. Sure enough, there were leeks, potatoes, onions, carrots and cabbage, all in neat, weed-free rows, and probably Emma's work.

I pulled a leek, then went to the fence, beyond which I could see the ragged tops of a clump of big parasol mushrooms poking up among the coarse grass. I was reaching through when a shout from Emma brought me up short.

'No! Juliet, not those!'

'Don't be silly, they're not poisonous!'

'I know that, but they're on the Paxham-Jennings' land. You'll never hear the end of it if you're caught.'

'Who's going to catch me? Anyway, they'll just go to waste otherwise.'

'That doesn't matter, believe me. His keeper passed just before you arrived, and he could still be around. Mr Marsh, the human gorilla.'

'Oh, come on!'

I reached quickly through, to break off the cap of a button, then another.

'Juliet!'

She looked genuinely shocked as I turned to walk back towards her, and was glancing at the woods and the area of scrub beyond the fence. Only when I'd been hustled back into the caravan did she break into nervous giggles, only to break off and dart a glance from one window.

'He can't be that bad!'

'Oh, he is, and it would just make things worse between Dad and the old man.'

'Sorry, I wasn't thinking.'

'Don't be, but please don't do it again. It would be just my luck if you got seen.'

'I won't. Have you got a pan?'

She had, and we were soon eating what had to be the best omelette I have ever made. There was simply more flavour, even than those I'd done with the ingredients Gabriel Blane had taken such trouble to select. For all his experience and equipment and determination, at the end of the day he had to operate on a commercial scale. I didn't.

Emma concentrated on her food, wolfing it down without comment until she'd finished, and only speaking when she'd swallowed an entire mug of Piesporter.

'Great.'

'Any time. Now, just give me a second, and I'll feel ready to look at the cottage.'

She gave an understanding nod and left me to finish my omelette. I did feel ready, but I was glad she was with me, because the way my feelings had been building up before, eventually the melancholy would have won and I'd have ended up in tears. Now I was sure I could handle it.

We walked across, Emma chattering happily, until I reached the door, when her tone became suddenly serious.

35

'I've tidied up, a lot, the personal stuff . . . pictures, you know. I hope you don't mind?'

'No. Thanks.'

She'd been right. I didn't want to wallow in my grief, but from the moment I pushed the door open I was having to fight not to. First it was the smell, so familiar across the years that I might as well have been a little girl again. As I stepped inside, I could almost hear Granny's voice, calling to me to wipe my feet and put my coat on the proper peg.

I stopped, my lips pursed, right on the verge of the tears I'd been so sure I could hold back. Emma put her arm around my waist, but said nothing, just waiting until I had got control of myself. I shook my head to clear it, and marched into the sitting room, where I'd lodged on a camp bed during my stays. It was unchanged, the wall-paper, the carpet, the chairs, every ornament, different only in that it no longer looked lived in. Even the books were as I remembered them: old paperbacks and even older clothbound novels, some ancient cartoon annuals from an artist called Giles and bound volumes of old magazines.

The bathroom was the same, with the huge cast-iron bath I'd been able to float in without touching the sides, and probably still could. So was the scullery, the ancient mangle still in place beside the washing machine. The pantry had changed, but only because it was nearly empty, with only a few of the jars of jams and pickles and jellies that had once filled every shelf. There was a microwave in the kitchen but the old iron stove was as I remembered it. I took a moment to peer up into the huge old chimney, through which I could see the sky, along with the big iron hooks Granny had always threatened to hang us from, by our collars, if we misbehaved. I had genuinely believed that was what they were for, but now

I knew their true purpose, a thought that once more drew me back from the edge.

They were for smoking meat, hams in particular, and it was a use I intended to put them to, probably for the first time in a hundred years, or seventy at the very least. I'd never thought about the architecture of the place before, but the kitchen, scullery and what was now the bathroom were very old indeed, and had probably been a complete cottage originally, with the living quarters in the loft. The sitting room, bedroom and the tiny hall had been added much later, probably in the late nineteenth century, maybe even in the 1920s. I began to think of all the people who must have lived there before, whole families, presumably labourers.

I found myself making a face, and wondering just how much knowledge had died out with such people. A hundred years before, a girl like Emma would never have tasted wine, but been drinking cider made on her own farm. They still had the orchard, where the infamous fight between John and Mark had taken place, but it was now planted with neat lines of small trees, undoubtedly of eating apples.

'Are you all right, Juliet?'

'Sorry, I was dreaming. Miles away. I usually am.'

'That's OK.'

Only the bedroom was left, Granny's inner sanctum, and the room I was least familiar with. She had always been very private about it, which had inevitably fascinated me. One thing in particular had pricked my curiosity: a carved wooden screen with brilliantly coloured parrots embroidered into the panels. I had vaguely understood that it was meant for undressing behind, and had wondered what terrible secret she had that needed to be so well concealed. I didn't actually know if she had used it at all.

It stood as before, smaller than I remembered it, but that was true of everything. Everything else was the same too, even my sense of guilty intrusion. I tried to shrug it off, telling myself I was being silly, but still found myself being careful not to make a noise as I closed the door behind me and turned back to the hall. Emma was waiting.

'If you're OK, I'll get out of your hair. Dad'll be finished with the tractor soon.'

Suddenly the last thing I wanted to do was get rid of her.

'No, don't ... I mean, stay, if you want. That is, you're welcome to leave the caravan there and use it whenever you like.'

'Are you sure?'

'Yes, absolutely. I'd like you to. You're fun.'

'I will then. It gets pretty cramped at home, sometimes. I'd better go back for now anyway, if you're OK, just to tell them what's going on.'

'I'm fine. I'm going to have to get used to it.'

She shrugged and smiled, then turned for the door. I watched her go, until she disappeared behind the hedge. With the sudden quiet my sense of dejection threatened to come back, but I forced myself to concentrate on something else, what I needed to do with the cottage, and what I could do.

They were two very different things. I'd have to run to the expense of a professional to check on the structure, the wiring, the plumbing and other such tedious necessities. Once I'd done that, I could get on with the more interesting part, making it my home.

Just about everything had to change. Not the basic structure, that was sacred to me, but everything that reminded me of Granny, otherwise I'd just spend my time moping, which is not good. In fact, it was a wonderful opportunity and one I'd always wanted to indulge. I could completely reorganise, keeping what was good from the old and adding what was good from the new.

The kitchen would be my first task. I'd stick to wood and tiles to keep the atmosphere, also dark colours, because with the broad south-facing window, there was always plenty of light. Aside from that, it would have to be functional, with a minimum of purposeless ornament and everything from the ancient meathooks to a state-of-the-art stove in full working order. Some of the equipment would have to come from catering suppliers if I was to indulge my ideas for home produce. With a little effort, I could get the washing machine in and so leave myself the whole of the scullery for storage, also the pantry, which was cool enough to make an acceptable cellar.

In the bathroom, decisions were not so easy. I liked the huge bath, but the rest was drab and cheap, cream-painted brick and fittings from some time in the 1970s. The only sensible thing was to put the bath in the centre with a shower fitting above it and tiling at least halfway up the walls, and add accessories as best I could. At least I didn't have to worry about the window, as it looked out onto my own garden. In the shared house the bathroom window had been frosted glass, but we'd had to keep it permanently closed, as the block behind seemed to be a rest home for elderly peeping Toms.

It had been annoying enough at the time, but the memory put a smile on my face as I turned my attention to the bedroom. There, I could afford to be a perfectionist, indulging my love of all things old-fashioned to the full. Her bed was a hideous iron-framed thing, very plain. I didn't like the idea of sleeping in her bed anyway, so that could go. In its place I would get a genuine old four-poster, complete with drapes, white linen, woollen blankets and cover, goose-down pillow, nothing artificial. That wasn't going to leave a great deal of room, but I could sit on the bed to use my dressing table, which would also be antique. The wardrobe was good, and after a moment's hesitation I decided that it could stay, and that the dark corner created by its bulk was actually a good feature. That was where I would put the screen, which was far too fine an object to get rid of, or even sell. I'd use it too, although not for the sake of modesty, but to tease some expectant boyfriend as he waited for me on the bed. My only concession to electricity would be the light, and at the thought of never again having to be woken by my radio alarm I found myself breathing a sigh of relief.

Retro is all very well in its place, but in the sitting room I was going to have to have some modern comforts. I couldn't do without films, or music, or an Internet link. So it made sense to have one big bank of equipment against a wall, but with something to cover it when not in use. What I really needed was a sort of gigantic writing desk, but to the best of my knowledge no such thing existed. A screen was more practical, or even two, latching in the middle, an idea I liked because it would give the room hints of both secrecy and eccentricity. A couple of big, comfy chairs, preferably leather, and a decent bookcase would be needed too.

The little hall was simple, just a matter of redecorating, and that was about it. Simple.

Not so simple, as I perfectly well knew, having ignored such minor problems as the fact that I don't drive, let alone have a car, and that my parents live a hundred and fifty miles away in Manchester. I didn't know anybody local at all, except Emma. Still, it had to be done, and I was determined to see it through, and also to make the break with my old life completely, and immediately. So I spent the night in a bed and breakfast in Newbury, where

I didn't have to explain myself or risk being lectured on the pain the trout I ate for supper had suffered. In the morning, I badgered Dad into helping me collect my things at the weekend and bringing them down to Berkshire.

3

The next few weeks were chaos. I was in London, Newbury, Oxford, Reading, Bristol and Manchester; at auctions, markets, antique shops and car boot sales. I spent hours online, searching for everything from furniture to a special thermometer for checking the temperature at the heart of a roasting joint. I spent more hours in shops, in a most wonderful shopping spree because for the first time in my life I didn't always have to look at the price first. I'd never had so much fun.

Inevitably, I got sidetracked a few times, and ended up with a number of things I hadn't intended, including a case of Romanée-St Vivant with the old Marey-Monge labels, an early Beardsley print showing a louche young man with fantastic black curls and a set of cock and balls that would have put an elephant to shame and a pair of mid-Victorian combinations hung with yard upon yard of fine cotton lace. Aside from that, I got everything I needed exactly right.

I could have happily run a small restaurant from the kitchen, and it was everything I had hoped it would be. In my imagination the hams were already smoking in the chimney and the pheasants hanging in the pantry as I downed a glass of my own cider on the big old settle I'd discovered in the storeroom of a Bristol pub. I had even managed to resurrect the old bread oven at the side of the fireplace, which had been blocked off years before.

The screen for the sitting room had been the hardest thing to get right, but I had eventually settled on an embroidered drape, a curtain really, which provided all the eccentricity I could have wished for. It was crimson, and embroidered in dark gold, rich blue and black, giving it a distinctly baroque feel which I echoed in the remaining furnishings. The effect was so strong I didn't feel right in it unless appropriately dressed, or naked.

In the bedroom, I went for dark wood and pale fabrics, with acres of muslin and linen and coarsely woven wool, to create a truly sumptuous effect. The screen worked beautifully as the sole splash of colour, and I was hopeful that to even the most dull-witted of men it would suggest the possibilities of disrobing rather than anything prudish. Not that anyone could be in much doubt. My Beardsley was the only picture, adding a bold erotic touch to remove any hint of the defensive or fusty.

The highlight was the bed. It was a huge thing, seven feet wide by six-and-a-half feet long, from the 1880s, and originally commissioned for an alderman from Leeds. The posts were attenuated statues, caryatids, I suppose, and to judge by their drapes, or lack of drapes, possibly the four goddesses: Hera, Athena, Artemis, and Aphrodite. The boards continued the pagan Greek motif, intricately carved with a jumble of grapes, vine leaves, fawns, nymphs and grinning imp faces. Once polished and fully draped, it was simply the most decadent thing, and the perfect place to make love, ideally to some real animal of a man.

That was the one fly in the ointment. Since my brief encounter with Teo I hadn't had any form of sex whatsoever. There hadn't been a lot before that either, not since I'd left college. I'd simply been too busy to really worry about men, and both Gabriel Blane's unwanted attention and the death of my granny hadn't helped. The shared house hadn't helped either, with the fact that every bump and squeal above minimum volume was likely to be heard by four others hardly conducive to letting myself go. Daring is one thing, but performing with friends within earshot is another, especially when they disapprove. Disapprove is too strong, maybe. Chloe had been cool, Sarah was with a steady boyfriend, but both Maggie and Heather had regarded unrestrained bonking as rather trivial, not really the sort of thing women intent on making a career for themselves should do. I suspected Roberta would have been shocked, but I hadn't stayed around long enough to find out.

At college it had been very different, with nearly four hundred of us in a huge student hall. There had been no shortage of parties, and no shortage of sex, so much so that I had come to take a man at the weekend more or less for granted. Most had shared my view that we were living for the moment, and to the few who had become possessive I had made it very clear that I wasn't becoming Little Miss Accessory to anybody.

Now, matters were different once again. My situation was stable. I wanted somebody reliable, yet I didn't want to sacrifice my lifestyle or control. That meant somebody intelligent and understanding, which was a bit difficult to balance against my desire for raw, masculine men. Not that I was exactly swamped for choice. The only men I ever saw other than shop assistants and workmen were Emma's brothers. Luke was married. Both Mark and Danny had steady girlfriends.

Sex might have been a bit of a problem, but friendship was not. Emma was an absolute angel. She attached herself to me from the start, and acted as my driver, handywoman, porter and shopping sidekick, not to mention goatherd, gardener, scullery maid and whatever the technical term is for a girl who looks after chickens. By the time I'd finished, it was as if we'd known each other all our lives, which we had, in a sense.

The only drawback to her company was that she added to my sexual frustration. She had a boyfriend, Ray, a huge young man with hands like spades who worked on their farm. He was shy, and completely besotted with her. For her own reasons she didn't want her father to know how far they went, and when she asked if I minded her indulging herself in the caravan I could hardly refuse. Not that I minded at all, morally, but they were noisy. She tended to giggle, and when she came she made a noise like a dozen piglets all trying to get at the same teat. I knew, because I'd been down to their farm and one of the sows had a new litter. Ray added the occasional deep grunt. The effect was to leave me feeling flushed and wet between my thighs, which was not comfortable when I had nobody to play with.

I finally moved in properly in the middle of October, toasting the event with a bottle of the Romanée-St Vivant. I had spent just over fifty thousand pounds, far more than I had intended, but it was worth every penny. I had created my own place, my home, in the way I wanted, without so much as a nod towards the dicta of modern fashion. I was almost tempted to invite Roberta down, just to see the look of shocked disapproval on her face, almost.

Emma had brought me a brace of the disputed pheasants, shot by one of her brothers, and I let her have a glass of the wine. She looked somewhat perplexed, the way most people are the first time they taste really mature fine burgundy. After a couple of sniffs and a doubtful sip she looked up at me.

'Is this all right?'

'Perfect.'

'It smells like shit.'

I just laughed, thinking of my wine tutor mumbling

about 'farmyard scents', 'earth' and *sous bois*. It wasn't entirely fair, because there was plenty of fruit to balance the tang, but Emma was nothing if not honest.

'Nineteen seventy-six, fuck me. It's expensive, yeah?'

'I paid nine-fifty for the case, at auction.'

'Nine pound fifty, for twelve of them?'

'Nine hundred and fifty. That's a good price.'

She didn't answer, but made a face, then took another sniff. We were standing in the hall, and she walked to the open door, tipping the glass.

'Hey, don't waste it!'

'I'm not.'

She tipped the glass further, to splash just a little of the wine on the flagstone in front of the door. Then she took a sip herself, very solemnly.

'You have to do that, or the house will be unlucky for you, and you can't use just any old crap.'

I realised she was pouring a libation. Immediately I wanted to do the same. It just felt right, respectful yet not fearful. It seemed much more appropriate than anything Christian, and so much more me. I stepped up beside her to pour out some of my own wine, just a drop, then more, most of the glass, in a sudden fit of pagan piety.

The rest I took into my mouth, to savour the complexities of the flavour as I let it run over my tongue and into my cheeks. It was truly exquisite, and so in tune with everything around me. The smell of autumn was more pronounced than ever. The sun was sinking slowly over the woods, casting a rich, golden light everywhere, with the shadows of the trees stretching out towards me. Even Emma's caravan seemed in place. For one magical moment everything was perfect: me in the autumn dusk, in my own cottage, my mouth full of the taste of fine wine. The libation was right too, an offering to whatever spirit made the golden evening so perfect.

Emma had turned back into the hall, as if what we had done was completely ordinary, and changed the subject.

'If you want pigs, you're going to have to build a sty. That means planning permission as there are no existing buildings, and they'll send some guy round to check you've followed regulations.'

'Oh.'

'Dad'll help, but the planning might be tricky. Paxham-Jennings will oppose it for sure.'

'Oh. Why?'

'They pong, and they're noisy. And you've got to think about slurry storage, drainage, all sorts of stuff.'

'I only want a few. Gloucester Old Spots maybe, or even wild boar. Couldn't they just forage? There's that big oak at the end of the wild patch, and I was thinking of planting cider apples, maybe Royal Wilding even.'

'You'd still have to meet all the regulations, unless you claimed they were household pets, I think. I'll get Dad to check over the regulations.'

'Thanks.'

It wasn't something I'd thought about. Stupidly, I'd assumed that I would be able to do more or less as I pleased, and that I would be able to ignore any inconvenient regulations. Somebody was going to notice an illegal pigsty.

I filled our glasses and turned my attention back to the wine. It was as good as ever, but some of the magic had gone. There was a devil in my paradise, a worm in my apple, a little man with a clipboard and a brain full of regulations.

Emma spoke again.

'Do you mind if Ray comes back with me tonight?'

I thought of the piglets.

'Sure, you know it is.'

'Just checking. We're going to the Royal Oak, do you want to come?'

I considered, thinking of drink and laughter and just possibly one of Ray's friends, then of cigarette smoke, the taste of stale beer and the sort of brief pre-emptive fucking I'd probably get. It was no way to baptise my wonderful bed, and I wasn't really in the mood anyway.

'Another time, thanks.'

'Cool, see you later.'

She swallowed her wine and walked off, so Emma. That was one of the things I liked about her. She wasn't going to get in a state because I didn't want to be with her every spare moment, or go to everything she went to. She didn't even expect me to like the same things as she did, but simply accepted what we did have in common.

I sat down on the porch, the bottle beside me, and gave the wine the attention it deserved after spending more years maturing slowly in the bottle than I had been on the Earth. I took my time, savouring every sniff and every swallow, but before long its glories had begun to fade as the air had its inevitable effect.

My last glass finished and the dregs added to the libation after a moment's hesitation, I got to my feet. I felt a little unsteady, which wasn't surprising after drinking three-quarters of the bottle. My feeling of discontent had gone, replaced by a lazy satisfaction, a touch of devilment, a touch of defiance. A walk seemed the perfect thing to do, to clear my head, and to explore, which I'd barely had a chance to do. Also, I wanted to think.

I took the lane, not towards the road and Bourne Farm in the valley, but past the garden, where the woods of the estate closed in on both sides. The lane was public, for all the PRIVATE and NO TRESSPASSING signs to either side, and led over the motorway, past Alderhouse and down into the next valley. There was a pub too, and I began to wonder if it would be able to provide anything worthwhile in the way of dinner.

It would mean having to walk back in the dark, but I didn't care. The sky was clear and the moon was waxing gibbous, so I'd be all right. I was enjoying myself too much to worry anyway, just walking drunk in the English woodland, warm and happy, with really no greater worry than what I would have for dinner. The pigs didn't matter, not all that much. Besides, I had a sneaking suspicion that once I'd got to know them, I wouldn't be able to bring myself to slaughter them, for all my free-range principles. I knew I wouldn't have been able to kill Harriet and Hilary, for certain, and pigs are just as intelligent and personable as goats. I could do other things, plenty of other things . . .

I stopped. It hadn't been the last time I'd walked the path that I'd ended up being made to apologise to Mr Paxham-Jennings, but perhaps the second or third last. I could remember it, in detail, including the place where I'd slipped into the wood after my bluebells. I was there now, where a track cut into the woods.

Then it had seemed ill used, little more than a path cut through the trees of the understorey with two deep ruts to mark where tractors occasionally went in. Now it looked completely deserted. The ruts were still visible, but grown with bright green grass. A fallen silver birch sapling blocked the path. The NO TRESSPASSING sign wasn't one of the new ones, but old, probably the very one I had deliberately ignored all those years before. The paint had flaked and one nail had rusted through, leaving it hanging at an angle from the beech to which it had been attached.

I paused, staring down the track and letting my mind run back over the years. I'd been in jeans, a baggy T-shirt and trainers. My hair had been short, and probably scruffy. Mum had called it my tomboy phase. I'd thought of myself as a rebel. I had been too. The other girls at school had all been into New Kids on the Block. I hadn't known what I was into, but it wasn't that.

Granny might have made me apologise, but I hadn't wanted to, or meant it. It had just made me feel more resentful. Now I felt a touch of that old bitterness. All I'd done was pick a few flowers out of millions. OK, I'd have left them alone now, as a firm believer in taking only what I need from nature . . .

Then again, at the time I'd felt I needed bluebells, and it wasn't as if I'd been stripping acres of the things and selling them. Besides, I'd been eleven!

The temptation to go into the wood was very strong indeed. The sign said I shouldn't, or at least it was obviously supposed to. What it actually said was N ESSPA NG, because most of the paint was gone. That was nearly enough, drunk as I was. What decided me was sheer nostalgia. I wanted to see if I could find the place I'd picked the bluebells, and other special places I could remember. There was the huge beech my cousins fool-ishly carved their initials on, the pond that was always full of newts, the great wire enclosures where the pheas-ants were reared and which it had felt so daring to approach.

It was all there. Maybe changed, maybe not, all within a quarter mile or so of where I was standing, and I was not going to let some bunch of stuck-up landowners prevent me from indulging myself. The estate was huge, and I wouldn't be doing any harm; certainly far less than their shooting parties anyway.

I spent a moment stood stock-still and listening, took

a hurried glance up and down the lane, and walked quickly down the overgrown track. It was muddy, and I immediately found myself treading on sticks to avoid leaving footprints and using branches to swing myself forwards – tricks cousin John had taught me. In no time, I'd lost sight of the lane, and was trying to work out how to get to the places I wanted to see.

It was not easy. The understorey was thicker than I remembered it, and more obstructive, yet seemed to be shorter. Before long I knew I had passed the bluebell place, or missed it, but the season was completely wrong anyway. The pond had to be further along the lane, because I could remember that the motorway had been visible through the trees from a bank beside it. Now the traffic noise was no more than a dull hum muffled by the trees.

I found the tree, suddenly, with a fresh and sharp pang of nostalgia as I realised where I was. Sure enough, the carved initials were still visible as green, algae-filled grooves. I was biting my lip, my alcohol-fuelled emotions boiling up inside me with my memories. It was a short walk through overgrown parkland from the cottage, but it had always seemed to take a great dramatic expedition through utter wilderness to get there, and to be a place of magic and mystery, spooky even.

The magic was still there, with the stillness, the dappled green and gold light and the woodland smells. It was a place apart, for me at least. Not only for me, as I discovered on rounding the tree. Somebody else had been there. There was a short marble pillar, green with algae like everything else, but perfectly upright. On top was a bunch of grapes, quite fresh.

My first reaction was shock, and I found myself glancing guiltily around through the trees. Finding myself as alone as ever, I moved closer, still with my ears straining for the sound of approach. The grapes were untouched, plump red globes, fully ripe. If no animal or bird had got to them it could only mean they'd been placed there recently, very recently. That made me edgy, but the real fascination was with why they were there.

I could only imagine that they were an offering, made in worship, or respect, but undoubtedly ritual, and far from Christian. I thought of Emma and her libation, a display of pagan belief made without self-conscious display. This had to be similar, and whoever was responsible had to share some of my most cherished feelings. To meet them . . .

Delighted by my discovery and full of strange, strong emotions, I moved on. I wanted to explore more, to build on the experience, maybe to glimpse my mysterious pagan. I knew I would reach the pheasant enclosures if I kept going for the same distance again. I moved forwards, feeling nervous, but determined to do it. I get like that, making myself do something, not because I know I should, but because I know I shouldn't, but can.

Even then, I don't think I'd have done it without the wine inside me. From what Emma had said, the keeper was giving any boys he caught on the land a clip round the head. While I couldn't imagine him treating a grown woman so rudely, I didn't want to find out I was wrong.

So I moved forwards carefully, bent low, and stopped to listen every few metres. When a pheasant called from right above me, I nearly jumped out of my skin, and it took all my obstinacy to go on. After just a few more metres, I could hear the noises of the other birds. I went slower still, to stop where a good-sized trunk had come down across the track, blocking it. Beyond, it was just a mess of black mud and decaying leaves, with deep ruts where vehicles had turned. There was a big oak a little way ahead, casting a dark shadow over some bushes. I moved to it and peered out cautiously.

It had changed. The enclosure had been a ramshackle affair, with a single sheet of chicken wire suspended from tall hazel poles and pegged into the ground along the bottom. That was gone, replaced by a much bigger structure, twice as wide. The fence was at least three metres and made of gleaming mesh on steel posts, more like the perimeter of an army barracks or a prison than anything I'd seen in the woods before. There were new feeders too, but one familiar feature was still there – an old caravan, much like Emma's, but half the size and green with algae.

We had liked to think it was where the keeper lived, lurking to catch unwary trespassers. In practice, it was only where the feed and equipment were stored, a rather disappointing discovery after John had tricked me into going to look inside. The way he and the others had painted it, I'd been expecting a den of evil, and the sight of sacks of grain and zinc feeders had been a major letdown. So I'd told them there was a bloody machete and a severed head. They'd run all the way back to the cottage.

I smiled to myself at the memory, and was about to duck back, mission accomplished, when the caravan door swung open and a man stepped out. If I'd thought the pheasant had startled me, then I hadn't known the meaning. A great rush of adrenaline hit me, and I found myself with my hand on my chest, my heart pounding so hard I could feel it through my coat.

He was facing towards me, and I couldn't back away without risking being seen. Pulling the collar of my coat up around my face, I squatted down in the shadow of the great oak trunk, hardly daring to breathe as I watched. He was roughly dressed, in muddy boots, jeans, a check shirt and an old tweed jacket. He was big, well over six foot, and muscular in a way that far surpassed the gym-toned sleekness of any of my male friends. Certainly none of them conveyed his raw masculinity. I felt that had Teo, let alone Gabriel Blane, been next to him, it would have been like seeing house dogs next to a wolf.

It had to be Marsh, Mr Marsh, as Emma always called him. I didn't know his first name. Toby Paxham-Jennings, I was sure, would not be so tall, nor so broad, nor so rough. Possibly there were other keepers and grounds-men, but it was hard to see the man before me as anything less than the leader of his group.

Everything about him suggested power and certainty, the way the big muscles in his arms and back moved under his shirt, the set of his jaw, his huge hands. Not only that, but the front of his trousers showed an impres-sive bulge, one it was hard not to stare at. There was no denying he was my type of man, and as I thought of how it would feel to be held in his grip, a shiver ran the length of my spine.

He was younger than I'd expected from what Emma had said too, maybe thirty, or thirty-five at most. His hair was roughly cut, a hank of dense black, mirrored by the shadow on his heavy jaw. All in all, he looked pretty rough, rough enough to make me feel more than a little vulnerable, for all his attraction. Yet there was no dog with him, and no reason he should see me, so long as I kept still, as he was busy.

In his hand he held a peculiar device, like a post for an electric fence, but with a cylinder attached to it, and a weight. This he pushed into the ground beside a tree and adjusted it with quick, exact motions of his huge hands. Only when he slipped a shotgun cartridge into the cylin-der did I realise what it was – a trap. A piece of fishing line stretched across the path confirmed my suspicions. If somebody walked down the path at night, they would push against the line, releasing the weight onto a firing pin, which would set off the cartridge into the ground. Thus it would alert him, and probably make the would-be poacher wet himself.

For all my uncertainty, just watching him work was bringing back the sexual arousal I had felt earlier. Not that I had the slightest intention of approaching him, not on his terms and on his ground. It was just too easy to imagine him demanding more than I was prepared to give, and he'd already given me quite a jolt. My heart was in my mouth, but that was better than his cock. Or was it? Maybe that was exactly what I wanted, exactly what I needed.

I bit my lip, hesitant, wondering if I should simply stroll forwards and introduce myself, perhaps claim I was a friend of Toby Paxham-Jennings. That would make him keep his cock in his pants if I decided I didn't want him, and if I did . . .

If I did, it would be rough sex in his caravan, down on the feed sacks, or bent over the little table, bottom up. Or, as I had no protection, I could offer to suck, as I had Teo, with his big cock in my mouth as I played with myself. That was better, really. No risks and the certainty of an orgasm. Yet I did want to fuck, and more badly than I had realised.

I couldn't go through with it. Normally, I'm pretty bold, but it didn't feel right, not there, not then. So I waited until he had set his poacher trap and, as soon as he had disappeared into the caravan, I moved slowly back into the undergrowth. Minutes later, I was back on the lane, smiling to myself for my little adventure.

It was getting on for dusk, with the sun now low behind the trees and broken into flecks of blinding yellow-orange light by the foliage. I decided to make for the pub, having had my fill of home-made omelettes for the time being, however delicious.

Without the revived childhood thrill of trespass I felt slightly silly for not speaking to Marsh. The excuse of being a friend of the Paxham-Jenningses would have worked long enough for me to get rude, and once I had, it would have been a very strange man indeed who wouldn't forgive me my little trespass. I'd followed my emotions.

It may be the thing to let yourself be led by your heart. Generally, I do, but there are times when I feel I ought to be able to rush a rational decision past what my body is telling me to do. One good example is when being propositioned by the handsome boyfriend of a close friend. That is definitely not a time to be led by the heart, which is basically animal instinct after all.

This time I had been, but it was hard to see my choice as inappropriate. There had been something animal about the whole situation, primitive, all to do with food and sex and territory – the basics. There was definitely something animal about Marsh.

There was also something animal about the way I'd instinctively perceived Marsh as a leader. It just wasn't true. He was an employee, and presumably did as he was told, by Donald Paxham-Jennings, by Toby, maybe by an estate manager too. I suppose, at base, a female wants to see her chosen mate as the dominant male. In reality, Donald Paxham-Jennings was the dominant male, but that didn't feel right. The Paxham-Jenningses led because they owned the land and employed Marsh; entirely civilised concepts.

Marsh seemed right for the grape offering on the pillar, too. I could imagine him singing lustily in church, then going to leave a gift at his pagan shrine, and not even being aware of the contradiction. Many people in olden days counted themselves Christian yet held pagan beliefs, even if they were called superstitions. Perhaps this was similar, an act of abstract veneration, or perhaps it was more, the deliberate worship of a woodland spirit in defiance of orthodoxy but not as a modern revival. That was a truly fascinating possibility.

All in all, it had been a strange, slightly frightening, but extremely exhilarating experience. My mood had diluted, and I expected reaching the motorway to break it. It didn't, but only made it stronger, as I looked down from the bridge onto tarmac painted into a ribbon of bronze by the setting sun and watched the cars and lorries tear past beneath me. Each had purpose, each was hurrying to a destination, home from work, delivering goods, all intent on her or his business, and nothing whatever to do with me. By the time I moved on, I had never felt more detached from the ordinary world.

Passing Alderhouse, with its grand Regency façade and brightly lit windows, only made my feelings of separation stronger, but the pub brought me back down to earth with a bump. I'd been imagining some kind of rustic dive, with red-faced old men wearing underchin beards swilling cider from tankards. What I got was a bright, modern bar with slot machines and a video game. Their idea of food went no further than scampi and chips, undoubtedly from the freezer, while the sulphated Central Valley mouthwash on what they laughingly called the wine list was simply not something I was prepared to put inside myself.

So I walked on at random with no more than a vague idea of where I was going. After maybe another mile I reached a village, Ilsenden, which I knew of but hadn't been to. The pub there proved more fruitful, providing me with a dish of mallard breast served in a rich sauce of mixed fruits. Something equally rich was called for to partner it, and, not wanting to buy by the glass, I ended up ordering a bottle of a Barossa Valley Shiraz. It was perfect, the heavy, peppery fruit balancing the intensity of the sauce and the strong meat flavour. Not to have finished it would have been a crime, and I left the pub with my belly feeling distinctly firm and my head spinning.

It had to be two miles back to the cottage, maybe nearer three, and it was fully dark. The moon was up, so I wasn't worried as I set off on foot, telling myself that I needed the walk anyway. At first it was awful, with every car that came past blinding me with its headlights so that I had to press myself into the hedge not to get hit, and to allow my vision to recover. From the lane onwards it was better, and I was soon feeling happy, and free, and more than a little naughty.

I kept thinking of Marsh, and how it could have been: rough and passionate; rude and animal. He was so big and strong that he would have been able to lift me onto himself with ease, or to hold me bent over, my body a toy in his hands. There would have been no hesitation, no self-obsessed worry about what we should or shouldn't do, just good, hard sex.

Had I met him in the lane I think I'd have demanded it then and there, down in the mud with me riding him, his cock deep inside me. I even stopped at the entrance to the track long enough to slip my hand under my coat and stroke the swell of my pussy lips through my jeans. I was wet, and my nipples were stiff, tempting me to take it all the way, and masturbate then and there. Only the distant noise of a car prevented me.

It was Emma and Ray, making for the caravan after a night's drinking, as I discovered when I reached the cottage to see the red tail lights of their taxi disappearing far down the lane. I could hear her giggling as I pushed open the gate, and my need grew abruptly stronger as I imagined them together, Emma fumbling at his fly in her eagerness to get his cock out.

She wasn't, but what she was doing came as quite a shock. The automatic porch light had gone on, and as I came into the garden I found them in full view, at the edge of the wild patch. She was squatting, skirt up, knickers down, her thighs spread as she relieved herself liberally into the grass, giggling as he watched and squeezed at his bulging crotch. They could hardly avoid seeing me. There seemed to be no inhibitions between them.

'Whoops! Hi, Juliet. Sorry . . .'

'That's OK. Hi, Ray.'

He turned, grinning. I busied myself with the door, allowing her to finish what she was doing and tidy herself up. I didn't go in, waiting to say goodnight when she was ready. She was still pulling her knickers up as she spoke.

'Come in, have a drink with us, yeah? We've brought some beers back.'

'No, I'd better leave you. You look like you need to be alone.'

'Nah, Ray had me in the loos at the pub, dirty boy! Still, don't stop him from wanting it again though.'

She prodded him. He responded with a shy, sloppy grin. I felt my sex tighten as the image of her bent across a toilet while he entered her from behind came up into my head. I wanted it myself, badly, and I knew I was going to masturbate for certain. Knowing them, it would be to the sound of grunts and squeals. Or I could get drunker still, and . . .

'OK, but come in with me. I'll open a bottle.'

'Sure.'

She took Ray's arm, pulling him towards me. He came, letting her lead him, as docile as ever, like a great lazy ox. I went in, flicking the lights on and pushing open the sitting room door. Like Emma, I was badly in need of the loo, and left them to it as I peed and tidied my hair. I had port, a straightforward LBV, and brought it in with some glasses.

They were on the sofa together, Ray casually fondling one plump breast through Emma's top, an open beer in his other hand. She gently slapped his groping fingers away as I came in, and nestled into his side as she took a glass from me. I filled one for myself and sat down, feeling nervous and happy and horny all at once. It was slightly awkward too, and I didn't really know what to say. Emma, as always, had no such problem.

'So, what have you been up to, Perky?'

It took me a moment to realise what she meant, and then I went bright red. My nipples were showing through my top, really badly.

'Emma!'

She just laughed and cuddled closer into Ray's side. Her eyes were bright with mischief, her full mouth a little open, her cheeks rosy with drink. Ray seemed indifferent, his bottle held up to his mouth, until his eyes moved slowly to my chest. I hate to seem naïve.

I put down my glass, took my top in both hands, and lifted, bra and all. As my breasts came bare I stuck my tongue out, and kept it out, while I let them have a good stare. Ray's eyes were popping out of his head. Emma dissolved in laughter. I calmly covered myself. She took a swallow of port and wagged a finger at me.

'Bad girl! You'll give him ideas.'

She slapped him on the thigh.

'Hey! What have I done?'

'Nothing, but I know what you're thinking.'

'What?'

'You're thinking what it would be like to take us both to bed, aren't you? Men!'

'I was not!'

I laughed. It was funny to see such a big man so easily teased by her. I was wondering if he would put up with it, but he accepted an admonishing poke in the ribs and went back to his beer. I was also wondering if what Emma had said had been true, and whether bringing it up had been entirely coincidental. She went on, ignoring him completely.

'They're all the same, aren't they? Every guy I've ever been out with, just about, has wanted me to get a friend involved.'

'Have you done it?'

'Juliet!'

I laughed, delighted to have embarrassed her in turn. She wasn't getting off easily either.

'Well, have you?'

'No!'

'No?'

'I have not!'

She'd gone crimson.

'The lady doth protest too much, methinks.'

'Eh?'

'Shakespeare, from *Hamlet*.'

'She's no lady.'

Ray laughed as he spoke. Emma turned on him, mouth wide, then slapped him again, hard this time.

'Ow! Hey!'

'You deserved that, pig!'

Suddenly, they were tussling together, Emma slapping and clutching at his clothes, Ray trying to get a grip on her, then succeeding. He lifted her, so easily, up onto his shoulder and stood up, leaving her with her bum stuck up in the air, her legs kicking and her fists beating on his back, protesting furiously. He look down at me.

'Time for bed, I reckon. Work in the morning. Night.'

He just left, ducking through the door and letting himself out, one handed, still holding Emma, for all her struggles. I couldn't help but laugh, and gave her a friendly pat on the head as I closed the door behind them. As I sat down again, her tirade ended abruptly in a slap, a loud squeal and sudden giggles. I picked my glass up, smiling to myself, amused but unable to completely rid myself of a pang of jealousy. He was quite obviously going to take her into the caravan for exactly what I so badly wanted – a good, hard fuck.

By the time I'd finished my glass, and hers, and taken the bottle back into the kitchen, they were at it. The caravan was creaking gently, and moving. It was impossible not to think of them – his big powerful body on top of hers, accepting the invitation of her open thighs. Or maybe she'd be on top. It seemed likely from the way she treated him. No, it wouldn't be either, or not for long. He would never get comfortable on the tiny bed, and for all his acceptance of her bossiness I had seen how easily he could handle her if he wanted to. He would have her bent over the bed, gone deep inside her from behind, holding her hips as he thrust into her, his cock pounding in and out, filling her, making her gasp and pant and squeal . . .

I shook my head, trying to rid myself of the images of them fucking. It would be pretty animalistic, just as I'd imagined it between Marsh and myself. Emma wasn't prissy about her body, and Ray certainly wouldn't be, for all his shyness. She'd think nothing of sucking his dick and swallowing, or taking his balls in her mouth, or sitting on his face to have him lick her, maybe even her bottom. They'd do what felt good, tangled together in raw, sweaty, uninhibited passion, fucking and sucking and licking until they'd both come.

They weren't the only ones who were going to be

coming. I was trembling as I readied myself for bed. And I was flushed, my whole chest red and prickly, my nipples rock hard, my pussy soaking. I stripped naked and climbed onto my bed, my hand brushing the twin bulges of Artemis's bottom as I slipped inside the drapes. I crawled in, under the warm blankets, to lie still in the darkness, biting my lips and letting my imagination go.

I was drunk, and they were too, but I was sure there had been intent to Emma's teasing. It might not have sunk into Ray's head, but I was sure that she'd been testing the water to see if I'd like to share him, and that she had done something similar before. She'd had more than enough opportunity to make a move on me had she wanted to, so I knew she was no lesbian, but she didn't have to be. She was full of mischief, and very confident, so I could well see that the idea of sharing her man might appeal.

It might have happened, as well. In fact, had it not been for Ray carrying her off, it might have been happening at that very moment. She might have told me what she'd done; maybe demanded some equally intimate revelation in return. I knew full well where that sort of thing could lead to from a drunken evening in college, me naked in front of two men, just as I was naked now, only kneeling on the floor of my room to take one man in my mouth as the other entered me.

I shivered at the memory. It had been so good, so daring, and maybe the naughtiest thing I'd ever done. Tonight could have been the same, only with Emma and I sharing Ray. It could have happened. I was sure of it. Maybe if I hadn't covered myself, if I'd stayed with my breasts bare, or taken my top off completely. Emma might have responded, perhaps to show the full heavy globes of her breasts in comparison to mine.

At that thought, I took them in my hands, cupping

them, my thumbs on my nipples. They made two good handfuls, but she was bigger, much bigger. Maybe she'd have teased him, as she liked to, making him judge between us to get him flustered. I'd have played along, going down to my panties to show off my legs, then bare, my bottom stuck out in the rude pose men love so much, an animal pose, my bottom pushed out to show my pussy, ready for entry.

My legs came up and open, spreading myself. I was wet, sensitive, two fingers slipping easily into my hole. Somewhere beyond the darkness of my bedroom, a shrill high squealing began. Emma was coming. I imagined watching, playing with myself as I was now, as they came together, Ray thrusting himself against the softness of Emma's bottom, from behind, as I'd pictured them. Or maybe she would have let me touch, even suck, take him between my breasts, into my sex.

Slowly I began to rub, not hard, just teasing my clitoris as my fantasy built in my head. By the time I was naked he would have had his cock out ready for us. She would have stayed in control, making sure he did as he was told, but encouraging me to touch him, to take him in my hand, my mouth, my pussy...

I stopped. It wasn't right. The fantasy was going in circles, and it wasn't truly what I wanted anyway. I wanted Marsh, in the woods, down on my knees in the tiny caravan sucking his cock, or bent bottom up over the sacks of feed with him deep inside me. Better still, we could have gone to the shrine, and stripped, to go naked in the dappled sunlight, to make love on the ground, offering our passion to the wood, dedicating ourselves as his come filled me.

That was right. I held the thought, thinking of myself naked in the cool woodland air, his cock deep in my body, him spunking into me. My own sigh sounded loud in the room as I started to come and I was rubbing hard at myself, my back arched, my bottom lifted from the bed, as everything came together in one long, tight surge of ecstasy.

4

I awoke to a medley of competing thoughts, the most immediate of which was that my head hurt. Pouring cheap port on top of strong red wine had not been a good idea, especially as I'd failed to open the window or even drink any water.

I was still smiling as I pulled on my robe. My failure had been due to being too turned on to think straight, and it had been quite a while since I'd felt that way. Not that I'd done anything, at least not with anyone else, but it had still been good. There had been a lot behind it too, and not all fantasy. Marsh was real, very real, and so was the shrine in the woods. I wanted to know more about both, and hopefully to make fantasy a reality.

There was a problem in that the last thing I wanted to do was alienate Emma in any way, and she hated Marsh. Still, if he and I were together perhaps I could persuade them to try and get along better. Certainly I wasn't prepared to abandon the whole thing on the off chance that I might get dragged into the local feud.

I washed and dressed as I considered the situation, choosing my heaviest boots, jeans and a thick dark-green sweater over my top. As I studied the effect in the mirror I was telling myself that the lack of bright colours had nothing to do with a desire to spend the day sneaking around the woods in the hope of seeing Marsh, honestly. It was merely a sensible choice for a clear autumn day in the country.

Whether I went into the woods or not, a walk was

definitely what I needed. It would clear my head and allow me to think about my plans for the future. From what Emma had said my original idea was clearly impractical. Livestock for meat was out, but that wasn't necessarily the end of it. I could buy from Emma's father instead, and just do the curing. He had at least some commitment to organic and free-range principles and was definitely moving in the right direction. The pigs were Berkshires too, which were undeniably regional however widespread the breed may be.

That was the sensible thing to do. I could source carefully, buy as I needed, and use my contacts to keep my margins worthwhile. Preparation would be the key, and I had the time and the knowledge. In fact it was better, as I could provide a broader range of products, including game. Nor would it just be meats. Pheasant, for instance, is too cheap to be worth dealing with in small quantities, but smoked or as a pâté it could well be worthwhile. There was certainly no shortage of pheasants locally. There were several roosting in my wild patch when I went across to the caravan thinking Emma and Ray might appreciate a decent coffee.

They were gone. Emma had left a note thanking me, and saying that she had dealt with the goats and chickens. Sure enough, the eggs were there, along with the milk pail. That left me with my own choice of what to do, an unfamiliar feeling I was hoping to get used to but which still seemed a luxury. So I drank fresh coffee at my leisure, three slow cups, as I wandered around the house and garden. I had to admit this left me buzzing slightly from excess caffeine.

What had happened the night before was a touch embarrassing, but not too bad. I knew I could handle it, and I was sure Emma could. Getting in a state over things you've done when drunk is pointless as the moment has happened, although it still makes for some cringeworthy moments. As I finished the coffee, I was smiling at my own lewd behaviour, and wondering about Emma's intentions.

The best bet was to ask her straight out the next time we were alone together. Some people like to do things but not to admit it, so can't talk openly. I try to avoid that, and Emma, I was sure, would be as honest with me as she was with herself.

As I finished my third coffee, I heard the thud of guns – one, then a volley, two more, then silence. It was coming from the west, presumably the Alderhouse Estate. If they were shooting it was presumably a party, which made it a very bad idea indeed to be wandering around in the woods. That meant I needed somewhere else to wander.

There was a map in the cottage. It was old, but accurate enough. The bulk of the estate and the area where they were shooting was within an irregular pentagon of land, roughly a mile up and down and maybe three-quarters across. Two sides were the lane, with the road leading past Emma's farm as the base, the motorway cutting off the top, and another road at the far side. That other road went past Alderhouse and down into Ilsenden. A footpath connected the lane and the road, running roughly parallel to the motorway and coming out beside the bridge. If I didn't dare risk the woods, I could at least explore that.

I set off, feeling daring and slightly guilty despite having no intention of doing anything even remotely illegal. As I walked I heard the guns, again and again, well off to my left, but getting closer. I could hear the alarm calls of the pheasants too, and the soft faint patter of shot passing through the tree tops, but thankfully not close to me.

The evening before I hadn't noticed the footpath, nor could I remember it. What it turned out to be was the narrow path leading past the newt pond, which I had never realised was a public right of way. Without the map I wouldn't have realised, as there was no sign and it was badly overgrown. It had to be right, though, because there was a huge red and white notice, SHOOTING IN PROGRESS – PLEASE USE ALTERNATIVE ROUTE.

I looked at the map. There was no alternative route, unless one counted the motorway or went all the way round by Ilsenden. That sounded like the Paxham-Jenningses through and through, doing their best to make the footpath obscure, then closing it unnecessarily. After all, if anyone shot towards it they would also be shooting over the motorway. I stuck my nose in the air and walked boldly past the sign, only to stop. Marsh might be around, and if he ran into me it was hardly going to make for a good start to a relationship. Then again, he was male, and once he realised what I wanted... He might even allow me to suck his cock by way of apology. I giggled.

As I started down the track, I was smiling at my own dirty mind. I found myself going cautiously though, and was relieved when I reached the far end without meeting anybody. The path came out beside a bridge where the road went under the motorway, which now ran on an embankment across the head of a shallow valley. I paused, peering out from among the trees as a car passed, then nipped past a second notice and down to the road.

The guns were louder now, but there was no patter of shot, meaning I had come around behind the line. I set off down the road, walking slowly and peering into the woods on my left. The mixture of dense scrub understorey and great trees gave way to a stand of squat pines with dark alleys running between them to a sunlit track just visible at the end. As I rounded a gentle corner a

Land Rover came in sight, then a cluster of parked cars where the track turned up from the wood. They could only belong to the shooting party: Mercedes, BMWs, various 4X4s, a Jaguar. A bored-looking youth with a shock of ginger hair was sitting on the back, presumably having been told to keep an eye on the guests' property.

I walked past to where the pines gave way to an open field with a cottage in one corner. It was much like my own, a little bigger and square, but of the same red-brick and flint mix, and brown tiled, only with gabled windows looking out from the upper rooms. In the garden were rows of cauliflower, a criss-cross of bean poles, and the plump yellow-green shapes of marrows beneath their leaves. An old twisted plum tree stood in one corner with fat, dark-skinned fruit still on the boughs. I immediately wondered if it was Marsh's cottage, which seemed likely, but as I came past it I found myself in full view of the shooting party.

They had their backs to me, a couple of dozen men strung out in a line across the field beside numbered posts. Most were in ostentatiously new tweeds or padded jackets; many wore hats and a few were seated on shooting sticks. Beyond them was a broad sweep of open field, the grass the brilliant green of a wet autumn, stretching down to a fence and the woods, with a stream running beneath the trunks of magnificent beeches.

Nothing much seemed to be happening, until a pheasant suddenly burst from the woods, squawking in raucous alarm. It was a cock bird, so fat it could barely run, let alone fly, but it was trying, neck extended, wings flapping in desperation. For all my belief in killing to eat, I was firmly on its side, and found myself biting my lip in anticipation as it finally managed to heave itself into the air. The first man missed completely, the second as well. The third didn't, hurling the unfortunate bird into the undergrowth in a burst of feathers.

It wasn't something I particularly wanted to watch, not with the odds so heavily stacked against the birds. My principle is that, as omnivores by nature, it is absurd to refuse meat, and that if we are prepared to eat meat, then we should be prepared to kill the animals we live from, if necessary. To do otherwise is hypocrisy, yet I regard killing for amusement as barbaric. I was sure the pheasant would be eaten, yet I was having difficulty in justifying the way it had been killed.

I began to move on, pondering the moral philosophy of blood sports as I went, when the shooting party began to break up. The Paxham-Jenningses were sure to be there somewhere, and I paused, wanting to see how the stuck-up little boy who had looked down his nose at me so haughtily had grown up. He'd been skinny, and I was imagining some sort of monocled twit, a sort of modern-day Bertie Wooster. One or two of those I could see certainly fitted the bill, although none actually had a monocle.

Reasoning that I had a perfect right to walk along a public road, and to stop and watch rich men getting into their cars if I pleased, I turned back, walking more slowly than ever. The party was walking parallel to me, and drawing closer, allowing me to get a good look. One had to be Donald Paxham-Jennings, an older man, red-faced, just as I remembered, but with his moustache now grey-ish-white rather than salt-and-pepper. The son was less easy to pick out, until I realised that he had to be the one who had hung back to speak to the beaters as they walked up from the woods.

Not that he fitted my image at all but, when someone addressed him by name, I had him in my sights. I stopped by the hedge, feeling rather self-conscious. He was perhaps six foot, not heavy, but broad at the shoulder and long-legged. His face was in profile, somewhat aquiline, with a strong chin and mouth; not bad at all really, if he lacked the brute solidity of Marsh. I nodded to myself, my preconceptions abandoned, and a touch annoyed that he hadn't turned out to be a buck-toothed, chinless pillock.

It felt a bit foolish to turn round a second time, so I continued, reaching the cars as they did. It occurred to me that I could perfectly well introduce myself, perhaps ask if they had a surplus of pheasants. After all, I needed stock, and the estate was right on my doorstep. That in turn might be a route to Marsh, if rather a mundane one after my exotic sylvan fantasies of the night before.

As I approached, I caught their conversation. There was a mix of accents: braying upper-crust, R.P. English, estuary English, then county Berkshire stronger than Ray's, in a deep bass. It was Marsh himself. He was leaning on a fence, his strong face set in a calm confident detachment that verged on contempt. There was nothing servile about him whatsoever, and his remark had been delivered not as flattery or respectful small talk, but as a criticism of technique. It was not as servant to master, but as expert to dilettante. Donald Paxham-Jennings might be his boss, but Marsh quite clearly regarded himself as master of his own domain, the woods and fields to which he was attached in a way they could never be.

Suddenly, I felt weak, lost for words and lost for action, and could no more have approached him, or any of them, than I could fly. It was a long, long time since I'd felt that feeling – the last time at school, waiting outside the village shop in the hope that a certain boy would pass and finding he was already there.

I hurried past, sure he would notice my blushes and

how flustered I was, telling myself I could not possibly have fallen in love with a man I'd not yet spoken to. Not me, not like that. But yet, despite the cool air, I was flushed hot across the whole of my face and chest as I walked on up the road. I didn't even know where I was going, except away to think. I would have taken the footpath, but as I reached it one of their cars was passing, and a moment later a group who had chosen to walk came into view.

All I could do was walk on under the motorway bridge. I felt a complete fool, but I couldn't bring myself to turn back and walk past them. Angry with myself, I stopped to put a foot up on the bank and retie my laces. They would walk past, and I could go back, nipping into the woods as soon as it was clear.

I realised Marsh wasn't among them as they approached, but Toby Paxham-Jennings was. He was near the back, and gave me a polite greeting as he came up, as had several of the others, but stopped, excusing himself to them and addressing me.

'I, er . . . I'm sorry to trouble you. You're not, er . . . Jean Sutton's granddaughter, are you?'

'Yes, I am.'

'I thought so. Toby Paxham-Jennings.'

He had extended a hand. I took it as he went on.

'I'm so terribly sorry. I was at the funeral.'

'Oh, I see. Thank you. Sorry, I didn't recognise you.'

'No reason you should, of course, no reason at all. Juliet, isn't it?'

'Yes. Hi.'

'You've moved into Jean's cottage, so I hear?'

'Yes. I . . . I didn't know you were a friend.'

'Why, yes, certainly. She was my nanny for what, four years?'

'Oh. I didn't know.'

'You'd have been a baby, not even born at first, I don't suppose. So, how are you settling in?'

'Very well, thank you. It's beautiful here.'

'Absolutely. Look, you must come to dinner. Friday perhaps? We've quite a party.'

'Um . . . yes, why not. Thank you.'

'Splendid. Seven-thirty for eight then, black tie optional as it's the season.'

'I'll be there.'

He hesitated, smiling as if he wanted to say something more, then gave an abrupt nod and walked on, turning to smile and wave after a few paces. I still had my foot up against the bank and my lace undone, so made a careful job of tying it, then the other, so that he and the others were out of sight by the time I'd finished.

I hadn't done badly, I felt. However feudal he was about his property he had been pretty friendly to me. If his eyes had tended to stray towards the shape of my breasts beneath my jumper, that was normal, and his sympathy for my granny had seemed genuine. He also had to be an excellent contact for pheasant, and perhaps other game as well. The dinner would be interesting for its own sake, and it seemed likely that Alderhouse had both a proper tradition of English food and a good cellar, or at least possible.

My thoughts turned back to Marsh as I reached the entrance to the footpath. The notice was gone, something I assumed would be his job. It didn't take Sherlock Holmes to work out that meant he was on the path ahead of me; he might also turn back towards his cottage after collecting the other notice. I would meet him.

The thought put butterflies in my stomach. I started down the path, telling myself to grow up and that it would be perfectly easy to speak to him, even proposition him if I wanted to. I did, and I was telling myself I should as I walked, and wondering what had happened to me. I'm the girl who asks for what she wants, and generally gets it, not the one who sits in the corner looking shy and gets nothing. I told myself I'd do it, as I had with Teo, hand to crotch in an offer no man could possibly mistake.

I didn't. I bottled out completely. He came past, just as I'd expected, and he acknowledged me with a feral grin as his eyes moved to the swell of my breasts, fixing on them as he passed. I said nothing, but was left pink-faced and shaking, my nipples rigid to attention. Most men glance at my breasts, some talk to them, most look guilty or get embarrassed if I meet their eye or make a remark to show I've noticed. Not Marsh. He'd stared, and I'd wanted him to. No, I'd wanted him to pull my top up and rip off my bra, to hold them and suck them and lick my nipples, to strip me and put me on the ground and mount me – to fuck me. He was just such an animal, his response to me so primitive. It was making me dizzy, and when I had reached the far end of the footpath I took a moment to recover myself, leaning on the motorway bridge to watch the traffic and trying to work out what to do.

Marsh was single – I knew from Emma – which was one good thing at least. Logically then, it seemed likely that he would be interested and that I could approach him. He couldn't be gay, not a man like that, and not after the way he had looked at me. Possibly I'd be a bit slim for him, his earthy sexual instincts more attuned to the earth mother type. Again, the way he'd looked at me suggested otherwise. I could do it, but I knew I wouldn't.

I'd spent nearly half an hour staring vacantly out over the motorway before I was brought back to earth by hunger. All I'd had since the evening before was coffee, and in the meantime I'd walked a good four miles and masturbated myself silly. Toby Paxham-Jenning's shooting party had been heading back for lunch, and they'd had the right idea. Marsh, I assumed, would also be sitting down to something hearty in his cottage.

Omelette tempted again, possibly mushroom, and I began to cast about for parasols on the short grass where the bridge began. It was an ideal site, in theory, but there weren't any, only some Russula I didn't recognise and wasn't going to risk. There had to be something, though. Chanterelles were possible, or horn of plenty, even ceps. With so much mature beech and oak, there had to be a fair chance of the rarer cep species, some of which are even better than the basic penny bun. If there were enough, they would make the perfect ingredient for my game pâtés.

I began to walk back towards the cottage, looking as I went, but it wasn't really an ideal habitat. The understorey was perhaps twenty to thirty years old, grown up on what had once been open parkland with scattered trees. The old wood, and the big oaks and beeches, were a fair way off, deeper in.

Marsh would be at lunch, or tidying up after the morning shoot. The beaters had presumably been hired and would be gone, or in the pub. Besides, I had now met Toby Paxham-Jennings. I was still feeling less than sure of myself, and moved cautiously into the woods with my normal guilty glance up and down the lane.

The young trees closed around and above me and, within moments, I was out of sight of the lane and any other point of reference. I wasn't worried. The track I'd used before, and so often in childhood, was a good two hundred metres to the east. That put the pheasant enclosures about a quarter-mile south and a touch east, with the main stand of old woodland south and south-west. All I had to do was walk in a straight line for about five hundred paces.

I tried, and ended up at a boggy area between a stand

of pine and the thick young growth after just three hundred. Somewhere I had gone wrong, but I could see the top of an impressive copper beech well to my left, and made for it. It was one of those at the bottom of the field where they'd been shooting, which meant I'd been walking south-west instead of south. I didn't understand how, but it didn't matter. Ahead of me was the line of great trees, magnificent with their silvery trunks and great sprays of dark copper or silver-green foliage. Behind them was the old wood, big oaks and beeches, with none of the ornamental species that marked the old parkland, and hollies beneath. It was ideal, and sure enough, there they were – fat, glossy penny buns and *Boletus appendiculatus* with their brilliant lemon-yellow spores; also pheasants.

They had simply been left where they'd fallen, presumably for collection later, yet it hardly seemed likely they'd be left lying in the woods for hours if they were intended for sale. An article I'd read came to mind, on how some estates simply ploughed the surplus of a day's shoot into the fields. The market price had been so low, apparently, and the profits from what the shooting party paid so proportionately high, that selling the pheasants simply hadn't been worth the extra effort and expense. This 'over-bagging', as it was called, had struck me as an appalling waste then, and it did now.

It also struck me that if they didn't want to take the birds, then I might as well. Recipes involving pheasant and ceps were already evolving in my mind as I began to gather up both birds and fungi. At The Seasons, we'd generally made a sauce and either served the birds roasted or filleted out the breasts for baking. Both dishes had been excellent but, with more time and no customers to worry about, I could afford to experiment. One possibility I had to try was cutting slits into the breasts and poking in bits of cep, then barding to hold it all together, and roasting. Pâté was another, and made best use of the bird, while filleted breasts layered with ceps and wrapped in pastry also appealed.

I was like a child in a sweet shop. In no time, I had more ceps than I could conveniently carry, and pheasants too. I peeled off my jumper, ignoring the autumn chill as I converted it into a crude bag. There was still more than I could possibly hope to carry, but I determined to get everything I possibly could, piling the pheasants under a low-hanging holly as I stuffed my jumper with ceps. A truly decadent culinary possibility occurred to me as I eased an especially plump penny bun from the ground.

When working with two distinctive but complementary ingredients, the real art is to blend the flavours in such a way that the pleasure of the whole exceeds that of the sum of the parts. It is the same when matching wine and food, but by no means easy to achieve. With the ceps and pheasants, I could fillet and marinate, but that probably meant taking the meat off the bone, which I prefer not to. Possibly I could make the incisions in the breasts before hanging, poke the bits of cep in and allow the flavour to infuse as the pheasant meat came to proper ripeness. It might work, it might not, but there was no reason not to try. Alternatively, I could . . .

I froze. There was a man in the field, at the first of the shooting posts. He was bent low, picking up the spent cartridges. I cursed myself for not keeping a proper look-out as I moved slowly back behind the trunk of the huge beech nearest to me. I was just in time. I heard a man's voice, strangely muffled through the trees, and a laugh in response. It had to be the beaters, come to collect the pheasants. Immediately, my heart was in my mouth. I slunk back and ducked low in among the holly bushes, clutching my jumper. Again the voices sounded, nearer, and as I flattened myself to the carpet of prickly leaves beneath me, I saw them.

There were three men, two of the beaters, and Marsh, walking along the bottom of the field and collecting those pheasants which had fallen there. My every instinct was telling me to run, but I knew they would hear me, the crunch of brittle holly leaves beneath my feet, the snapping of twigs. I stayed down, waiting until they had passed my hiding place. I knew they'd come back, through the wood, to collect more pheasants. They would see me, or find my cache. The man collecting cartridges was still in full view, but I had to go.

I crawled back, my stomach fluttering, my teeth clamped hard on my lip, ignoring the pricks of holly leaves on my hands and bare arms. Behind the holly, I risked rising to a crouch, shuffling crabwise, all the while having to fight to keep down my panic. More trees shielded me, and denser holly as I crept up the slope, until at last I could no longer see the green of the field. I rose, walking, taking in air in long, slow breaths.

It had been close, but I was away, needing only to reach the lane for absolute safety. All of them would be helping clear up after the shoot, I hoped, but I stayed alert, moving carefully and keeping to cover. I reached the track, crossed it, and pushed on into denser undergrowth close past the shrine tree, and to the lane, emerging from the overgrown track. I didn't stop, but hurried back to the cottage to spill my cargo of stolen ceps out onto the kitchen table. Only then did I rest, hands spread wide as I leant on the table, admiring my haul and grinning to myself for what I'd done.

I felt wonderful, exhilarated, daring, mischievous. It had been stupid of me not to pay full attention to what was going on around me, but I had kept my cool and escaped. Not only that, but I had escaped with an amazing crop of ceps, enough to keep even The Seasons going for a year. That was good, wonderful, but the true thrill had been in the chase.

If I thought I'd been buzzing after three cups of strong black coffee, then I hadn't known what it meant. My fingers were shaking, I couldn't stay still and I couldn't stop grinning. It was just so good. Strangely, I got an erotic thrill out of the whole thing, even more so than when I had propositioned Teo in the kitchens. My sole regret was that I had left the pheasants, and while it was a minor loss compared to my triumph, I found my pride stung. By the time I had made myself the biggest, most extravagant four-egg penny bun omelette, I had decided that I would get them back. They were well hidden, six of them, not enough for the beaters to miss, or so I hoped.

The omelette was every bit as good as it should have been. I savoured every mouthful, and there was no denying that the taste was better for the knowledge that the crucial ingredient was stolen. Maybe it's a lifetime of being taught respect for property and authority, maybe I'm just a bad girl, but it was satisfying to a level I had never experienced before.

Finished, I sat down in my baroque sitting room to plot. My expedition hadn't been planned, and I could see I'd made mistakes. I'd been far too recognisable, for one thing. Marsh had seen me clearly, maybe near the cars, and definitely when I passed him on the footpath. He'd had a good view of my face, and knew what I'd been wearing. He knew I was female, slender, five foot nine, fair skinned with dark straight hair worn long. I could almost see the 'WANTED' poster. If he'd seen me, even glimpsed me, all he would have had to do was compare notes with Toby Paxham-Jennings and I would have been sunk. There would be no doubt, if no actual proof.

If I was to go again, I'd have to do better, to make sure I wasn't seen, and that if I was, I wouldn't be recognised. That meant drab clothing, camouflage gear. I didn't have any, but that was all the better. Nobody had seen me in that style, yet it was popular enough, which would tend to point suspicion elsewhere. I could pick some up in Newbury, or maybe even Reading, just to be on the safe side. I could go further. If I put my hair up under a hat, and chose a jacket and trousers a touch too large, I'd be able to disguise the shape of my hips and bum. My chest might need binding and I'd have to do something to my face, but with a bit of effort I would be able to pass for a boy – a poacher boy!

When there's skulduggery afoot, the culprit is always assumed to be male. If he proves to be a she, surprise and shock are expressed and a Svengali is sought for to explain her depravity. If I could play on that, I would be safe just so long as I wasn't caught, and for all Marsh's height, he was built for power rather than speed.

It had to be done.

I spread the remaining ceps to dry in the pantry, briefly consulted my telephone directory, rang for a taxi and snatched a quick shower as I waited for it. The shop was in a Reading backstreet, sandwiched between a greasy-spoon café and an industrial unit. The front was so hung with military gear I could barely see the window display, and inside were several young men lounging around a counter, everyone in full camouflage gear, including webbing belts, all sorts of leather and canvas straps I wasn't at all sure of the purpose of, and in one case a helmet covered in netting.

If some people's idea of a good time is to pretend to be soldiers that's fine by me, and they certainly looked pleased to see me, although I wasn't sure if that was because I was female or merely a customer. One, taller than the others and with a mop of unruly blond hair, stood up.

'Can I help you, miss?'

'Yes. I want to buy some camouflage gear.'

He must have been expecting me to ask directions, because his face lit up and for a moment his eyes even moved up from my chest. The others took notice too, almost scrambling over themselves in their eagerness, which was amusing, and satisfying too. Tall Blond responded.

'What are you thinking of? Field? Desert? Polar? Or are you after an army style? You'd look great in German greys.'

'She'd look great in a old sack,' the one with the helmet on chirped up and they all laughed dirtily.

I gave him a smile as it was, after all, intended as a compliment, ignored the temptation to enquire what he thought I'd want polar or desert camouflage for, and explained my needs.

'Something for woodland, and for this season. Maybe a bit like the colour of my sweater?'

'Going paintballing?'

'Yes.'

I'd answered quickly, without really thinking about it, because I could hardly explain that I wanted the outfit to make myself a better poacher. The one who'd asked, a stocky youth with sergeant's stripes on his jacket, made to say something else, but was interrupted by my Tall Blond.

'Good colour, sure, but you need to break your outline up. I've got just the thing, but . . .'

He stopped, looking embarrassed for no obvious reason. The fourth of them, a skinny individual with braces on over his camouflage shirt, chimed in.

'It's all blokes' stuff, the woodland. We've got field in girlie style, if you want?'

'No thanks, woodland is what I need. What colours?'

Tall Blond answered me, a little more confident now.

'The best are black, rusty brown and dull green. Those work 'cause you've got to stay down low, see, to blend in with the ground as much as the foliage.'

'I see. That sounds about right. Can I try on some trousers and a jacket?'

'Sure ... yeah, out the back.'

He pushed through a doorway closed off by a camou-flage-netting drape hung with plastic ivy. I followed, catching a remark from Braces as I went.

'You want to watch him, love. Half a chance and he'll have more than just your trousers off.'

Helmet and the Sergeant laughed. Tall Blond told them to shut up, his immediate desire to defend me really rather amusing. There was no cubicle, not even a draped-off area, just lines of clothes racks packed together and each one hung with army gear of every conceivable type, from drab-looking work suits to smart dress uniforms. Tall Blond pulled one rack out from among the others, almost upsetting them in his eagerness, and made a slightly embarrassed gesture to them and quickly left the room.

His attitude was really rather sweet, as if I was some fragile and temperamental animal, but it was Braces' remark about getting more than just my trousers off that had stuck in my head. Braces was brash, a typical Jack the lad, and just the sort to boast about his conquests and make up extra ones to order, or all of them. My Tall Blond was shy by comparison, and it was easy to imagine Braces telling him how to behave with women, perhaps even boasting of what he would have done with me. It was just an idle thought, but it put a smile on my face as

I pulled my jumper up and off, then sat down on a chair to do my bootlaces.

The clothes they suggested looked ideal, especially to achieve my boyish look, and by good fortune I wasn't even going to have to explain why I wanted male clothing. Once I was down to my bra and knickers I chose a set, only to find I couldn't get the trousers up over my hips properly. My second choice was better, although still a little tight over my bum, while I was going to need a belt to make the waist. The jacket was pretty baggy though, and I was sure it would conceal my chest.

There was a tall dusty mirror at the far end of the room, stuck to a door, but not a great deal of light, with a dim light bulb and a few streaks of bright sunlight filtering through from the main shop. I stood to admire my look, and as I did so, one of the little spots of sunlight reflected from behind me winked out, appeared again and winked out once more. Only then did I realise that the boys in the shop were strangely silent.

Immediately I was sure they were watching me change, one of them anyway. My first reaction was annoyance, then embarrassment, mainly at the way I'd been wiggling about trying to get the over-tight trousers up, with my bum sticking out right at my watchers and only covered by pretty brief knickers.

Somehow I was absolutely sure it was Braces who was watching. It just had to be, he was that type. He would boast about it too, which was much more annoying than being watched. After all, I'd just been in knickers and bra, so what?

So he was probably going to be wanking his little cock over what he'd seen, describing my body to his mates and generally being smug, maybe even saying he could have had me if the others hadn't been there. That really was a bit much, and even as I shrugged the jacket off again I'd decided to burst his bubble. It just had to be done. I called out.

'Could you come in, please?'

My Tall Blond appeared, just as I was pushing my trousers down, and did the most wonderful double take. I went on, as if undressing in front of strange men was the most natural, ordinary thing in the world.

'This is great, just what I want. How much for the set?'

'Thirty-six quid.'

There was no time for subtlety or flirting. I pulled myself up on tiptoe to whisper into his ear.

'How about a nice suck of your cock instead?'

As I drew back, I gave him a wink and a smile. He just stood there, red-faced and gaping like a cod, but he was not trying to get away. I was laughing inside as I pulled the chair around to make absolutely sure that all Braces got to see was his friend's rear view and my head bobbing up and down, and sat down. Tall Blond sighed deeply as I drew his fly down, either in pleasure or amazement.

It might have been Braces who was watching, but my boy had been thinking about me. His cock was already half stiff, with a big, meaty head poking out from the foreskin. He was very smooth too, his skin deliciously silky, and it was no hardship at all to pop him into my mouth and start sucking.

In fact, it was a serious pleasure and, as he grew in my mouth, I was rapidly starting to feel naughty. I do like cock sucking, the taste of man, and the feel of that firm, stiff shaft in my mouth, and the knowledge that any man who I do it to will be an absolute puppy dog for me. Now, I wasn't just sucking on a good-looking young man's cock, but I was being watched by his jealous friend, friends even. That made it so much better, and so did the situation, with him in his combat gear and me in nothing but my panties and bra. It was so naughty in fact that he was fully hard while I had one hand between my thighs, stroking the front of my panties.

I had to come, and I couldn't see why I shouldn't do it. Braces would be so jealous, knowing that I'd not only sucked his friend off but got horny over doing it, horny enough to want to come myself. I'd make a show of it, really rub it in, make sure he knew exactly what I was doing but never got a really good view. Still sucking, I put my hands to my breasts, stroking to feel my nipples through the material of my bra, then pulling it up to spill them out into my hands, bare and heavy and sensitive.

Being bare felt better still, and it was the work of an instant to push my panties down to my knees, but no more, because I wanted the feel of being in dishevelled clothing, showing everything, yet not nude. My Tall Blond saw, and made to open his jacket, but I stopped him with a gesture. That was best, me near naked and him in combats with his cock and balls stuck rudely out of his fly for me to play with.

I moved closer, once more slipping my hand between my thighs, this time to the soft warm bulge of my cunt. Cupping one breast so that I could stroke my nipple, I began to masturbate, and to think of how naughty I was being, sucking a man's cock as his friends watched.

He was getting excited, moaning and pushing himself into my mouth, but I badly wanted to come first, still with his erection to suck on. Bracing myself, I began to rub harder, revelling in the feel of cock in my mouth, his heat, his excitement. He reached down to grab at his shaft and tug, furiously, full into my mouth. I tried to protest, pulling back, only for his cock to jerk in his hand and fill my mouth with hot, thick sperm, one eruption, then another, as I sucked it back in my mouth, still rubbing myself hard as I let him drain himself into me. I had to come, then and there, and I was still rubbing as he stood away, grinning down at me happily.

'Wow, that was great!'

'Fucking right!'

I nearly jumped out of my skin at the second voice. Tall Blond had moved back, and behind him were the others, all three of them, staring lecherously at me as I sat there with everything on show, my fingers still pushed deep between my pussy lips. It was Braces who had spoken, and he was in front, squeezing a very obvious bulge in his uniform trousers. Tall Blond spoke, coming to my rescue.

'Hey, you guys, this isn't a peep show!'

Braces answered him.

'No, it don't get that good in peep shows. Come on, babe, I . . .'

Tall Blond stepped between me and them, my knight errant. Helmet spoke.

'Aw, go on, look how up for it she is!'

They were mesmerised, like puppies whining for a treat. That decided me. I didn't want a knight errant, because I didn't want rescuing. I wanted to come, and I would be fully in control of what happened. I beckoned to Helmet.

'Come on, then.'

Tall Blond was gaping at me as he moved out of the way. Helmet came forwards, Braces with him, the sergeant behind, all three struggling with their flies. Out came their cocks, three hard poles of male flesh sticking out from among the straps and buckles of their gear, filling my head with fantasies of being molested by soldiers as I obligingly opened my mouth. Helmet put his cock in and I was sucking once more. Braces' eager hands found my breasts, squeezing and fondling, then pulled my hand onto his erect cock. The sergeant took me by the ankles, spreading my legs as he sank down to push his face into my pussy. I pulled Braces closer, to take his cock in my mouth, giving him his turn, all enmity forgotten, holding both of them and wanking them into my mouth and right at my face, the air thick with the smell of cock and excited girl.

The sergeant was being really dirty, holding my thighs up and licking me from my bottom hole to my clit, but I didn't care, the sensation far, far too good to resist. It was going to make me come, that was for sure, at any moment, my pussy tightening every time he touched at the top, bringing me higher and higher, until I could stand it no more and grabbed his head, forcing his lips hard against me to make him lick my clit.

Helmet came, deep in my mouth where I'd been rubbing his cock on the inside of my cheek, a second helping of sperm, which I swallowed even as Braces got there, right in my face, just perfect, as I started to come. I cried out in pleasure as Helmet's cock slipped from my mouth, and both of them were milking themselves over my face as I hit the most wonderful climax, my whole body taut, each splash of come vivid in my mind as it landed on my skin.

I was snatching at my pussy even as I came, pushing the sergeant away to get my own fingers where they were needed. He stood, his erect cock rearing between my thighs, and just came, all over my cunt and all over my hand, leaving me to rub his sperm into myself as I went through my orgasm, with both the others still rubbing their cocks over my face and in my open mouth.

In the end I insisted on paying for my camouflage outfit, but that's just me. My little encounter left me feeling strong and thoroughly in control, which was just as well considering what I was going to do. I had bought a jacket and trousers in a broken pattern and colours to suit the autumn woods: black, rusty brown, dull green. That wasn't all. I'd added a drab-green balaclava and gloves, a torch with an adjustable beam and a thick belt. The rest of my accessories came from a garden centre: a sack and several balls of green twine.

The sun had already begun to sink behind the woods by the time I got back, but the moon was going to be full and I had decided to wait until nightfall anyway. So I took my time, going over my plan step by step to see if I had missed anything. It was risky, but that was the whole point. Confident or not, the thought of what I was about to do put a lump in my throat, but there was no way I was backing out. The risk was calculated, and worth it, for all I knew full well I was really doing it for the buzz. My little incident in the changing rooms had given me a cheeky confidence and I wanted to add to it by carrying out my plan that night.

By the time I was dressed and ready, I really looked the part. If I'd met myself unexpectedly I'd have screamed. Just stepping outside was a thrill. It was dark, just, with a fat moon already above the trees. There was a risk of cars in the lane, and I had no idea if Emma was planning to come up after work, so I slipped directly into the woods. It was darker still beneath the trees, near pitch-black, but I had it all worked out. There was an old field boundary, with bigger trees on a ridge of earth, and I followed it, only flicking my torch on occasionally to check the map.

There was apprehension at first, instinctive, at the dark loom of trees and the sudden noises: the unexpected bark of a fox in the distance or the clatter of a roosting pheasant's wings. As I pushed deeper in, it faded, until I myself felt part of the woodland night. My sight had adapted, and I stopped using the torch, but moved forwards with slow, even motions.

Again and again I stopped, seeking any sound that did not fit in, any hint of torchlight through the trees. There was nothing, and my confidence grew slowly until I was certain that I was the only human being out in the woods. Marsh would be in his cottage, Toby with his guests, leaving the woods to me. All I had to do was follow the gentle slope I had reached down to the stream, turn right until I found the line of great beeches and my pheasants, and return as I had come.

That was how I planned it, and how it would be, but as I moved slowly through the darkness, my imagination had begun to weave a different story. In it, Marsh would be in the woods, coming back from his shrine, his head full of pagan thoughts, and lust. He would meet me, but there would be no angry accusation, no mumbled excuses. We would both know. Not a word would be spoken as he led me by the hand to the great tree. We would strip naked, heedless of the chilly night, to have passionate, unrestrained sex down on the leaf litter in front of his altar.

It was enough to make me briefly touch myself between my legs, my eyes closed as I rubbed myself through my camouflage material. For a moment I considered masturbating, for the joy of being bare and naughty in the woods, to give my orgasm in honour of the spirit of the place. Only the cold stopped me, but I promised myself a long, lazy session once I was home.

I reached a path, a section I didn't know, and crossed carefully, wary of Marsh's traps. That sparked a new, and dirtier fantasy, of being caught and given the choice of sex or being marched straight to the police station. I would choose sex, and get it, rough and hard, down on my back in the mud of the path with Marsh's cock pumping between my open thighs, deep inside me.

That was too much for me. I just had to do it, cold or no cold. The ground dropped away beyond the path, a bank, and I could hear the gurgle of the stream below me. Down in the dell I was completely sheltered, yet that did nothing to diminish the delicious sense of daring as I pushed my trousers and panties hurriedly down to my ankles and sank into a squat, the air cold on my bare bum, my skin prickly with goose pimples as I slipped one hand underneath myself to stroke.

I closed my eyes, knowing I had to be quick as I focused on my fantasy. He'd catch me, find I was a girl, make his dirty suggestion. I'd accept, and in moments I'd be down on his cock, made to suck him hard with my breasts pulled out and my trousers and panties down to show off my body. He'd stiffen quickly, his cock growing to a vast, rigid pole of flesh in no time at all, so thick I could barely open my mouth around it, his taste thick, animal.

The moment he was hard I'd be pushed over onto my bottom in the mud, my thighs spread as he mounted me, his heavy, powerful body settling onto me, his monstrous cock probing for my cunt, finding the hole, slipping up me, filling me right to the top of my head, pumping furiously into me as I gasped and screamed beneath him, and coming, filling me with spunk, huge amounts of it, a quantity only a man so, so virile could possibly make, to leave me fucked and gasping in the mud . . .

I came, and had to bite my lip hard to stop myself from screaming, then clutched at a nearby tree to keep my balance. That just made it last longer, on and on as I teased my clit with little flicks, each and every one bringing me a new, tiny peak as the fantasy ran over and over in my head, caught and fucked by Marsh, rough and hard in the mud.

When I finally managed to get my senses together and tidy up, I turned along the stream, moving north and watching for the field they had been shooting in. Soon I could see it, a broad wash of moonlit silver through the trees, with Marsh's cottage a square black bulk beyond, unlit.

That made me pause, wondering if he was out on an evening inspection of the woods. It was possible, but I was sure he'd take a torch, and that I'd see him in time to hide. Only if he had a dog would I be in trouble. I knew he might, and paused, wondering if I should go back. Yet the silence was near absolute, broken only by the faintest of noises among the trees and the dull, background drone of the motorway.

I moved on, reaching the open wood where the ceps grew. I moved forwards slowly, biting my lip, my eyes flicking again and again to the cottage. I began to think of excuses instead of erotic fantasy, each less likely to impress anyone than the last. Halfway, I began to examine the weird dark shapes that marked the holly trees.

They had looked different in the day, and my anxiety grew as one after another drew blank. I began to wonder if the beaters had taken my cache after all, but went on, until at last I was sure I was beyond the point at which I'd fled. Frustration welled up, but I was determined, and began to search again, this time risking brief flashes of my torch. The third tree I tried was the one – the pheasants were exactly as I'd left them.

Working by touch, I began to push them into my sack, quickly filling it, with the longer tail feathers still poking from the neck as I tied it off. I had my haul and turned back, smiling to myself in triumph only to freeze at a sudden shout from behind me.

'Who's in there?'

I jerked around, just as a torch came on at the top of the field, the beam powerful enough to send patches of rich yellow flickering among the trees around me. I got down, flat. It was Marsh, in his garden, the beam coming from beyond his hedge, bright, then blinding as it swept over me. I stayed down, praying he would give up.

No such luck. I heard the creak and clack of a gate being opened and closed, and he was coming, striding down across the field right towards me. Excuses forgotten, erotic daydreams forgotten, I flicked my torch on and ran.

'You, stop!'

It nearly froze me, just from the command in his voice, but I forced myself on, hurling myself between two huge beeches and into the deep wood. Again he shouted. Again I just ran harder, pell-mell across the thick leaf litter, holly branches lashing at my legs. Abruptly, the undergrowth got thicker, forcing me to slow. Fear took me, a tight feeling in my throat, and panic as I heard the splash of his boots in the stream.

He was gaining fast, his torch on my back, as I struggled with the branches and brambles. Then the way was open as I hit the track, nearly going down as my foot sank into soft black mud. Ahead was dense scrub, impenetrable. Marsh was just metres behind me. There was no going back. I dashed down the track, knowing I'd be in full view when he reached it, sure he was stronger, faster, sure he could catch me. Ahead was the enclosure, pheasants scattering in a flurry of feathers, calling and clucking. Something touched to my waist, taut for an instant, then gone.

An ear-splitting roar caught me like a blow, my muscles jerking in shock. I tripped, went down, my fear turning to raw terror as for one horrible moment I thought I'd been shot. Even as I sprawled in the mud, I realised that I had only set the poacher trap off, but it didn't matter. I was caught, slipping in wet muck as I struggled to rise. Marsh was yelling out behind me, closing, snatching at me even as I found my feet, his fingers brushing my arm.

Burning pain slashed across my buttocks. I screamed, staggered, caught myself and I was running again, in blind panic, my muscles on fire, my heart hammering. I passed the caravan, leapt the fallen tree. Marsh cursed, crashing after me into the undergrowth, too big, too heavy, his jacket catching as I ducked low to nip in among the young trees, and I was free.

I didn't stop even to catch my breath until I was back in the cottage with the door securely bolted behind me. Then I just collapsed down on my knees on the hallway floor, gasping for air as my pounding heart gradually slowed. There was fear and shock, but it died slowly to leave me grinning. I'd done it, I'd outrun a full-grown man six or seven inches taller than me and as strong as an ox. Suddenly, I was elated, feeling a rush of triumph at my escape but, as the raging tide of adrenaline that had sustained me slowly began to ebb, I realised that I had not come off entirely unscathed.

The pheasants were gone, and my sack, although I couldn't remember when in the chase I'd lost them. I was scratched too, but not badly. My gloves and balaclava had protected me. Several places on my body stung, but none were bleeding. My knee hurt where I'd gone down after setting off the poacher alarm. My bottom was worse, smarting badly where he had caught me with his stick.

I winced as I finally climbed to my feet. I needed to change, just in case Marsh was suspicious of me and decided to investigate. After all, he knew I had watched the end of the shoot. I also badly wanted a bath, and to inspect my bottom. The taps on, I went into the bedroom to undress, turning my back to the big mirror on the wardrobe door as I pushed down my trousers and panties.

He had caught me hard, full across both cheeks, leaving a long red welt. It stung, and I spent a moment rubbing it ruefully before I realised just how silly I looked with my trousers and panties at half mast in full camo kit and a resentful pout on my face. Not that I didn't have a right to pout.

The man I had set my sights on, the man I had fallen in lust with, to be honest with myself, had not only chased me through the woods, but taken a stick to my bottom. What might have happened if he'd caught me didn't bear thinking about. Possibly he'd have beaten me, possibly pulled my jeans and panties down to do it, possibly . . .

He'd gone too far. Rough sex is all very well, but nobody treats me like that. That I'd been pinching his stuff was no excuse. He was not the man for me after all. That hurt, and my emotions were in turmoil as I finished undressing and climbed into the bath. It was hard to come to terms with, when I had deliberately provoked him, in a way, and when he had seemed to hold so much promise. Harder still was accepting the reaction of my body. I was aching for sex.

As I lay in the hot scented water, slowly letting my aches and pains die away, I was trying to tell myself that my excitement came from the thrill of the chase and my escape, not from having some over-muscled oaf take a stick to my bum. I knew I was kidding myself, and again and again found my fingers sneaking down towards my pussy.

I never did it, even in bed, just too proud to give in to my feelings and rub myself to the orgasm I so badly needed.

5

I had two days to recover before dinner with Toby Paxham-Jennings. I spent them quietly, mulling over what had happened and the implications.

Mainly, I tried to reason away my resentment of Marsh. I told myself it was my own fault for poaching, but I still couldn't justify what had happened. I told myself he wouldn't have lashed out at me if he'd known I was a woman, but I couldn't be sure. I even told myself it had been a deliberately sexual gesture, unacceptable, but basically rough foreplay, like the way some men like to spank a girl's bottom. I knew that was rubbish.

The conclusion was always the same. Marsh was too primitive for me, too much the animal. To accept that meant I wasn't capable of handling the consequences of my own fantasies, and that galled. I had wanted to be as he was, the female counterpart to his untamed masculinity. I still did and, if I accepted that what had happened was my fault for going poaching...

It was a circular argument, with no solution. That didn't stop it from going round and round in my head.

The after-effects of my poaching foray were much the same. On the one hand, I felt I'd taken a stupid risk for very little. On the other, I'd given myself an adventure I knew would always be a happy memory. I tried to tell myself I'd stick to the one foray, and not do it again but, even as I watched the sun sink down behind the trees on the following evening, I was wishing I was out there again.

I might have given in and gone, despite being sure Marsh would be on the lookout, had not Emma turned up. She was on her own, greeting me with her big open smile, and I immediately decided to tell her about Marsh and Toby Paxham-Jennings. Not the poaching though, a secret is no longer a secret when two people know it. I came straight out with it, at least once I'd said hi, made coffee, asked after Ray, teased her about the way she squealed and generally avoided the topic for a half-hour.

'I have a confession, Emma.'

'I hope it's a dirty one. Tell.'

'Not that dirty. I went for a walk yesterday, and saw Marsh, the keeper. He's gorgeous.'

'Ian Marsh! He looks like a gorilla!'

'He does not!'

'He does so! Juliet! And there I was thinking you were such a sophisticated young lady.'

She had put on an accent, in imitation of mine. I stuck out my tongue. She shook her head and went on.

'Don't do it, Juliet. He's not your type.'

'I know. I'm not going to, but I can't help but fancy him.'

'Just don't. The guy's an arsehole.'

'Why? I mean, sure, he's a bit rough and ready, but –'

'Where do you want me to start? He's a real pig. He shot at Danny once –'

'He didn't!'

'He did. Not at him, over his head really, but it's a fucking stupid thing to do. He's supposed to have got a girl pregnant too, when he was seventeen, Luke says.'

'OK, message received, I'm best out of it. There's another thing. I'm going to dinner at Alderhouse tomorrow night.'

'You're joking!'

'No. I met Toby Paxham-Jennings. He invited me.'

'Bogus Tobus? Oh my!'

She paused to fold her arms across her chest in mock disapproval.

'So, Juliet, let me get this right. Of the two guys I said were bad news, you fancy one and you're going on a date with the other?'

'Not a date, not exactly. It's a dinner for the shooting party.'

'A date. He fancies you, face it.'

'I don't think he does, he –'

'Oh, yeah, sure! That lot are so stuck-up you'd think they had flagpoles up their arses. If he's asked you to dinner he fancies you.'

'It's not like that. Granny used to look after him.'

'I know. She said he was a spoilt brat.'

'He seems to think a lot of her.'

She made a face, paused to sip her coffee, then spoke again.

'So, are you?'

'Am I what?'

'Going to shag with him.'

'No! He's ... oh, I don't know. I can't get Marsh out of my head. You say he's called Ian.'

'Yes. Forget him, Juliet. Shag Bogus Tobus.'

'Why? I thought you hated him? You're always putting him down.'

'Sure, but if you hitch up with him, then when he gives Dad a hard time you can put his blow jobs on the ration.'

'Thanks a bunch, Emma.'

She laughed, and went on. 'What you should do, if you really want to shag yourself silly, is come down to the Royal Oak with me. Some of Ray's mates are all right. We have a great time.'

'I might, some time, thanks.'

'Ray's coming up later. All right, yeah?'

I nodded, and so was treated to the now familiar medley of pig noises that evening while I tried to sort out my emotions.

The next day I didn't even bother to get dressed, leaving Emma to deal with the animals while I wandered around the house in a bathrobe. The ceps were drying nicely but, each time I inspected them, it was impossible not to think of the rest of the crop going to waste beneath the great beeches because the Paxham-Jenningses didn't have the knowledge to make use of them. Again, I think I would have ended up going out had I not had the dinner invitation.

I wanted to shine, or at the least stand out, and it was a chance to wear one of my extra purchases, a beautiful silk dress from the 1930s. It was in sheer gossamer, sewn with silver thread into a spider's web pattern, completely see-through, but with a lining of the palest dove-grey silk. The first impression was of elegance, but it was actually distinctly provocative, with the centres of the webs positioned to focus on the wearer's breasts, lower regions, and, at the back, her bottom.

Silk stockings worked beautifully, and I had also picked up a pair of long lace gloves, which not only matched the dress perfectly, but would hide the tell-tale scratches from my poaching expedition. I had to wear the Victorian combinations underneath, nothing else would have been right and, for all the lace around the legs, they were light enough not to show through. A grey silk shawl, silver leather slippers and a tiny clasp bag completed my look, but left me with the practical problem of getting there.

My footwear was less than suitable for a three-quarter-mile hike down a muddy lane, yet I wanted to arrive in style, and could hardly change out of walking boots in the hall. Making a taxi come five miles to take me less than one seemed silly, so I got Emma to give me a lift in the tractor. Fortunately nobody saw and, at precisely a quarter to eight, I was climbing down from the cab onto the strip of tarmac outside their driveway.

I'd only ever seen the front of Alderhouse from the lane and my impression was of a big, block-shaped building, pretty well symmetrical, save for the spread of ivy and Russian vine across the face. Closer, and better able to study it, I realised that there was a large, single-storey wing hidden by trees, and a much newer building in behind.

Like so many local buildings, it was mainly built of brick and flint, but the cornerstones and steps were of stone, sandy in both colour and texture. The ivy and vine, yews and ornamental pines added to the air of old-money respectability, which for all I knew was genuine. As I walked through the gates, a final touch was added by the sight of a male peacock strutting proudly across a section of lawn.

Toby Paxham-Jennings greeted me himself, in full black tie, from brilliantly polished leather shoes to neatly tied bow. He was full of smiles, and slightly shy, which made me wonder if Emma wasn't right after all. Toby's mother, Elizabeth, was also there. A tall woman, taller than me, very elegant, and I thought slightly chill, until she greeted me with the warmest of smiles. I was ushered in, my coat taken by a maid, and kissed on both cheeks by Donald Paxham-Jennings. For one horrible moment, I thought he was going to make some embarrassing remark about my childhood misdemeanour but, if he recognised me, he kept it to himself. He still made me feel small and, as they ushered me deeper into the house,

I kept expecting him to round on me and deliver a sharp lecture on the subject of my lack of respect and general moral delinquency.

The dining room was in the new part of the house – a long, high-ceilinged chamber lit by two beautiful chandeliers, beneath which the mahogany table was spread with silver, crystal, immaculate white linen and a gorgeous array of flowers. It was hard not to be impressed, and I found myself hoping that the food and wine would live up to the decor.

The company certainly did. If the house spoke of old money, then the opposite was true of the guests. Like their cars, they were shiny, expensive and new or, at least, less than ancient. They seemed to have raided the City, as one after another I was introduced to bankers, brokers, and people who did complicated things with money that I didn't even want to try and understand. Only two were female, both prime examples of slim, blonde everywoman, and both from the City.

That left enough good-looking, available and wealthy young men to send your average Bridget Jones clone into multiple orgasms. Many were also suave, witty, fashion conscious and intellectual, not to say vain, arrogant or self-obsessed. By contrast, Toby was positively earthy, and after my second glass of *Grande Marque* champagne I found myself wondering if he was such a bad choice after all. He could at least engage me in conversation, or rather, in conversation I actually wanted to listen to. There were place cards, and mine was next to Toby's right at the centre of the table. Maybe Emma was right!

So I allowed him to steer me among the others, and made no effort to play down the implication that I was with him. When the time came to sit down, he even held my chair out for me, an unexpectedly courteous gesture even from him. Impressed, and looking forward to being served a fine meal rather than cooking one for a change, I sat down.

I was to be disappointed, not by Toby, but by the food. They'd hired caterers, who plainly thought they knew what they were doing, or at least were keen to give that impression, but didn't. We started with squares of salmon fillet, very simply and neatly served with slices of lemon and lime, and pretty well tasteless. The wine was a Gewurztraminer from the biggest of the Alsatian co-ops, and worked only in that it had as little flavour as the salmon. I refrained from commenting, telling myself it would be impolite and that as the food wasn't actually inedible I should be grateful. That was until Toby commented on it.

'Hmm, delicious. Simplicity is the key, don't you think, Juliet?'

I couldn't resist the bait.

'I'd agree, with really good salmon, yes, but this is farmed ... sorry, I don't mean to be rude.'

'Oh.'

There was disappointment in his voice, hurt even, and I was immediately trying to justify myself.

'Sorry, Toby, that was rude. Before I moved into the cottage, I was training to be a chef, and when it comes to quality I'm afraid I'm a bit of a fanatic ... a snob, maybe.'

Immediately, he was all smiles, and trying to take the blame onto himself.

'No, no, not at all. I see what you mean, and, well, yes, a good rod-caught salmon, excellent.'

'It would be better.'

'Yes, but it's all down to what's practical. We use a catering firm in Reading, and they're certainly efficient, but what with having to work in bulk –'

'In bulk? This isn't bulk, Toby. There are only, what, twenty-five of you?'

'Twenty-three, twenty-six counting family, then there's the occasional guest such as yourself, and a –'

'Let's say thirty. That's not bulk catering. Bulk catering is when you're supplying a school or a hospital or something. With a group like this, I might be a bit stretched on my own, but with one assistant it would be easy. As for the ingredients, they're just cutting costs, or you are.'

I deliberately made it a joke, finishing with a light laugh, which fortunately sank in.

'Not us, that's for sure. Our reputation relies on providing luxury, and we charge accordingly.'

He leant close to continue.

'I sometimes think half these people wouldn't come if we didn't.'

I nodded in understanding, having seen flash customers walk into The Seasons and demand 'the most expensive champagne'. With that attitude, it's very tempting indeed to put the prices up – right there. Toby's mouth flicked briefly into a conspiratorial smile.

Suddenly there was a bond between us, a sense of shared feeling. I found myself smiling back as a warm flush spread across my chest. The man beyond him asked a question about the next day's shoot and Toby turned to address him, leaving me to myself.

The main course was served, this time a choice, with roast leg of lamb or pheasant, along with some vegetarian pap. Both meats were served from the bone at table, and I chose the pheasant despite the slightly squashed shape of the bird betraying the fact that it had been frozen. That seemed bizarre on an estate set up for shooting and, once I'd taken a mouthful and committed infanticide with a *Cru Bourgeois*, I questioned Toby.

'Why freeze your pheasants?'

'The pheasants? Oh, these aren't from the estate. The caterers bring everything in themselves.'

I could only laugh, barely able to believe what I was hearing. Toby spoke again, now a little defensive.

'It's in the contract.'

'In the contract?'

'Yes.'

'So, you have what, fifty, sixty pheasants shot every day, and –'

'Over a hundred often enough. We breed our own, you see. The keeper releases enough to keep us going, just before the shoot, and the beaters drive them towards the line, at an angle naturally. You can't go around shooting the help these days, you know.'

He gave a dry laugh, cut it off abruptly and spoke again.

'Sorry, not funny. One of Daddy's jokes.'

'Whatever. So you take several hundred pheasant in a week, but you're eating frozen birds? What do you do with your own?'

'Sell them, if we can, but there really isn't the demand, so it's hardly worth the trouble. Our keeper gets rid of the rest.'

It was as I had feared. I shook my head, but without the anger I'd expected. Warmth, food, wine and male attention made the sharp reaction I'd felt in the woods impossible. Toby was oblivious.

'Not good then, the pheasant?'

'Frozen meat is never good, Toby. Freezing destroys the cell structure. And it hasn't been hung properly. Sorry.'

'Don't be. So what would you do?'

'Simple. Hang them properly for a start, then prepare, trussed and stuffed, perhaps with penny buns, bard –'

'What are penny buns?'

'Ceps, *Boletus edulis*, you know, surely?'

'Yes, but they're French, aren't they? And hideously expensive. There are some limits to the budget!'

'French? No . . .'

I stopped, realising that he had no idea that his estate was alive with the things.

'OK, so maybe the ceps are a bit ambitious, but stuffed anyway, then barded with fat bacon, roasted with the breasts downwards to keep the meat as moist as possible, and serve.'

'With a sauce?'

'Just their own gravy if they're good enough, although with the birds on your estate the fat would need skimming off. You ought to put your birds on a diet, you know.'

It was supposed to be a joke, but his answer was deadly serious.

'Oh, no, they have to be like that. Otherwise the guests never hit enough to keep themselves happy.'

'Oh.'

'So you only use sauces for inferior meat?'

'I wouldn't go that far, no. Anything really good should be allowed to show its own flavour, unless you can achieve more by combining something to make it better still. But yes, with poor meat I'd use a sauce. Let's say I had to use bulk production turkey, which is about as tasteless as meat gets. Rather than presenting the meat for the sake of its own flavour, I'd use it as a vehicle for a sauce.'

'That's jolly clever.'

'It's hardly original! Think about horseradish sauce, for instance. It traditionally accompanies beef because it used to be the only thing strong enough to hide the flavour of off meat. It would be completely wrong to serve, say, a good rolled sirloin with horseradish.'

'I adore horseradish.'

'Me too, but in the right place.'

He nodded thoughtfully, then went on.

'So ... er ... if I dare ask, what did you think of the wine?'

'I don't think I should answer that.'

'Go on, I'm already shell-shocked.'

'Er ... rubbish?'

'Really? Rubbish?'

'Maybe rubbish is a bit strong, but with the champagne you're paying most of your money for the brand name. The salmon didn't have the flavour to match the Gewurztraminer, which I find a sickly combination anyway. The Médoc was good, but wasted.'

'Well, you certainly don't mince your words! I'm interested though. Why was the Médoc a waste?'

'It was too young. In ten years' time it would have been delicious. Claret needs to mature; it's in the nature of the grapes. Cabernet Sauvignon, Cabernet Franc, even Merlot – they're are all thick-skinned varieties with high pip-to-pulp ratios, and therefore a lot of tannin. That means if you're going to get any real flavour out of them the resulting wine will need time to mature. There are modern techniques to get around the tannin, but you always end up with boring wine, all fruit and no real character.'

'So what would you have served?'

'Now that's the problem. I know what I'd like to have served, but it would be prohibitively expensive. You'd be better off having a wine list with everything individually priced.'

'That's a thought, but we charge an inclusive fee, and everything comes from the caterer's list.'

'At a huge profit, no doubt.'

'I expect so. Look, I know this is a bit sudden, but I

don't suppose you'd be interested in working for us at all? As catering manageress? I freely confess I don't really know what I'm doing.'

'Thanks, but no. Believe me, I would have snapped that up like a shot just a few weeks ago, but not now. I've had it with work, at least with working for other people. No offence.'

'None taken. You're a woman after my own heart, Juliet. Do you know, in my grandfather's time the estate brought in enough income to support the family and a dozen servants. He spent his time as he pleased, shooting, hunting, taking long walks. He used to collect moths.'

He finished with a sigh, not, I was sure, out of sympathy for the moths, or any desire to collect more himself, but for his grandfather's lifestyle. He went on, as plates of cheese and bread were put out, French style, after the main course.

'Inheritance tax, they call it. Why can't they be honest and just say banditry?'

I didn't answer, taking some Stilton and a piece of French bread. I was feeling that he was being a little selfish by yearning for a lifestyle where it took a dozen underpaid servants to allow one man to do nothing more serious than persecute moths. I tried to be jolly instead.

'You seem to do well enough, even if you haven't managed to find a decent caterer.'

'Well, not bad, I suppose, but it's not the same. The estate is owned by a limited company now. That way we won't have to worry so much, although I don't quite know how it all works. So how about yourself? You've set up a rustic idyll, have you? Won't you get bored?'

'Not so far.'

'So what do you do to keep yourself amused?'

I hastily put a dangerously large piece of Stilton and bread into my mouth, being pretty certain that admitting to having taken up poaching on his land as a hobby was not the answer he was hoping for. He waited politely for me to finish my unladylike mouthful.

'This and that. It's still an adventure for me, just not having to get up in the morning. Well, not for work anyway. I have two goats and eleven chickens . . .'

I'd been going to go on, but again his attention was distracted, and he went back to playing host. I finished my bread and cheese instead, which left me pleasantly full, but it was still a shock to discover that there was no pudding. Instead, we went straight to port, with Toby and his parents politely dividing the group into smoking and non-smoking sections. Ignoring the temptation to show off by taking a cigar, I joined the non-smokers. Toby had taken his cigar, but pushed it into his pocket and followed me, obviously not keen to leave me to the attentions of other men.

He was interested, he had to be. I wasn't sure, but I didn't mind the attention, not just from him but several others. Already pleasantly drunk, warm and replete, I was soon feeling full of mischief and more than a little horny. In no time I was teasing Toby, flirting with the others but always coming back to him. By the time the party had at last begun to break up, I had three offers, and he was beginning to look very flustered. I was game, maybe, but I wanted him to make an effort if he wanted me, at least to fend off a few rival males. Eventually he managed to corner me on my way back from the loo. He was holding my coat.

'Are you ready to go home, Juliet?'

I was taken aback, having been expecting to stay until the end and then be cajoled into going to bed with him. Suddenly I wanted what I had merely been allowing myself to be led towards.

'. . . do you . . . do you want me to?'

He looked puzzled. I sighed, all thoughts of being seduced abandoned.

'OK, but . . .'

I didn't finish. As he slid my coat around my shoulders he gave me a meaningful squeeze.

'I'll see you back, of course.'

I understood, or I hoped I did. At my cottage we would be alone, completely. Then again, he might just be being gallant. I hoped he wasn't. I hoped he wanted me naked and willing and eager . . .

He led me out, steering me by my arm to the Jaguar parked among the other cars. I slipped into the seat as he held my door, and lay back, thinking naughty thoughts about sex in cars and what it might be nice to do if it took a bit of encouragement to get him indoors.

The drive took moments, neither of us speaking, in what I dearly hoped was silent expectation. At the cottage, he parked, got out and came to my door. He looked uncertain, and I wasn't having it.

'Could you . . . could you carry me, please, Toby. I'll ruin my slippers.'

He smiled and ducked down. I was lifted into his arms, easily, but dissolved in giggles as he nearly fell trying to shut the car door with a foot. He grinned, and used my bum to barge the gate open.

'Hey!'

'Better bumped than muddy.'

He set me down in the porch. The light had come on and we were looking at each other, just inches apart, his hands still on my waist and hip. For a moment there was something between us, and he was going to speak, but hesitated. The moment broke, and what he did say was not what I wanted to hear.

'I'm sorry you didn't enjoy your meal.'

'Oh, I'm sorry, Toby. I did ... the company anyway, thanks.'

There was one of those moments, each looking at the other, neither quite sure. Then he kissed me, just gently, no more than a peck, but on my lips. A warm feeling ran through me, from my throat, down over my chest and tummy, right to my sex. I had to do it. I wanted to do it, and it had been too long. If he was going to be shy, then I couldn't.

'Would you like to come in for coffee?'

'Not for me, thanks.'

'Would you like to come in and go to bed with me?'

He didn't answer, and for one awful moment I thought I'd got it all horribly wrong. Then he came forwards and suddenly I was in his arms, his mouth pressed to mine. I responded, opening my lips to the bruising pressure, trying to slow him even as my body responded, and pulling away as he took my bottom in his hands.

'Not here, Toby. Inside.'

He nodded, grinning, but his hand found my bottom again as I pushed the key into the lock. I let him grope, feeling horny and flattered by his open, boyish enthusiasm. The door came wide and, even as we tumbled through, he was reaching for me again, this time to take hold of me from behind. He cupped my breasts, holding them firmly, as his lips found the nape of my neck. With that kiss I was his, but I managed to pull away, not so drunk that I would risk my beautiful dress.

'In the bedroom, Toby. Be patient and let me get undressed.'

'Shall I, er ... wait outside?'

I shook my head and reached out, to take him by his tie and pull him gently into the room. The tie worked loose, but he came, and I drew him to me, to kiss him again as my free hand found his crotch, to squeeze at the reassuring bulge of his cock and balls. I felt his Adam's apple bob as he swallowed, and found myself smiling in delight at his reaction. Stepping back, I put my hands to the straps of my dress and shrugged it free. He watched, his eyes fixed on my body as I let the dress slip from my shoulders.

Standing in a puddle of gossamer, I began to tug loose the laces at the front, letting my breasts push the cotton and lace apart, then fall free and bare. Again he swallowed, and his hand moved to his crotch to adjust what I could see was an uncomfortably stiff cock. I smiled and nodded to his crotch.

'Your turn.'

He grinned, mostly lust, a touch of embarrassment, but his hands went straight to the fly of his dinner suit. It buttoned, and I found myself licking my lips as they came loose to let him push one hand in and pull it all out, cock and balls too. He was a good size, if not huge, and beautiful, smooth and pale and straight. I reached out to take him in my hand, feeling how hot he was, how hard he was. His hands went to his jacket, but I shook my head.

'No, like this, please, just showing.'

It was best, with him so well dressed in immaculate black tie, but with his erection and two plump balls sticking out from his trousers. As I stroked him I went down, stepping carefully from my dress to nuzzle his cock with my face, drinking in the man smell, until I could hold off no more, and took him in my mouth.

His taste filled my head as I began to suck, revelling in the feel of having a cock in my mouth. I began to play with his balls, feeling the taut, heavy sac and teasing him with my nails. It was bliss and it would have been so easy to take him there in my mouth and drink what he had to offer as I rubbed my pussy. I wanted more though – I wanted the lovely cock in my mouth put inside me properly, into my cunt.

I rose, letting him slip from my mouth, to look into his eyes. He took me into his arms, holding me close, his hands going to my neck, to tickle, then moving lower. I cuddled into him as he began to stroke my bottom. My combinations had slipped to my waist but he made no effort to get them off, instead putting his fingers to the buttons at the rear. His hard cock was pressed against my belly, hot and solid, adding to my delicious feelings as, one by one, the buttons on my panel were opened, baring me. The last one came loose, the flap fell away, and my bottom was in his hands, his strong fingers caressing my cheeks, stealing between them. He touched my anus and I shivered with mixed apprehension and desire as I wondered if he would expect to bugger me. Then his hands were on my hips and he was trying to turn me around and, at the same time, steer me to the bed.

There was no question of how he wanted me, only what he hoped to do. I could say nothing, but gave him my best arch look and went with the pressure, down over the bed with my bottom stuck in playful display, his to enjoy as he pleased. His first response was to make a deep, guttural noise in his throat, pure passion, then to speak.

'Beautiful.'

I couldn't help but giggle, for the sheer passion in his voice at the sight of my bottom showing bare through the unfastened panel. It was a nervous giggle though, and I could feel the little hole between my cheeks twitching in my alarm. My pussy was ready, open, and badly in need, but my strongest need was to surrender. His hands found my bottom, to cup my cheeks, stroking, patting, slapping gently, and abruptly hauling them wide as his control snapped completely. I gasped as every rude detail of my bottom and sex was abruptly put on show, and again as his cock pushed firmly between my thighs to find my entrance. I pushed back to let him in, my mouth coming open with my pussy as the head of his cock nudged in.

It was my turn to show my feelings as the full, thick length of him slid into my body, stretching me, opening me, only to pull gently back. He pushed again, deeper and harder, and again, and again, faster and faster, until I was clutching at the bedclothes and panting for breath. He'd taken my hips and was holding me as we fucked, pulling me to his body, jamming himself into me, the hard muscle of his legs and belly slapping over and over on my naked bottom. For one awful yet ecstatic moment, I thought he was going to come in me and then he was out and hot fluid was pattering down on my bottom as he finished himself off over my cheeks. I slumped forwards, panting, dizzy with pleasure, my hand sneaking back to where it was wanted even as he spoke, puffing.

'I . . . I'm sorry.'

'Don't be. I don't mind. That was nice. Just let me –'

'No . . . to come so quickly . . . I –'

'That's fine, Toby. Just let . . .'

His hands took my legs, and just rolled me, over and up, presenting himself my open sex. There was no hesitation. He smiled, got to his knees, his tongue found my clitoris and I was in heaven. My hands went to my breasts, cupping them, running my fingers over the stiff, sensitive bumps of my nipples. He'd done it before, the tip of his tongue flicking at my clitoris, so fast, so firm . . .

It took just moments. I felt my pussy squeeze, my thighs tighten, and I was there, moaning aloud in my ecstasy as I came. He didn't stop, licking faster and harder as my back arched tight and my toes curled in, bringing me up and up until I could bear it no more, and screamed, a full-throated shriek of pure rapture. My legs locked around the back of his head, trapping him to me, and I was bucking on the bed, rubbing myself in his face, my fingers locked onto my breasts, my whole body agonisingly, beautifully tight and so, so sensitive as the orgasm tore through me.

I nearly fainted, my vision going to red at the high point of my climax, which broke only just in time. Toby rose as my legs came slowly open, and stood, smiling down on me, his upper lip marked with a faint white moustache of my juice. I thought of his dad's bristly white effort and giggled, opening my arms. He came in, cuddling me to himself, kissing my neck, then my mouth. I responded, lost in a golden haze of satisfaction.

6

Toby didn't sleep with me. He was expected to be back, to do his share of all the bits and pieces required of him as host. I would have preferred him to, but I didn't mind, content to cuddle together for a hour or so before he left, with the promise of more. When I finally did go to sleep, it was with a contented smile on my face.

Typically, for me, I felt less good in the morning. Toby had made it clear he wanted a relationship, and I was simply not ready. If I was with him I could hardly do a Lady Chatterley and shag Ian Marsh, and I wanted to. I wanted more than just sex, too. I wanted to understand what lay behind the keeper's rough exterior, what drove him to make offerings to a pagan deity, to share his love and understanding of the deep woods.

Being Toby's girlfriend would mean I could wander around the estate at will and, while I'd thought that was what I'd wanted, I'd been wrong. It wouldn't be the same. What I really wanted was the thrill of the forbidden, of trespassing, of poaching. If stolen food tastes sweeter, then the same food given free is sure to lack savour.

If he saw me, Marsh wouldn't chase me with sticks. On the surface, he'd be respectful, distant, polite. Underneath, he would have the same contempt for me I had perceived in his attitude to the shooting party. Once I'd identified myself with his employers, it would be far more difficult to achieve any intimacy with him, even if it wasn't sexual – maybe impossible.

Toby was nice though and I didn't want to hurt his

feelings. I didn't want to reject him at all. I did need space and, as I sat down with my robe wrapped around me and a coffee in my hand, I was thinking wistfully of college days and uncomplicated shagging. It had been so simple, with everyone more or less in the same boat; no real social barriers, not all that much jealousy. I was still thinking when Emma knocked on the window. She was holding a basket of eggs, which she put on the table as she came in.

'Coffee?'

'Yeah, slacker. What time do you call this?'

'Eleven thirty-six.'

'Good party? So what happened with Bogus Tobus?'

'Could you not call him that –'

'Ooooooh!'

'Emma!'

'So you shagged him?'

'Yes.'

'Oh, Juliet! I bet he's kinky. What's he into? Weird stuff?'

'No, he's –'

'I bet he tied you up ... No, not him, tits, I bet it's tits. He wanted to suck on you like a baby, any money!'

'No he did not!'

'Gags then? He gagged you, yeah?'

'I wish someone would gag you!'

'Bum spanking, then, and I bet you let him!'

'No! He was really sweet ... a bit obsessed with my bum, yes –'

'I knew it.'

'No, he didn't smack me or anything like that. I thought he was going to ... you know, ask for anal.'

'Up the bum? I knew it, dirty bastard.'

'No, I thought he would, 'cos he wanted me bent over.'

'They all want it doggy. That doesn't mean they're going to stick it up your bum!'

In my experience it usually did, but I could already hear her delighted laughter if I admitted it, and contented myself with sticking my tongue out at her. She went on, barely pausing, as I poured her a coffee.

'So what? Is this a big deal? Do I start saving for the toaster?'

'Not the toaster, no . . . but seriously, Emma, he's pretty keen, maybe more than I can really handle just now.'

'So keep him on a string and don't piss in your own kitchen.'

'Sorry?'

'Go out with him, and do as you like when he's not around. Who's to know, as long as you don't do it in a stupid place, like pissing in your own kitchen. Haven't you ever heard that one?'

'No. But it's not that simple. I –'

'Want to shag Ian Marsh, you said.'

I shrugged, not wanting to go into it any deeper. She finished spooning sugar into the coffee I'd given her and began to stir it. When she spoke again, she was serious.

'Marsh is bad news, Juliet. Dangerous.'

'He's rough, yes, but maybe there's more to him.'

'There isn't. Take it from me.'

Again I shrugged. She was right, he *was* dangerous. He had put a stick across my bottom, a completely unacceptable thing to do. I knew that, I was sure of that, but it didn't change my underlying instinct. I could deny myself him, but I still wanted him. I wanted him because he was dangerous.

It was only then that I realised Toby must have seen the welt on my bottom. What with the drink and my arousal, I'd forgotten all about it. The pain had died to a dull ache when I sat down on it, but there was a bruise, and Toby had had a good look, more of an inspection really. With just the light coming in from the hall it had been dim, but I knew he'd been enjoying the view. He'd seen, he had to have seen.

He hadn't said anything, but then, why should he have? He had no reason to think I'd been beaten, and would probably have been too polite to say anything if he had. More likely he'd assumed I'd had a fall, perhaps on a step. Yet if Marsh mentioned that he'd caught a poacher a blow with a stick . . .

It wasn't likely. So far as I could tell the relationship between Toby and Marsh was very much professional. Marsh was taciturn, and it was hard to imagine him describing an encounter with a poacher in such detail. It was still worrying.

Emma took a swallow of coffee, then spoke again.

'Tell him straight. Say you like a good shag but don't want to commit yourself. Tell my Ray that and he'd be well happy.'

She was right. The only thing to do was be honest with him. I would go up to the house and speak to him, making my position quite clear.

Only it would look really arrogant to try and lay down the rules when he hadn't actually said anything specific. I still wanted to go, to talk. I needed to be subtle, perhaps to encourage him and yet at the same time make it plain that I valued my freedom. Some men would go for it, others wouldn't. I wasn't sure about Toby.

'I'm not sure, Emma. That might just upset him, and I don't want that.'

'Then bollocks to him.'

I sighed. She was trying to help, and I had to admire her upfront, in-your-face attitude. Unfortunately, I just could not see Toby accepting an open relationship, least of all with me shagging his gamekeeper. I still had to talk.

Emma stayed for lunch, sharing the eggs flavoured with the ceps, fresh goat's cheese she'd made herself and herbs from the garden. By the time we'd finished and she had gone back to work, it was early afternoon. From the conversation the night before, I more or less knew the routine at Alderhouse. There would be a shoot in the morning, on one or other of three lines. Lunch followed, and the afternoon was left open, for shooting clays, rabbiting or just enjoying the facilities at the house: fishing in the lake, tennis, snooker, croquet or whatever.

I knew Toby would have finished lunch and presumably be playing host. It was dry, but very grey and, with luck, I could catch him at home. I dressed quickly in a red jumper and tight jeans, just right to show my figure without being blatant. That seemed right, and was certainly right for the weather, with a stiff breeze shaking the trees and rolling heavy clouds in from the west.

It certainly cleared the last of the cobwebs from my head, and I had soon decided that I should follow Emma's advice. After all, if he was too flaky to cope, then our relationship was sure to be a disaster anyway. I simply cannot handle men who demand constant emotional support.

I got as far as the motorway bridge before I met him coming the other way. It's odd, but there can be few more awkward moments than the first time two people meet again after their first shag. We'd parted with a kiss and cuddle. I'd been naked and not in the least embarrassed. Now, I found myself colouring up and biting my lip, but it was nothing to his reaction. He was grinning like an idiot, and could barely speak.

'I, er . . . um . . . was just coming to see you, to, er . . . thank you for last night . . . I mean, not that . . .'

He trailed off. I managed a smile.

'My pleasure.'

'We ... er ... said we'd, er ... doing something together.'

'Yes, sure. What were –'

We were interrupted by the clack of metal on wood directly behind us. Toby went abruptly quiet and the expression on his face changed. I turned, to see a man at the entrance to the footpath – Ian Marsh. Toby stepped past me.

'All done, Ian?'

'All done, sir.'

'Good. Juliet, this is Ian Marsh, who keeps for us. Quite a character is Ian.'

Marsh gave me a polite but extremely perfunctory nod. Toby spoke.

'Nothing last night, Ian?'

'Nothing, sir. I've put out two more traps, one down the side of the big enclosure, one a way down where the track used to come up this ways. That's where he came out.'

'Thank you, I'll be careful. Ian had a poacher a few nights ago, Juliet, after the pheasants from the shoot. He'd nabbed a whole bag of them!'

I had to ask. 'You caught him, then?'

Toby laughed.

'He got clean away, too fast for Ian here, I'm afraid.'

'I'll have him.'

Marsh's answer was firm, aggressive and supremely confident. The cheeks of my bottom tightened in reaction, the bruise twinged. I wanted to know more, but didn't dare ask anything specific, or risk giving away that I knew more than I was supposed to.

'Do you get many people poaching here then?'

Marsh answered first, his voice low and gruff.

'No.'

Toby expanded on the comment. 'Not any more. The locals have learnt enough respect for Ian to stay away, and there are plenty of easier pickings for the gangs who come out from the towns. This one's a cheeky sod, though. Do you know what he did?'

The question was rhetorical, I hoped.

'No.'

'He hid in the woods during the shoot, right under the guns, behind a tree. Ian found the marks of his boots. Then, once we'd gone all gone in for lunch he hid six under a holly tree and came back at night, thinking nobody would see. Ian saw his torch.'

'I did. Kid he was, nothing more. I'll have him, if he's the guts to come back.'

'A regular Sherlock Holmes, Ian is. From the size of his boots and his height we reckon he must be fourteen or so.'

I nodded thoughtfully. As I'd suspected, to them, poachers were men.

Marsh nodded, and left with the notices. Toby waited briefly before he spoke again, with a great deal more confidence than he had shown before.

'Sorry about that. As I was saying, we should go out, somewhere special. How about The Seasons? Even you won't be disappointed there.'

'The Seasons? Um ... I don't know ... I, er ... I'd love to go out somewhere, Toby, but not The Seasons.'

'No? But I would have thought it was exactly your thing. The chef, Blane, is a genius.'

'So they say, still –'

'Surely you're not going to tell me he's not up to scratch!'

His tone was close to mockery, as if it were comic for a silly little girl like me to even think of criticising the wonderful Gabriel Blane. For a moment, my anger flared, but I held it back, spilling out the only thing I could think of.

'It's not that, Toby. It's just that I'd rather be alone with you, not in a crowd. Come to me. I'll cook for you.'

'That's sweet ... I'd like that, of course, but I want to treat you. Let someone else do the hard work – Britain's top chef! The last time I was there, I had grouse served with slices of truffle under the skin and a sauce of wild blackberries. You would have loved it.'

I'd made it, sometimes, and eaten it. It was good, but a fairly basic recipe, and would almost certainly have been prepared by Anna anyway, along with the others. Blane was unlikely even to have supervised. It was phoney as well, or at least not to the standard Blane liked to claim. He used Chinese truffles and the blackberries were varietals from a farm in Kent. I wasn't going to point that out.

'I like to cook, Toby, and I can do as well as Blane.'

His answering smile was amused and more than a little condescending, the response of an indulgent grown-up to a little girl pretending to be a princess.

'I can, try me!'

He didn't answer immediately. I could tell what he was thinking. He wanted to tell me I couldn't possibly achieve Blane's standards, that I was getting way above myself. Not being a complete idiot, he didn't, but the little nod he gave before he finally replied said it all.

'Very well then, you're on, but I insist on contributing.'

'No, leave it to me, everything.'

'Well ...'

'No male chauvinist piggery, please, Toby. Just let me treat you.'

This time his smile was sincere.

'Monday then? The shooting party goes back Sunday evening and we get a new lot Friday.'

'Make it Wednesday then, there are some things I need to get. I'd better go now, I promised to meet my friend Emma in Ilsenden.'

'Emma Thompson, from Bourne Farm?'

'Yes.'

'Oh, right. See you later then.'

He stepped close to kiss me, and I responded, but my feelings were more than a little mixed as I walked away.

Having told him I was going to Ilsenden, I had to at least continue that way, and he walked with me as far as the house. I continued, sure he'd see if I turned back. I had no idea where I was going, but I was content just to walk and think. It was a complete lie about Emma, but it revealed one thing: Toby didn't approve of her. Again, he'd been tactful, but again his true reaction had shown in his face. True, there was a bit of a boundary feud between their families, but that was no reason to look down on her. His remarks about Blane rankled too, and I was determined to show him he was wrong, and to get one over on him at the same time. Not only would I surpass anything Blane could do, but every single course would feature something stolen from the estate, without exception.

Toby's behaviour wasn't the only reason I wanted to pinch things from the estate. I wanted to prove to myself I could do it too. Marsh had been so sure of himself, so dismissive. That had annoyed me despite the fact that just being near him made me feel wet. Having actually spoken to him, my feelings towards him had become stronger than ever, and more ambiguous. He displayed a raw, crude aggression I should have despised, yet which spoke straight to my instincts. At once, he made me want to walk away in contempt, and to offer myself for entry.

I tried to tell myself that Toby was far more suitable for me, far more my type of man. It was true, in a sense.

Certainly my mother would have agreed. Toby was a bit arrogant, but basically nice, and safe, with just an edge of rudeness in bed to make him interesting. Marsh was anything but nice, dangerous even, but so intensely male, and so mysterious.

Without that air of mystery he would have been just one more big lunk, a slab of man-flesh appealing to my own base instincts but no more. There was more, I knew. He worshipped at a pagan shrine, and that meant a depth far beyond what his exterior suggested, and an understanding of his link with nature that echoed my own feelings. I knew it was foolish, but I wanted to be involved, to get closer, even if only to challenge him, to force him to notice me.

So I was going poaching again, and this time I would plan thoroughly.

I did, as I walked back to the cottage in a big easterly loop, taking nearly an hour. The first thing I had to consider was what was available. It would have to be regional, and seasonal too, so I'd be following Gabriel Blane's philosophy, which was only right if I intended to outshine him.

At minimum I would have to offer the conventional three courses, but that was not enough. Blane usually offered four, so I would do five ... no, six. That meant I could use a classic English formula, with soup, fish, game, a main course, dessert and cheese. That meant I needed to pinch six separate ingredients from the estate.

The soup was simple enough. I had excellent vegetables in my own garden and could steal some parasols, or chanterelles, even *Conocybe*, which might make the after-dinner entertainment interesting. Fish was not so easy. I could buy something and put the stolen ingredient in a sauce, but that didn't satisfy. The lake behind Alderhouse was stocked for the guests, with carp mainly, but even if I ended up serving goldfish I was determined it would come from there, and get Chamborded.

Then there was the game. There was no point in taking pheasants as they wouldn't have time to hang properly, and in any case I had the brace Emma had brought me. They'd been just about ready anyway, and were now filling the pantry with a good, rich aroma, so would do nicely as my game course. I could experiment with one, and serve the other. Not that they counted as poached. Luke had shot them on his father's land, which was his right. The ceps did count, and I could use them in the same way Gabriel Blane used the truffles, cutting slices and feeding them in under the skin of the breasts and thighs.

If my game course mimicked the grouse recipe, and was perhaps less grand, I would need something both exotic and exquisite for the main course. That way I could present Toby the pheasant, serving it with a fruit sauce and allowing him to believe it was the top of my form and not quite to Blane's standard, then amaze him.

The question was, how?

To start with, I needed meat. There were plenty of animals in the woods, Ian Marsh for one, but cannibalism would be pushing my luck and human flesh is said to taste rather dull anyway! My principles also kept foxes and badgers safe, as both are supposed to be inedible. I was sure there would be fallow deer, and possibly munt-jac, but I didn't dare risk borrowing a gun with Marsh around, and I just couldn't see myself hunting one down with a home-made spear. There was no time to hang the meat anyway. I briefly considered hedgehog baked in clay, but realised I was too soft to do it. Rabbit was simply too dull; hare better but not easy to catch.

Eventually I put the problem aside to focus on the last two courses. For dessert there was only one choice. Emma and her brothers had scrumped quinces. So could I, just so long as there were any left on the tree. If not, I could revise my plans, but the chance of serving a steamed quince pudding was far too good to pass up. Cheese was simple enough. Emma was using the goats' milk to make her delicious soft goat's cheese. Serving it with slices of fresh – and stolen – apple would round the meal off perfectly.

By the time I got back to the cottage I was beginning to baulk a bit at the sheer scale of what I was trying to do. For a moment I considered setting it aside as a hopeless pipe dream, or scaling it down, but the memory of Toby's knowing little smirk and Marsh's arrogant certainty wouldn't go away. I am nothing if not obstinate.

So I spread my map out on the table and began to plot, marking the boundaries of the estate, the locations I needed to visit, my best routes for access, the places I knew Marsh had set poacher traps, and more. With just four nights and a waning moon I needed to get a move on, but I also needed to scout.

I'd need daylight to get the fungi, but I could stick to the borders of the woods, where there was sure to be something edible. Sunday would do nicely. It seemed sensible to try and do the fruit and the fish at the same time, but I had no idea where either the trees or the lake were. That meant a visit to Alderhouse, which was easy enough to arrange. I would go and see Toby on Monday once the shooting party had gone and make my raid that night.

It was going to be risky so close to the house, and I knew I'd have to approach from the back. I could safely assume that there would be no poacher's traps in the actual garden, and it seemed highly unlikely they'd have the lake or fruit trees alarmed. Dogs were a problem, or at least a potential problem because, while I hadn't seen any, it seemed likely they had some. That wasn't the only noisy animal either . . .

Suddenly, I had my main course, a centrepiece to surpass anything Gabriel Blane had ever done – peacock.

I would serve it in the medieval style, a cock bird, with the feathers set in full display. I could bard and lard with dry-cure bacon. The giblets would go with some of my ceps towards the richest possible stuffing. I had beech-wood, I had calcareous soil, just possibly I could even find summer truffles to go with it, creating a dish at once so extravagant and so utterly delicious that Toby would be left speechless.

There was only one drawback. Toby might not be the sharpest card in the pack, but if one of their peacocks went missing and I served him peacock just two nights later, even he was sure to spot that something was going on. Finally I had to abandon the idea: not the recipe, which was a must, but serving it to Toby. I'd invite my parents instead and show Dad that I hadn't entirely wasted my education.

It was a nuisance though, because there was simply nothing else that could be guaranteed to be beyond what Gabriel Blane had achieved. He had served lampreys, swan, even ortolan if the rumours were true. In fact, he had probably done peacock, if not to the full medieval recipe. I had to face it. He had served everything.

Only he hadn't. There was one thing he would never be able to serve. Suddenly I had my main course.

It was perfect, and put me right in the mood for my first expedition on the Sunday morning. Emma had slept over in the caravan, and I chatted to her and Ray over coffee, bacon and eggs. Only when they were safely gone did I start to prepare.

In broad daylight, and with Marsh on the lookout, I

had to be clever. I needed some sort of fungi other than ceps, and fruit. The fungi was just a matter of patience. The fruit was trickier. I couldn't use blackberries because Blane had for his grouse and most now had the devil in them. Most other soft fruit was over. There would still be apples and pears, and a few of the latest varieties of plum, such as the ones in Ian Marsh's garden.

It was risky, very risky, but to succeed would be so satisfying. So I dressed in my full poaching gear and stuffed a baggy jumper and my longest, loosest skirt into a bag, along with various bits of equipment. I could hear the shooting in the lower field about Emma's dad's property, and I knew it would mean Marsh either had to come up through the woods or along the road to get back to his cottage.

Taking no chances, I followed the route I had taken before, along the old field boundary, and got lucky. The bank was thick with moss and fungi, including chanterelles. Deeper in, there was a plump young Chicken of the Woods growing on an oak, not something I'd have thought of, but good. I cut it free and wrapped it carefully in cloth, then continued until I could peer out at the road on the far side of the shallow valley. I waited, crouched down among the thick bushes, listening to the guns until they at last fell silent. Ten minutes later, some cars went past, then Marsh appeared, walking along the road. I moved quickly, down to the enclosure and along the side. Just as Marsh had said, there was a poacher trap set up, well concealed between the wire and a straggling thorn bush.

I put the safety catch on and quickly scooped puddle water into one of the pheasant feeders. A quick search found me a log a touch lighter than the water-filled feeder, and I joined the two with a line. With agonising care I suspended the log directly over the tripwire on the poacher trap, positioned the feeder and twisted open a tiny hole where the zinc plates overlapped. As water began to seep slowly from the feeder I took the safety catch off once more.

I ran up the track and into the concealment of the stand of young pines. There I stopped, just short of the road, to pull on my jumper and skirt, peel off my balaclava, shake out my hair, and he was a she once more. Only then did I move slowly closer to Marsh's cottage, until I could glimpse the door while I ducked down safely among the pine trunks.

Again I settled down to wait, knowing perfectly well what was about to happen, but I still jumped when the cartridge went off. That left me with all the adrenaline I needed, and I was fidgeting and biting my lips as I waited for what seemed an eternity before Marsh's door swung open.

He came out, stick in hand, face set in determination, and loped off down the track and out of sight. I started forwards immediately, checking the road, jumping down from the low bank, and trying my best to look casual as I strolled the road and nipped into his garden.

There were the plums, big, red, more than fully ripe, doubtless packed with flavour, and a good three feet out of my reach. I was not giving in that easily. He had a trestle by the door. I hauled it over, to climb up, balance precariously on the top, snatch at the nearest plum, and lose my balance, coming down hard on my bum in the wet grass as overripe fruit rained down on top of me.

I grabbed up as many as I could and stuffed them into my bag, leaving quality control to a more convenient moment. Returning the trestle, I made for the gate, certain that the entire Paxham-Jennings clan and all their guests would be choosing that moment to visit the keeper's cottage.

They weren't and, a moment later, I was out in the road, unseen. I glanced at my watch as I set off up the road with my precious cargo. From the moment I'd first seen Marsh to leaving his cottage just fourteen minutes had elapsed. It had felt more like fourteen hours.

I got my rush, with a vengeance, and it was a real struggle not to skip and sing and generally make an exhibition of myself as I walked up the road. Mr oh-so-confident Ian Marsh would be scratching his head in the woods while I strolled off with my loot. At least, he'd be scratching his head until he found the remains of my timing device, after which he'd be hopping mad and rushing around in circles trying to find out what had happened while he was distracted. Given the amount of plums I'd brought down when I fell, he would probably figure it out, and he was certainly going to be on the alert. That didn't matter. The last place I was going was into his woods.

Monday started easily enough. I walked over to Alder-house in the morning and spent a pleasant couple of hours with Toby and his parents. Rain was threatening, but it took only a slight hint to persuade Toby to come outside for a cuddle on the pretext of showing me the garden, or rather, to come outside and show me the garden on the pretext of having a cuddle. It was a nice cuddle too, with his hands on the nape of my neck and curved under my bottom, tickling and kneading as we kissed.

I'd have gone further if he'd wanted to, and if it had been safe, but I couldn't see Donald and Elizabeth Paxham-Jennings being best pleased if they found me down on their son's cock in the garden. So I contented myself with a teasing stroke and squeeze at his crotch and whispered into his ear that I'd be in my combinations on Wednesday. That was too much for him and, an instant later, he'd pulled his cock out and folded my hand around it.

'Toby!'

It was a protest, but I was already tugging.

'What about your parents?'

'Damn my parents, I want you to myself!'

'Toby, don't be gross!'

'I want to be gross, Juliet, I want to be very gross indeed.'

I couldn't help but giggle at his sheer passion, and gave in completely, tugging at his cock and glancing guiltily around. We were behind a hedge, and couldn't see the house at all, but I was sure we would be caught. Toby seemed confident, though, and took hold of my breasts, stroking my nipples through the wool of my sweater, then trying to pull it up. Again I protested, imagining the hideous embarrassment of being caught topless in the garden by his parents, but he was getting persistent and I was getting horny.

So, out came my breasts, my sweater and top tugged high and both pulled free of my bra to leave them sticking out in a froth of satin and lace. Toby made a purring noise and went straight down, burying his face between them, kissing and licking, taking one nipple in his mouth, then the other. By then, I was past protest, feeling too horny and too naughty to care about anything but my pleasure. Even as his hands found my bum I didn't stop him, and all I could manage was a low moan as my jeans were unfastened and tugged quickly down over my hips, my knickers going with them.

Toby went down too, kissing my tummy, burrowing his tongue into my navel, and lower, to kiss my pussy mound, to bury his face in my sex as he took me by my bottom. I closed my eyes in ecstasy as he started to lick, his tongue flicking over my clit again and again, as if determined to get me off as fast as possible.

That was just fine by me, and I took my breasts in my hands, stroking my nipples as he licked and thinking of how rude we were being, and of how I was, bare from my neck to my knees in his garden, being licked. He was holding my bottom apart, as if showing the rear view of my pussy and my bumhole to some confederate, and that sparked the fantasy I needed. Like in the army shop, there would be somebody watching me.

Only it would be Marsh. They'd have agreed to fuck me, to share me, and they'd do it. As Toby licked me, Marsh would come up behind, his huge cock ready in his hand. More manly or not, he was the employee, and he'd have agreed to have my bum while Toby fucked me. So up it would go, pushed into my bottom hole as Toby licked me to keep me too high to resist and, once he was all in, he'd lay back, spreading my thighs for Toby to mount me, the two of them sharing me, their cocks in both my holes . . .

My mouth came open in a cry of ecstasy as I came despite my best efforts to hold back. Toby kept licking, and squeezing my bum, until I was done, then rose, grinning, his lips white with my juice, his erect cock still straining out from his fly. I felt weak with reaction, but I made to go down, meaning to suck him. He had other ideas, and pulled me close, to press his cock between my breasts. I took them in hand, to fold them around his erection as he began to fuck my cleavage, my body still shaking from my orgasm.

I was determined, though, to give him the same pleasure he'd given me, however awkward, and stayed down, jiggling my breasts around his cock as he pumped himself between them, faster and faster still, panting and grunting, as come erupted from the tip of his cock, high into the air, to catch my face and splash down over my breasts and back into my cleavage. He finished himself off in the now slimy slide he'd made of my breasts and we were done, giggling together like naughty kids as we quickly tidied up.

The rest was simple and not nearly as exciting. A brief stroll revealed the quince, in a small orchard enclosed by hedges. It was well hidden, but also offered no easy escape, which meant no torch. I made a careful note of a thin place in the hedge and counted the trees to fix the position of the quince in my head, all the while making light romantic chit-chat with Toby.

The lake offered every opportunity for escape, also good cover. It was set at the bottom of a shallow slope, obviously artificial, and designed to enhance the prospect from the rear of the house. Two follies, a picturesque bridge and several spinneys made it look rather twee, but were ideal for my purposes. Beyond was open parkland, ending in a hedge, with woods and the spire of Ilsenden church visible beyond.

My reconnaissance done, I allowed Toby to steer me back to the house, both by my arm and my bottom, and accepted his mother's invitation to lunch. They served duck with rice and green peas, simple and really very good, while we discussed topics as diverse as family history, cellaring wine, dogs, cats and carp fishing – mainly carp fishing. Elizabeth Paxham-Jennings bred Burmese, and there were no dogs.

There was still a lot to do clearing up after the guests and, despite a clear hint that I could join them, I made my excuses. They had been so friendly it was making me feel a little bad about my intentions, and as I walked back afterwards I was having to tell myself it was just mischief and that no real harm would be done. I even considered telling Toby after the event, but decided that would be taking it too far. I was not going to stop in any case. I was having too much fun.

After doing a little computer time, I spent the afternoon propped up in bed, going over the map and trying to pick holes in my plan. I also slept a little and, when I awoke, it was dark. There was a moment of panic and disorientation when I thought I'd slept through the night, but it was barely eight o'clock. I got up, into my bra and knickers, to eat two big slices of bread liberally spread with Jersey butter and home-made strawberry jam, and then dressed. As before, I put on my jumper and skirt over my combats, and stuffed my gear into a very girly shoulder bag.

Outside it was dank, and quite chilly. I set off, with that same delicious thrill of anticipation and daring. Just before I reached the motorway, I saw lights coming towards me and hastily took cover in the bushes, determined that nobody should see me if at all possible. A Land Rover passed, the driver visible only as a dark profile within, but I was sure it was Marsh.

I stayed down, praying he hadn't seen me. The Land Rover went on, the red tail lights disappearing, the sound of the engine fading, and rumbling to a halt. He'd stopped. For a moment I stayed frozen in place, my heart hammering. He couldn't have seen me, he had continued too far down the lane. I heard his door thud shut and my nerve broke.

Running light-footed down the lane, I crossed the bridge and on, past Alderhouse, before I stopped. Even then, I hurried on, constantly glancing back in the expectation of seeing the lights of his Land Rover. The hedges were high and thick, and I had no way off the lane, but he never came. He was out though, looking for his poacher – for me.

Just the knowledge that Marsh was out there, hunting me through the night, was enough to set me trembling with excitement as I made for Ilsenden. Cars passed on the road, but not his, and I made the village still sure I hadn't been seen by anyone who mattered.

There was now a wet mist in the air, and I saw nobody as I skirted the churchyard and hurried down a lane towards the rear of the Alderhouse estate. I passed a cluster of modern houses, climbed a field gate, and another, and I was behind the park. There was a ragged hedge, in which I stripped off my jumper and skirt and concealed them within a plastic bag. The bag hidden, I climbed the single strand of barbed wire and I was on their land, looking across to the well-lit windows of the house. The lake, the gardens, all were in blackness; even the huge old trees in the park were hard to pick out. Still, I moved warily from tree to tree, skirting the bottom of the lake and up, to arrive behind the hedged orchard.

All was quiet, black and wet. I pushed through the hedge, then counted my trees. The quince was low, the fruit easy to find, even groping in the dark. I took several, enough to be sure of sufficiency, but hopefully not to be noticed. A tree to the left provided apples, and I was done, already elated as I slipped back down towards the lake.

I was not finished. It was nearly ten, and there were plenty of lights still on in the house, on all three storeys. That meant they couldn't see out, but I could see in and, when Toby came to shut his curtains, I was given a flash of a surprisingly well-muscled torso, a thrill both erotic and illicit. So he'd gone to bed, and his parents were hardly likely to come out on such a filthy night. I was full of confidence as I chose my spot by the lake, on the little bridge where it sloped down away from the house. It was perfect, above shallow water and with a smooth flat surface to enable me to select my gear by touch alone.

There is a knack to nocturnal carp fishing. A little bread should be used to draw them into the bank, then something smelly as bait, preferably something including nice, rich fish oils. I'd gone for anchovies, which I reckoned even the dimmest carp would be able to smell clean across the lake. I had no rod, but a strong line, which I dangled over the side and wrapped around one finger.

How people can spend entire weekends fishing is beyond me. I waited, hugged into myself and grew slowly colder, with the thrill of the hunt dying away gradually to be replaced by boredom. One by one, the lights in the house went out, leaving me in total blackness, the green glow of the hands of my watch the only thing I could see.

I was beginning to shiver, and to wish I'd gone to a fishmonger. I'm an obstinate little pig though, and I stayed, thinking about how I'd prepare the carp and feeling a little sorry for it. I've always felt it's hypocritical to eat meat and not be prepared to kill, but this was the first time I'd put my principles to the test. I'd brought a length of lead pipe left over from the bathroom refit to make the end quick, and also just in case I met any man who had funny ideas about girls out on their own. It was not going to be easy to use it.

Time wore on, with the damp slowly soaking through my clothes until I was beginning to worry about hypothermia. I stood, absolutely certain nobody was going to see me, and at that instant the line twitched. I froze, dead still, half risen from the bridge. Again the line twitched and pulled, firmly, then hard. I had a big one. I held still, letting it take the bait, then hauled. It came, the water beneath me heaving and splashing as my prey began to struggle. Guilt washed over me, but still I pulled, the line jerking frantically in my hands, the noise so loud I was sure I'd be heard from the house.

Then I had it, its full weight on my line, then on me,

as it came over the parapet with an unexpected jerk and I fell back. I grappled for it, felt the long, powerful body thrashing in my grip and, at the same instant I realised I'd caught a pike, its teeth locked in my hand. I screamed in pain and panic, snatched for the lead bar and I was beating at the thing, all guilt gone, all mercy gone, determined to kill.

I did, after hitting my arm and leg and screaming blue murder without a thought for who might hear. Maybe it just died of suffocation, I don't know, but the moment I'd prized it loose and stuck my bleeding hand in my mouth for a good suck, the reaction set in – pure triumph. It was huge, a great vicious thing the length of my arm, a monster that dragged ducklings to their death, a predator. I'd killed it, caught it and killed it, and now I was going to eat it. Never in my life had I realised I was capable of such murderous glee.

Common sense finally got the better of me when a light went on in the house. It was on the first floor, and probably just someone going to the loo, but it put an abrupt end to my primitive frenzy of bloodlust. Gathering up my things, and the pike, I retreated back across the park.

It was gone eleven, but I was cold and wet and in no mood to hang around. I dressed in the hedge and hurried back to Ilsenden, with half the pike protruding from my bag. A dead giveaway. There was only one thing to do – wrap it in my jumper, call a cab from near the pub and hope that the driver had the decency not to comment on my fashion sense and the smell of fish.

7

On the Tuesday morning, I was thoroughly pleased with myself. I'd got away with it, and I had everything I needed. As I got dressed and made coffee I was singing happily to myself and when not singing, I was finding it impossible not to smile.

Looking back, it had been immense fun. The cold, the fear, the pain, all were forgotten. I'd done it. I'd also learnt something about myself. When it came down to it, my civilised veneer, my qualms and principles, vanished very quickly indeed. It felt good to have killed the pike, and I suspected that the pleasure of eating something I had not only poached but killed myself was going to bring to me a whole new level of taste experience.

Now it had to be perfect. I had the food, and it had also cost next to nothing. The wine was going to be a very different matter, but I was determined not to cut any corners. I would serve champagne and a carefully selected wine with each course. Not that I actually expected to drink three and a half bottles myself, but I could also vacuum some for later. Nowhere local was going to be able to provide what I needed, so I went up to London.

The smell hit me as I stepped off the train at Paddington: exhaust fumes, dust, oil, and hamburgers. There was noise too, constant loud noise, and the press and bustle of the crowds, and drunks demanding money as they ogled my chest, and tourists with vast rucksacks blocking my way, and the horrible machines that swallow tickets and snap shut before you can get right through...

Immediately, I was wishing I was back in the country, and my brief journey to South Kensington did nothing to change my mind. I have never liked cities, but until that moment I had never truly appreciated just how foul they are, and London is no exception. It is, however, the wine capital of the world, with a greater variety available than any other city, bar none. I knew where I wanted to go, fortunately, and had finished in just over an hour. For the champagne I avoided the overrated *Grand Marques* and went for a pure *Grand Cru* vintage *Blancs de Blancs* from Mareuil itself at eight years old. Wishing to balance delicacy with flavour, I chose an Albarino from Rias Baixas for the soup, and a Meursault Perrières for the pike, no expense spared. It was impossible to find anything better than my Romanée St-Vivant for the pheasant, which was a relief, given the prices of comparable wines. That was hard to follow, but I managed to find a Ribero del Duero *Reserva* Especial I'd tried before and knew to be spectacular. A thirteen-year-old organic Saussignac caught my eye to go with the pudding, and after some thought I decided to finish off with Armagnac, a single estate from 1972 I simply could not resist. Loaded down, and more pleased with myself than ever, I turned for home.

Two hours later, I was back in the cottage, at the computer, and trying to type one-handed as I worked out the sequence I'd need to cook in. It was not easy, with an immense amount of preparation to do, while my left hand was next to useless. For one thing I had to skin the back of the pike, which would have been slow work at the best of times. Then there were the pheasants to be plucked and prepared, and most difficult of all, the grand centrepiece, which was going to be nearly impossible to do on my own, never mind one-handed. By the time I'd completed the schedule, I was seriously considering drafting Emma in to help.

It meant telling her what I'd been up to. She might have been pretty rustic, but she was not stupid. If I lied I'd need a story Baron Munchausen would have thought twice about telling. She was bound to twig, and I didn't want to risk spoiling our friendship. On the other hand, I could not see her keeping a secret for five minutes, least of all one she would enjoy so much.

In the end I decided against it. I set to work on the pike as I was intent on allowing the flavour of the excellent dry-cure bacon I'd picked up to work into the flesh for as long as possible. That meant skinning the back and flanks, larding the flesh all the way down to the bones, then barding. An hour later I'd changed my mind and rang Emma.

She'd finished her work and came straight up, bouncing happily into the kitchen and stopping dead at the sight of the monstrous pike laid out on my kitchen table.

'What a monster! What does he weigh?'

'Twenty-three pounds.'

'Twenty-three! The boys just have to see this, Luke's never –'

'No, no, no, nobody else is to know, Emma!'

'Why not?'

'Because it's poached.'

'Poached? Where from? Not Alderhouse?'

'Yes, last night. I was after carp, but –'

'Oh, wow, you are the best. The cheekiest! But, if you've been shagging Toby, why'd you need to poach from his lake?'

'Because he's coming to dinner tomorrow, and I don't want him to know that all the food has been pinched from his land. It's complicated.'

I told her, everything. She took it in mingled amazement and giggling delight, along with gasps of shock as I described my close encounter with Ian Marsh. When I'd finished, she sat back in her chair, mouth open.

'You are something else, Juliet!'

I shrugged.

'And I thought you were such a good girl.'

'Not me.'

'No, not you. Oh, I wish I could tell the boys, they'd love it!'

'No, Emma. A secret, just between you and me.'

'All right, but you don't have to worry. The boys all do it.'

'On the estate?'

'No way! Not with Marsh around. I tell you, you were lucky he just whacked you with a stick. The man's a fucking pyscho!'

'I can run faster than him.'

'You can't run faster than a charge of birdshot. Then you'll really know how it feels to be hit in the arse!'

'Do you think he'd do that? You can't just go around shooting people, Emma.'

'Well, I wouldn't risk it, no way!'

'You're right. I'm not going to do it any more.'

'Come out with us sometime instead.'

'I will. Just now, I badly need your help. The pike bit me.'

'Well, you've sure got your own back on it!'

'I'm skinning it. I need to for my recipe, pike Chambord. It's French, originally from the Loire Valley, the Sologne. There are good fish in the ponds there, around Chambord, where some king, François the First, I think, set up.'

'They taste of mud, don't they, carp?'

'Exactly, so you cleanse them, then skin the back, sew

fat bacon into the skin and cover it with more bacon. That's what I'm doing, and I need you to hold the pike still while I cut. OK?'

'Sure.'

'Thanks. There's more too. I need you to . . .'

I explained in detail, running over the entire dinner menu as we set to work on the pike. As I expected, she was more than happy to oblige, accepting it all with giggling delight.

Gabriel Blane never, ever serves anything he hasn't experimented with extensively. Usually he'll try a good half dozen variations on any particular dish before it is presented to the customers. I didn't have that luxury, and could only manage to share the hen bird of my brace of pheasant sewn with ceps in a plum sauce, with Emma. She finished by splitting the thigh bones between her teeth and licking the sauce from the plate, which had to be a good sign. It didn't convince me I'd surpassed Blane's classic grouse dish.

By the time she left the pike was in the fridge, larded and barded, the bacon juices seeping slowly into his flesh. The cock pheasant was also ready. I collapsed into bed, my head still full of details, but I was asleep as soon as I'd hit the pillows.

I'd had a chance to test the pheasant, I'd done Chambord before, and the rest was all first principles. Except for the Chicken of the Woods soup, which was entirely experimental. I was prepared to give it to the goats if it didn't work, but it did, producing a richly scented, distinctly fungal soup unlike anything I'd tried before.

That was my first task in the morning. Others followed, in precise sequence, each course and each wine needing its own special care. For lunch, I snatched bits from the leftovers spread around me and got on with it.

Emma arrived at two and I left her to tidy up while I took a long, hot and very well-deserved bath.

By the time I got out, the kitchen was spotless and everything arranged almost to my satisfaction. Together we arranged the sitting room, putting out linen, heavy horn-handled cutlery and my pre-war Czech glass and setting black iron candlesticks around the room. The effect was rich, more baroque than ever, highly individual, and would have sent a minimalist screaming from the room. For my purposes, it was perfect.

I left Emma to it and went to get ready, shaving my armpits and pussy, depilating my legs, and making all the subtle adjustments that take so much time and pain and which men seem to take for granted. To Toby, an only child and from public school, I could safely assume that women simply come smooth.

A touch of perfume, deliberately understated, a yet more subtle touch of make-up, a silver band to confine my hair, and my groundwork was done. Dress came next, and that, for once, was simple. Stay-ups, my silver slippers and a long, figure-hugging number of deep-red velvet that went with the decor in what was now the dining room. It was strapless, and tucked and puffed across the chest, making a bra impractical. My nipples showed through it, but then, it was a romantic dinner, and I had no knickers on either.

Emma gave a nod of appreciation as I came out of my room to ask her to help with the zip. I felt ready, with my insides fluttering just a little and a warm feeling between my legs. It was going to work.

One more thing remained to be done: chanterelle Velvet Down, done with Jersey butter, arrowroot, pheasant stock and whole chanterelles. Everything else was ready, and my timing was perfect. No sooner had it thickened than we heard the sound of Toby's car. Emma made herself scarce, disappearing into the scullery as the doorbell went. I opened it to find a huge bunch of tiger lilies, with Toby behind them.

I wasn't the only one who had made an effort. He was immaculate, in full black tie, given a splash of colour by a red silk cummerbund that exactly matched my dress. It was just the image I wanted – smart, old-fashioned, formal, but with just a hint of eccentricity. I kissed him and ushered him in, taking the flowers to quickly place them in a pair of vases to add both their scent and beauty to the dining room.

'Thank you, Toby. They're beautiful. Now, sit down, and everything will come to you.'

I went for the champagne, held ready by Emma in the scullery, brought it in, twisted the cork free and poured. Toby had been looking around.

'Well, this has changed a little.'

'It suits you.'

'Haphazard and slightly unbalanced?'

'I was going to say dark and mysterious.'

'I can go with dark and mysterious. You won't find this in a Home Tips column anyway.'

'No, I'll bet you won't. You like to be different, don't you?'

'I like to be me.'

I took a sip of the champagne, which was everything I'd expected, deliciously fresh, with just a hint of that biscuity richness that comes only with time. My insides were fluttering harder, and badly needed the rush of alcohol, so I took a most unladylike swig as Toby swivelled round to admire the screen. He spoke again as he turned back.

'I wish I could live like this.'

'You do. Alderhouse must be ten times the size, and it's full of beautiful things.'

'Yes, but there's no privacy. There are always guests and whatnot. It's more like a hotel than anything. Besides, how many twenty-five-year-old men do you know who still live with their parents?'

'A few. Apparently, when there's a serial killer about, the first thing the police do is check up on all the men over thirty-five who still live with their mothers.'

'Thank you, Juliet. Hmm, I must say, there are some delightful smells coming from your kitchen. What have you got for us?'

'You'll see, and I want you to be truthful, Toby. If anything's not as good as the food you had at The Seasons, you're to tell me, OK?'

'Oh . . . I didn't mean you to take that to heart, Juliet.'

'I have. Just say I can be oversensitive, but promise to give me your true opinion, and tell me if you think he could have done better.'

'That's not easy, he does have the reputation for being able to do anything. This champagne is superb though, I'll hand you that one.'

'It is, isn't it? But that's just a matter of knowing what to buy, and how to serve it. The credit belongs to the *vigneron*, a Monsieur Henri Blin.'

'Yes, but isn't cooking all about knowing what to buy, and how to prepare it, of course? I mean, we have the gods to thank for the fruits of the earth.'

'You're right, mainly, but personal flair matters as well as just learning what's what.'

'But, surely, any recipe you create I can recreate, just as long as the instructions are explicit and I follow them exactly.'

'Not in practice. You wait. More champagne?'

'I will, eagerly. Please, yes.'

I poured, and refilled my own glass. Already the bubbles were getting to me, making me light-headed, and confident. There really is nothing like champagne to kick an evening off. Emma needed her share, so I retrieved the bottle as I stood up.

'First then, Chicken of the Woods soup.'

It was ready, hot on the stove, and it took me just moments to fill the bowls and bring them through, then nip back to swap the champagne for the Albarino. Toby had waited, but dipped his spoon in as soon as I'd filled his glass. I tasted my own, praying it had not undergone some ghastly transformation during the day. It hadn't, but retained the slightly sour, slightly peppery tang of the fungus.

For a while we ate in silence, Toby apparently as rapt in his enjoyment of the food and wine as I. Only at a sudden thud from the direction of the scullery did he look up. I made a dismissive gesture.

'Just my goats, Hilary and Harriet. They always come to the back door when I'm cooking to get the scraps.'

'I remember the goats. You're keeping them, then?'

'Yes. Emma Thompson looks after them, mostly. I let her have half the milk in return.'

'Share-cropping, eh? Hmm, this is delicious. I must say, I've never tasted chicken like this.'

'It's not chicken. It's a fat yellow fungus. You must have seen them in the woods.'

'A fungus? It's edible? I mean, obviously it is –'

'I'm afraid not. It's deadly poisonous. Didn't I mention that I'm a witch?'

For one delightful instant he thought I was being serious, but on the word 'witch' the expression of utter horror his face had been working into faded to a wry smile.

'You have quite a sense of humour, Juliet.'

'Sorry, I couldn't resist that. Of course it's edible, silly. Do you really think I'd poison you?'

'No, of course not, but there is something about you —'

'I'm murderous? Evil?'

'No, no, nothing like that ... mischievous, maybe. Not that I mean —'

'Not at all, that's sweet. Thank you. I'm flattered.'

'Really?'

'Yes, I'd hate anyone to think I was too serious, or prim and proper.'

'I don't, believe me.'

'Maybe "correct" would be a better word, as in "politically correct", or maybe "lifestyle correct". You know, the way you're expected to like certain things, to have certain things.'

'I know what you mean. You should see some of the stiffs we get at the parties. You're never that. After all, what could be more out of fashion than being traditional?'

He'd hit the nail on the head, and I couldn't help but smile. I leant forwards to touch glasses in a silent toast. As I went back to my soup, I was wondering if he himself had enough of a sense of mischief to understand what I'd done, even appreciate it. I was beginning to suspect he might, but I didn't dare say anything, not wanting to risk spoiling the moment.

The soup done, the bottle close to empty, I made another quick swap with Emma. First I brought in the Meursault with the bread and butter, and then the pike. He was laid out in all his glory on my largest platter, his huge jaws wide around a lemon, the barding crisp along his back, like plate armour. Toby could only stare.

'A whole pike! Goodness, Juliet, that is ... is ... I'm lost for words.'

'Don't say anything then. Just enjoy him. Take a little bread and butter, add just a drop of lemon. Take your time, and with the wine too.'

'I shall.'

I served him, taking a steak of pike from the back above the rib cage. The meat was pink from the bacon and succulent, looking perfect. It was truly excellent, although there was no denying the added pleasure of devouring my adversary. The Meursault was also superb, scented with apricots and mealy – if anything, too rich for the fish. Toby ate in reverent silence, paying full attention to every mouthful and every sip of the wine. I watched him, just to be sure his reaction wasn't put on, and allowed myself a quiet smile when he completely failed to notice my attention. When he finally did look up, it was to throw me a polite but definitely enquiring glance.

'A little more?'

'Please, yes. It's wonderful.'

'Thank you. Don't overdo it though, this is only the fish course.'

'There's more.'

'Naturally. Did you have fish at The Seasons?'

'Yes, once. Lamprey. It was amazing what he'd done with it . . . Sorry.'

'Don't be. I'm sure it was excellent.'

I'd served him his second piece, and he went back to eating as I finished my wine. When he was done, he gave me a big smile and patted his stomach, a man well fed and completely at ease. I cleared and swapped, bringing in the pheasant and carving it at the table, a breast and a leg each, with two tiny potatoes and a little red cabbage arranged around it.

Again we ate in silence, each concentrating on the pleasure of our senses, neither feeling the urge to make chit-chat and so take our attention away from where it mattered. The recipe had worked beautifully, and the wine was a perfect accompaniment, yet even to myself I had to admit that Blane's grouse and truffle counterpart was even better. I still enjoyed every mouthful, and finished the bottle. When I at last looked up, Toby was dabbing his lips with his napkin.

'Superb, exquisite, what can I say? I don't know if you can do better than Gabriel Blane, Juliet, but you could certainly give him a run for his money.'

I smiled, happy to let him think I was flattered. There was still a little wine in my glass, so I paid attention to that, sipping and rolling it around in my mouth to leave my palate with a warm, soft wash of red fruit and rich earth. Toby sat back, looking thoroughly content and at ease, only to start at a sudden bleating mixed with frantic squawks.

'What's that?'

'My animals. Something's wrong. Could you check, please? These slippers . . .'

'Of course.'

He made for the door. I jumped up, followed, leaning out as he stepped onto the porch and the light came on, bathing him in brilliant white and plunging everything beyond the hedge into utter darkness.

I nipped back inside. I had seconds. Emma was already in the dining room, and paused an instant to tug my zip open before snatching up both plates. I shrugged the dress from my shoulders, to let it fall and step free. One slipper came off, and the other. Emma came back as I rolled my first stay-up off, to throw a fresh linen drape over the table. I scrambled on, cocking up my leg to peel my second stocking down, and off. Emma grabbed my clothes, bustled out, and came back laden with the wine and the sauce. I composed myself, naked and serene.

My pose held just as long as it took her to start pouring the chanterelle Velvet Down. It was hot, and stung, leaving me gasping as it pooled between my breasts, heavy and viscous, running only slowly across my flesh. I swallowed, and gritted my teeth as she did my breasts, my nipples immediately coming erect, to stick up through the dark brown sauce and pieces of mushroom. My tummy was done, my thighs, and my pussy, leaving me coated in warm, thick sauce. I had served the one dish Gabriel Blane could never ever have presented Toby, or anyone else – me.

Emma vanished. There was silence. I waited, the Velvet Down trickling ever so slowly down around my body. The door clicked. Toby's voice sounded.

'Nothing. Probably a fox. I . . .'

He stopped dead. I didn't move, but lay absolutely still, letting him drink in the sight of me served naked for him. I could see him, just, from the corner of my eye, staring in amazement. Slowly his expression changed, to delight, then lust. He stepped closer and, very calmly, reached for a napkin, which he tucked into his collar.

I could feel myself trembling as he leant forwards, first to kiss my mouth, firmly, sensually. I responded by instinct, my tongue pushing up to meet his, but he drew away, to kiss lower, on my neck, with his lips, then his tongue, to lap at a runnel of sauce. I felt my sex tighten as he began to feed from me, moving to between my breasts where the sauce had formed a thick pool, to lap at it and take the pieces of chanterelle up with his lips. Every touch sent a shiver through me, little electric jolts that grew as his kisses moved to my breasts.

He was in no hurry, enjoying his food, teasing me too, the touches of his lips and tongue moving ever closer to my nipples, but never reaching them. My instincts began to take over, my muscles reacting, my mouth coming open in a long sigh. He put his mouth to mine again, to feed me a piece of chanterelle, and went back to my breasts as I ate.

My pleasure was still growing, higher and higher. Soon

my back was in a tight arch, my breasts thrust up to him, and still he teased. I began to moan, with the knees to lift my thighs and open myself to him rising, until I had begun tossing my head and squirming against his mouth. At that, at last, his mouth moved to the peak of one breast, to nip off a piece of chanterelle, exposing my nipple. His tongue touched my flesh, then again, licking me, lingering on my erect bud, slowly teasing the sauce off with tiny flicks, then sucking, to feed from me with real passion, real urgency.

I pushed up, my mouth wide in ecstasy, my eyes shut, my fingers locked in the tablecloth. The whole of my nipple was in his mouth, sucked in deep, to the point of pain, his teeth nibbling on the bed. I cried out, my thighs and bottom squeezing in my helpless reaction as a jolt of pure pleasure shot through me. Already I wanted to come, but he moved back, leaving me shaking, my breath now quick and deep, my sucked nipple straining up, so taut it hurt.

Slowly I came down as he stepped around the table, until once more his mouth found my flesh, on the other breast. Again he began to feed, and to tease, bringing me slowly back up, until once more I was gasping and shivering to his every kiss and lick. Suddenly I could stand it no more. My thighs came up and open, spreading myself wide, nothing held back, offering myself to him in lewd, uninhibited display. He took no notice, save to put his mouth to my nipple, suckling on me as I squirmed my bottom on the table in desperate need for entry.

Sauce began to run down over my sex, warm and wet, coating my lips, filling my open, ready hole, and lower, to tickle my bottom hole and pool beneath me, between my cheeks. Still he suckled, cool and purposeful, completely in control as I wriggled wantonly beneath him, spread out in sauce – his to enjoy, his to eat. Just a touch, the slightest touch, where it mattered, and I was going to come.

He stopped, to leave me gasping and splay-legged, my breasts pushed up, my pussy thrust out for entry. His finger touched, below one breast, to take up the sauce from the shallow groove of flesh. As I opened my eyes I saw him pop the finger into his mouth. I was still shivering, on a plateau of ecstasy, just waiting to be taken up to that final, glorious peak.

My mind slowly came back into focus as he wiped his mouth and poured himself a glass of wine. It felt so good. I was in a pool of warm sauce, bits of chanterelle tickling my pussy and bum hole, my breasts licked clean but my belly wet, needing only a little more attention, that final act, to bring me to climax. It was going to happen too, beyond doubt, but not yet, not until he had had his fill of me.

He lifted his glass, paused to admire the deep, garnet gleam against a candle flame. He sipped, swallowed and sipped again, filled his mouth and bent to my face to share, the rich red Duero spilling out, to run out over my lips and down my cheeks. I met his kiss, our tongues entwined, my mouth filling with the heady taste, and of him, and my own body.

When at last he pulled away, I met his eyes, saw the urgent, lust-filled look for a moment before he had bent again, to kiss my neck, my nipples, my tummy, and once more he was feeding. I held still, my legs open and ready, my pussy desperate for his tongue, tormenting myself even as he was tormenting me. The sauce was lapped from my belly and sides, Toby moving slowly down, each touch of his tongue sending a jolt to my sex. His lips found my belly button to suck, then burrow in, licking out the sauce. My muscles went tight, belly and bottom too, my pussy twitching, a sensation not far from orgasm.

He moved down, to lap up the pool of sauce on my lower belly, and further still, licking at the smooth skin on my pussy mound, slowly, teasing. My legs came wider still, held as wide as they would go, in straining invitation. He stopped once more, moved to between my legs. I closed my eyes, my breathing deep and even, thinking of how open I was to him, of what he was about to do.

My mouth was wide, my eyes shut, my pussy tingling. He took my thighs, his strong arms curling around them, to hold me ready. I pushed out, desperate, and his lips touched my sex, kissing my pussy, full on. His mouth went wide over it, his tongue poked out, and in, to lap sauce from my open hole. Again I was clutching the tablecloth and wriggling in his face, my clit like a point of fire between my legs, urgent for his touch.

Still he licked, feeding from my cunt, and more, utterly without inhibition, his tongue pushing down between my bottom cheeks, to lap sauce from my anus. My whole body went tight, just the touch of his tongue on that tiny sensitive bud enough to take me right to the edge of orgasm. Again he touched, burrowing a little way in, wriggling his tongue in the hole, and I was tossing my head in reaction and clutching for his hair, all restraint gone as I wrenched his head hard onto me.

His tongue found my clitoris, pressing hard, licking, then his lips, to suck the little bud in suddenly. I screamed, my sex, my thighs, my bottom cheeks, all going into frantic spasm as my orgasm hit me. My whole body went into a frantic, bucking motion, totally uncontrolled, writhing in an ecstasy so high, so sweet, that I never, ever wanted to come down.

I did, eventually, and slowly, even as he gently detached my clawed hands from his hair and got to his feet. All I could do was slump down, weak and shaking, yet full of a deep, deep satisfaction. After a moment I opened my eyes and managed a smile. He was looking down on me, his face smeared with sauce and my own juice, his hair dishevelled, his shirt front a mess.

He returned my smile with a wolfish grin, bent, and slid his arms under my knees, to take me firmly by the legs and slide me forwards, right onto his cock. I gasped as he filled me, taken completely by surprise. I hadn't even realised he'd taken it out, and now it was in me, deep in. He began to fuck me, pulling me back and forth onto him in time with his thrusts, with my body slipping in the mess of sauce beneath me.

I could only lie back and take it, overwhelmed by sensation. He was going to come, I was sure of it, deep in me, filling me with sperm, maybe making me pregnant, but I didn't care. I wanted it, whatever he chose to do to me, to give me. In moments I was clutching at the tablecloth again, then at my breasts, my flesh sticky with sauce and so, so sensitive.

He slowed, and began to undress, his cock still inside me, his eyes feasting on my body. He shrugged off his jacket, tugged his tie loose. I began to tease my nipples, showing off for him as well as keeping myself nicely high. As he unbuttoned his shirt, I watched, playing with myself lazily, but no more lazily than the motion of his cock inside me.

His shirt came off, his hands went to his trousers, opening the button to let them drop. Still he kept his cock inside me, pulling free only as he bent to undo his shoes. I stretched, purring, ready for whatever he wanted, whatever he needed. He stepped to my side, erect cock in his hand, gently masturbating himself. I opened my mouth, wondering if he'd like to pop it in. He grinned and picked up the jug of Velvet Down.

I stuck out my tongue, eager for the rude, decadent act I'd guessed he was about to perform. Sure enough, he pushed his cock into the sauce jug and tipped, to bring it out brown and dripping, thickly coated with sauce. I stretched my neck out, to take him in my mouth as he reached the table, sucking eagerly at the rich taste, not just of chanterelle and pheasant, but also of man, and of myself. His cock felt huge in my mouth, excitingly hard and slippery with sauce. I swallowed, sucking down the taste, and again as I turned onto my shoulder, now feeding eagerly from his body just as he had fed from mine.

He took me by the hair and by the hip, pulling me to him, gently. His hand cupped my bottom, fingers easing down between my slippery cheeks. One found my anus, pushing inside, opening me as I sucked him in, harder and deeper. I twisted up onto my knees, my energy surging back as I raised my bottom to the delightful sensation of being penetrated.

Immediately, he pulled free of my mouth, grappling with my body, slipping and sliding in the sauce, both of us laughing as he twisted me around. My knee slipped as his finger came free, but he caught me, to ease me down across the table, my face in a pool of sauce, my bottom lifted behind.

I knew what he was going to do, and my stomach was fluttering in trepidation at the thought. Not that I tried to break free, but stayed down, my eyes closed, focused on the feelings of my sex and anus as his thick, solid cock shaft came to rest between my cheeks. For a moment he rubbed, his balls pressing to my pussy, making me gasp as his hair touched on my clit. He stopped, pulled back. I forced myself to relax, my lower lip tight beneath my teeth. I heard him move, and a sticky sound . . .

Warm sauce spattered over my upturned bottom, suddenly, unexpectedly. I gasped and giggled as it trickled down the cleft of my buttocks to tickle the little hole between and fill my pussy. Then he sunk down, and was licking me, no longer little teasing dabs as before, but slurping up the sauce from my cunt, my bottom cheeks, and between. I cried out as his tongue found my anus, and then he was licking me, over and over, until I was gasping, clutching at the table and curling my toes with pleasure.

It went on until I was wriggling myself frantically in his face and not that far from a second orgasm. Then it stopped, he rose once more, and again pushed his cock into me. Taking my hips, he began to ride, harder and faster, wringing fresh gasps from my throat, all the while my head swimming with relief and regret that I wasn't to be given anal sex.

I was. He pulled free of my pussy. His cock-head pressed again to that tiny, sensitive ring between my bottom cheeks where I knew no man should be allowed to put his penis. I didn't care, I wanted it, for all my apprehension. Even as he pushed I had made myself relax, and when the moment came there was no pain, only a wonderful stretching feeling mixed with sheer delight at being so rude.

He pushed it in, all the way, to leave me breathless, gasping for air, my fingers locked in the sauce-smeared tablecloth. I heard him grunt in pleasure as his strokes grew abruptly harder and faster. His hands slid forwards, lifted me, to take my breasts. I twisted, struggling to find his mouth, to kiss him. His weight came onto me, our mouths met and he began to pump into me with a frantic jerking motion, pressing my splayed pussy right onto a twisted ridge of tablecloth.

I knew I was going to come on the instant, and so was he. He was pounding into me, his arms crushing me to him, his cock jerking back and forth up my bottom. Then it had begun and all reason was gone. We clung, joined, sticky with sauce, drunk and dirty, rutting crazily together, heedless of everything save for the pleasure we could take in each other's bodies.

My orgasm hit me and I was clutching at him, scratching at him, screaming and mewling and biting at his lips. At the very highest peak, I felt him jerk inside me and knew that he had filled me with his come. His whole body went rigid, locked to mine as he emptied himself into me, with my sex and bottom still contracting in orgasm, drawing what he had to give out into my body.

I'd hoped we would fuck. I'd suspected he might want to put it up my bottom. Still, I'd expected to find some comment, some little remark to make when it was all over. I didn't, completely overwhelmed by what he'd done to me, and by my own reaction.

8

After my night with Toby, my life settled down. We were together, and it was good, relegating my fantasies of Ian Marsh and rough, ritualised sex to the back of my mind and the occasional piece of private night-time amusement. Toby might have been less raw, less of an animal, but his blend of old-fashioned courtesy and open-minded attitude to sex kept me more than happy.

It stayed the same for the rest of the month, and into November. I gave up poaching as I could walk more or less where I liked on the estate, although the temptation was still there underneath. It would have been very risky anyway. Marsh had noticed the plums, and realised what had happened. He was furious, and took to stalking the woods at unpredictable hours, sometimes with his shotgun.

Toby never did realise that much of the food had come from his own land, and I didn't tell him. It never even seemed to occur to him to question where I had got hold of such a monstrous pike, which is not the sort of thing you can usually pick up at a fishmonger's.

There was no time to poach anyway, with a lot of things going on, and not all of them good. I could now fish the lake, pick my fungi at will and take as many pheasants as I pleased. With such good ingredients to hand, I began to put my plans into action. I had an enormous number of ceps, mostly penny bun, and began to experiment with pâtés, trying them out on Toby and occasionally the guests at Alderhouse. They went down well, so I settled on a specific recipe and made up a batch of samples.

Only then did I discover just how much I'd bitten off. The first problem was distribution. As I'd anticipated, the bad reputation Gabriel Blane had given me didn't matter when it came to buying fine food. They were eager to sample my wares, and eager to buy once they had. The problem was that I couldn't meet their expectations. Each and every one seemed to expect delivery at a moment's notice, and in tiny quantities. Walking to the Post Office everyday with a rucksack full of heavy parcels was murder and took ages, while the cost took a major chunk out of my profit.

I needed a car, and a driving licence too. I began to take lessons, first from Toby, which very nearly brought our relationship to a premature end, and then from Emma, which ended up with the front half of Luke's battered old pick-up in a pond. Finally I hired a professional, and more by good luck than skill I managed to pass first time.

That was not the end of my troubles. There was payment. I'd never had anything to do with the accounts at The Seasons. Deliveries had simply arrived and, I'd assumed, been paid for. To discover that every single restaurant expected to be allowed thirty days credit came as a nasty shock. By the beginning of December I had spent several hundred pounds and didn't have a penny to show for it. One morning I rang Ralph Brookman on his floating restaurant to discover it wasn't floating any more. An incident with a *flambé* and the wash from a big river cruiser had forced a hasty evacuation and left the boat a half-burnt wreck by the bank side near Marlow. He had owed me nearly two hundred pounds.

It left me in tears. Just over a month I'd been trading, and all I'd managed to do was work myself to exhaustion, worry my self silly and lose money. Quite simply, it was more trouble than it was worth. I could not do it. So I gave up, officially, making a pyre of all my stationary and packaging and setting light to it with a pot of paté on the top. It was small satisfaction.

As I was watching the last red flickers eat along the ashes, the garden gate banged behind me. I turned, hoping to see Emma, but it was the postman. There was a single, large envelope for me, marked Inland Revenue. I'd been expecting it, but that didn't stop me feeling increasingly depressed as I went into the kitchen.

I made coffee, ate a slice of bread and jam, made my bed, did the washing-up from the night before, fed the chickens, said hello to the goats, then told myself I was just putting off the inevitable. Back in the kitchen, I opened the envelope and pulled out the thick letter inside, bracing myself for the shock of a demand for several thousand pounds, maybe over ten thousand . . .

One hundred and seventy-six thousand three hundred and twenty-four pounds and thirty-one pence.

I sat there, staring at the piece of paper. It was impossible. It had to be a miscalculation. They had to have sent me someone else's bill. They had to have developed an unexpected sense of humour and sent it as a joke.

They hadn't. It added up to the penny. Set in a beautiful rural location, ten minutes' drive from the motorway junction beyond Ilsenden, my little cottage was being valued at just under half a million pounds. I could appeal, but I had a nasty suspicion that the valuation would prove accurate, or too low.

Finally I managed to motivate myself to calculate how big a dent it was going to make in my finances, and how much it would leave me to live on. The answer was, not enough. I could pay. I'd have to pay. I could even live on what was left for a while, a fair while if I was frugal. The bottom line remained the same. I would have to get a job.

It was that or sell up and move somewhere cheaper. That was unthinkable. I had put so much of myself into the cottage, and into becoming a part of the local life. I had Toby, undoubtedly the best partner I had ever had, and Emma, who, for all our different backgrounds, had become closer to me than any other friend. There was the land too, not just a slice of the country, but something that linked me to my childhood, that grounded me.

I hadn't felt much sympathy for Toby's opinions on inheritance tax. Now I did. He was the answer too. I at least had the option of catering for the estate, and now I was going to have to take it. That meant hard work, stress, trying to handle a relationship with somebody who was also my boss, but at least it was local and would let me stay where I was.

It was still an appalling shock. For a long while I sat there, numb, just waiting for the third, fourth and fifth disasters to hit me. They didn't, but they didn't have to. My dreams were in tatters.

I wanted to talk – to Emma really – but I had to find Toby, and I at least knew that he'd be sympathetic. One good thing about Toby was that I generally knew where he was. I'd heard guns earlier, from across the motorway, which meant they were shooting on the line in the woods across from the house. It was the smallest of the three, and the furthest, but I needed the walk to put my thoughts in order.

Outside it was cold, with frost from the night before lingering in patches of shade and my breath white in the air. It was bright too, and very still, leaving the late autumn colours of the woods sharp and clear. I set off, well wrapped up, melancholy despite the beauty all around me.

They were still shooting by the time I arrived, a party of fifteen, all male, which I knew to be a corporate booking. They weren't after pheasant, but clays, with Toby at the far end, and Marsh working the trap. I moved along behind them, Toby greeting me with his big, boyish grin.

'Care for a go?'

'Thanks, no. I . . . I've had some bad news.'

'Oh . . . Sorry. Er . . . is there anything . . .?'

'Yes. Can we talk?'

He had broken the gun and came close, his face full of concern. I handed him the letter. He scanned down it and shook his head.

'Iniquitous! A disgrace! Bunch of mealy-mouthed, thieving bastards!'

'It's just the way it works, I suppose.'

'No it's not. It's blatant robbery, that's what it is. The whole system's designed to push the old families off the land, pure and simple. Jealousy, that's what it boils down to. Damn hoi polloi! You're not going to sell up, are you?'

'No. It's not that bad, quite. I am going to need to work, though. I was wondering if you'd still be able to consider taking me on to do the catering. I'm sure I could cut costs, maybe even save my salary. I—'

'Say no more. It's done. Not this week, of course, because the caterers are on contract, but the next.'

'What about Donald?'

'He'll be all for it. He's been raving about you, keeps saying I should "Bag you before you get away". Maybe I should.'

He finished with a laugh, but there was a touch of nervousness to it. I immediately found myself wondering if he was really joking, or testing the water. I forced a smile, not knowing what to say, or what to think. He took me by the shoulders, kissed me and ruffled my hair.

'Cheer up, then! It'll be fun, and I promise not to take advantage of my position, well, not during working hours anyway.'

I smiled, for real, feeling at once grateful and somewhat bemused. It was hard to believe he could really be considering marriage, after so little time together. I certainly hadn't been, and I didn't know if it would have been right in any case when I was still having fantasies about his gamekeeper. The job was good, though, and I could feel the relief welling up inside me. Toby went on.

'That's better. Come on, take a shot. Pretend the clay's the chap who wrote the letter, the assessor or whatever the pompous bandit calls himself.'

It was childish maybe, but satisfying. I took the gun and stepped forwards to his post. Ian Marsh gave me a doubtful look as he fed a new clay pigeon into the trap. Toby handed me a pair of cartridges.

'Have you shot clays before?'

'I've never shot anything before!'

'It's simple. Keep the stock well tucked into your shoulder, like so. When you're ready, call for Ian to pull, point and shoot. Easy.'

He had loaded for me and pulled the gun to, leaving me feeling extremely unsure of myself. All fifteen of the party were looking at me, and Marsh as well. I lifted the gun, putting it to my shoulder, certain that the moment I pulled the trigger I was going to go down hard on my bum.

I called, the trap twanged and the clay pigeon appeared against the sky. I immediately jerked at the trigger hard, to set off both barrels in quick succession. Two deafening bangs left my ears ringing as the clay pigeon sailed serenely on to land at the far end of the field.

There was a light laugh from somewhere along the line. I felt myself go pink. Suddenly determined, I broke the gun, pushed in fresh cartridges from Toby's box and snapped it shut. Marsh already had another clay ready, and spoke.

'Just point, girl, and squeeze gentle.'

I nodded, put the gun to my shoulder and called. The clay shot into the sky. I followed it with the barrels, squeezed, and squeezed again, the clay exploding into pieces an instant after the double report. Ian Marsh gave a faint nod of appreciation and a warm flush washed over me, from my chest right to my pussy. It was definitely not the time to be thinking of marriage to Toby.

It was all a bit much. In the space of a few hours I'd changed from independent and fed up to not so very independent and with an offer of security, and dependence. I should have been happy. I felt confused.

What I wanted to do was talk to Emma, but Toby wanted me to come to lunch and I was in high demand with the shooting party. So I spent the rest of the day with sixteen young men, most of whom seemed to want to flirt with me regardless of my relationship with Toby. Perhaps I should have basked in the attention, and I did play the game by being nice and making sure I never gave anyone too much attention, but my heart simply wasn't in it.

I didn't stay for dinner, but Toby came to me later. We made love, a strange experience, with my body responding wholeheartedly but my mind elsewhere. Even though he was deliciously rude with me I never did come, simply too flustered to concentrate. If he noticed, he said nothing.

Emma was there in the morning, as always, and I

managed to get up early enough to catch her as she fed the chickens, throwing out handfuls of grain as they bustled out from their run. She gave me her big open smile, full of life as ever.

'Hi, Juliet. Going off somewhere?'

'No, I've given up, completely.'

'Yeah?'

'It was too much work, and that's not all. The tax people want a hundred and seventy-five thousand.'

'Ouch! Big, big ouch! Have you got it?'

'Just. I need to get a job.'

She made a face, sympathetic, but not really understanding. I could see her point. She worked all hours, doing everything from helping me out to ploughing, and barely received enough to be called pocket money.

'So what are you going to do? If you move away, I'll kill you.'

'Thanks, Emma. With friends like you –'

'Anytime.'

'I'm going to be catering at Alderhouse, from next week.'

'Neat. What a doss! You sure fall on your feet.'

'I suppose so.'

'You suppose so? Get real, Juliet!'

'It's not as simple as that. After all, Toby'll be my boss, in effect. That's not going to be easy.'

'Eh? I don't get you? So Toby's your boss, that's perfect. Any problem, give him a quick blow job and he'll be all smiles. Find me a man who can act the boss when his cock's in your mouth.'

'Very funny, Emma. Anyway, technically Donald would be the boss.'

'So suck him off too.'

'Emma!'

She laughed as she threw out a final handful of grain to the mass of chickens clustered around her feet. I went on, spilling everything.

'It's not just that, either. He said ... well, not said exactly, but implied, that he's considering marriage.'

'Oh? Who to?'

'Emma, will you be serious? I'm having an emotional crisis here!'

'Sorry, but I don't get you. So he wants to marry you? Great!'

'But that's the problem. I don't know if it is.'

'You have to be joking! You are unreal, Juliet. The guy's heir to a fucking great estate and one of the only businesses around here that can stand on its own feet. He's got a big house, he's a good dirty fuck and he follows you around like a puppy. OK, so he's a arrogant little shit too, but not to you. Marry the bastard!'

'He hasn't asked, and –'

'Then ask him.'

'No, it's not that. It doesn't feel right. You see ... you see, I can't get Ian Marsh out of my head.'

'So? If you want to play it dangerous, do. Marry Toby, shag Marsh and you'll be well happy.'

'You must be joking! It'd be a disaster waiting to happen!'

'Why? You just have to be cool. Why would Toby suspect, as long as you're getting down and dirty with him, and Marsh won't tell, 'cause then he'd get the sack. I won't either, just so long as you keep me up to date with the filthy details.'

'You make it sound so simple. Come on, Emma, how would you feel if Ray was having an affair?'

She made a face and shrugged, clearly none too keen on the idea. I knew I'd feel the same about Toby, even if I was having an affair with Ian. It's easy to argue that you shouldn't be jealous of a partner if you're up to no good too, but emotions don't work that way. She went on as we turned back towards the house.

'OK, so I'd feel bad. But you've got to get it together, Juliet. Forget Ian Marsh. He's a bastard, and you know it. Yeah, sure, you're into bastards and he turns you on, but big deal. You want it both ways, you do, to shag everyone in sight and feel good about it too. Life doesn't work that way.'

I didn't answer her, despite wanting to make an angry denial about wanting to shag everyone in sight. She'd only have laughed. She was right too. It may be the thing to believe that modern women can have whatever they want, but it's crap. Sometimes it's one thing or the other. I had to make a choice ... eventually.

'Coffee, Emma?'

'No, thanks, I've got a ton of stuff to do. Look, if there's a place going at Alderhouse, you know, doing the donkey work for you, I'd be up for it. I'm fed up with working my arse off for fuck all.'

'I'll ask, but –'

'Yeah, I know, but you know I work hard, and maybe you can persuade Toby, yeah?'

'I'll try my best, promise.'

'Thanks, Juliet.'

She leant forwards, kissed me and made for the tractor, which was parked directly across my gate. As she climbed up she turned back, waved, then called out.

'Hey, what was that place you used to work at, the posh restaurant?'

'The Seasons. Why?'

'It's gone bust.'

The roar of the tractor engine drowned out my immediate query, and in response to my frantic waving she simply threw a paper from the cab. I ran to pick it up, sure she had made a mistake.

She hadn't. The Seasons had gone down.

There wasn't much in the paper, but I could read between the lines. Basically, he'd bitten off more than he could chew, staking everything on the three new restaurants being a hit from their opening nights. It hadn't worked, and there was a most satisfying irony to the reason.

It had been one of his commonest, and most irritating, chestnuts that his name was the draw for The Seasons. It had proved to be true. The customers, most of whom knew next to nothing about how a restaurant operates, had always assumed that what they ate had actually been cooked by Blane himself. Of course, it very seldom had, but they didn't know that. With the new restaurants it was plain that he wasn't doing the cooking. He wasn't there to do it.

So they'd failed, all three. They had been losing money from the start, and at an alarming rate. Finally, the bank had decided that enough was enough, and the overall debt was simply too great for him to cover. By the time the bank, the taxmen and various suppliers had finished with him he had been forced to sell up. By the sound of things he didn't have a lot left either.

It was satisfying, and there was no denying it. OK, so I'm a vindictive little bitch, but it felt good. There was no doubt he would go on to make a fortune presenting a cookery programme on TV or writing recipe books, but it was still nice to know that he would have felt something of the same emotions as those he had forced on me.

Toby got his blow job, and Emma got her job. I would have probably been able to persuade him anyway, but it felt delightfully mischievous to go down on him to get my way. I know men think women do that sort of thing all the time, but I hadn't, simply because I'll never normally suck a man's cock unless I want to, or do anything else.

We started with the next shooting party, another corporate booking, this time for 22 people of both sexes. Some were even vegetarians, and I was forced to swallow my principles and provide a suitable alternative. Other than that, it was fairly straightforward. I sourced as much as I could locally and, with Emma knowing just about every farmer and smallholder in the district, that was quite a bit, despite being so late in the season.

I also introduced the practice of explaining the dishes and the philosophy behind them on the menu. It had been done at The Seasons, to an extent, and always improves people's appreciation of what they're eating. Gabriel Blane had always argued that it went further, and that people would not only accept things they would normally not have tried or enjoyed, but would actually like them more in a real, physical sense. Having watched our party wolf down my completely experimental goat's cheese washed with rough cider, I was forced to agree with him.

It also gave me an outlet for my own products, and a far more profitable one. Toby had no objection to me charging myself full price and paying upfront, just so long as it all came within the budget, which was generous. The first party alone allowed me to half my losses.

Of the twenty-two guests, eighteen sent emails complimenting the quality of their stay. Of those eighteen, fifteen mentioned me specifically. Toby was delighted, his parents were delighted and I was left feeling better about my professional abilities than at any time since discovering that Gabriel Blane was more interested in my physical talents than my mental ones.

The next shooting party was the Christmas one. It was different from the others, in that those focused on the sport. For Christmas, the sport was secondary, and it was really meant for those too idle or too busy to sort out their own celebrations. The highlight was the Christmas lunch, and I was determined to do it in style.

We had fourteen people, all wealthy, all single, and all expecting to be well entertained. Many were older, including no less than four very refined widows, one baronet and a retired wine merchant. Several had been in previous years, and Toby warned me that they were highly demanding.

Emma and I pulled out all the stops, both working all day every day and trying to sort out our own needs at the same time. There was no way I could get to my parents' on Christmas Eve, so she'd invited me to come down to the farm when it was all over. I'd accepted, Toby or no Toby, sure that at Alderhouse there would always be some professional call on my time. That was going to be the early hours of the morning.

My plan was to offer three courses, and three choices for each, varying from classic to inventive, which was as much as we could realistically do. After that, a spread of cheese, fruit and nuts could be offered, leaving the gluttons to feast until they dropped.

Smoked salmon was going to be expected, and I managed to get a side from one of the low-profile contacts of Blane's I'd learnt about while at The Seasons. It had been poached by a gang operating out of Glasgow, but was none the worse for that in my opinion, better in fact. I didn't tell Toby. A French classic, parcels of goat's cheese in puff pastry, made a straightforward alternative, with individual quail breasts set in a Sauternes jelly for the real gourmets.

As with the smoked salmon, so with turkey – something unavoidable. I managed to get a decent free-range bird and smothered it in barding to keep the flesh moist. For those with any real sense, I provided a stubble-fed Orkney goose, along with a carp Chambord for the eccentrics, something I was beginning to gain a reputation for.

Christmas pudding is so traditional that I could have done without options. I'd stirred them the moment I'd found out I'd need them, substituting a couple of weeks of maturation with a large dollop of single estate XO Cognac. To go with it, I had brandy butter and rum butter, made with Armagnac and a French golden respectively, along with cream from a Jersey herd. That should have satisfied anyone, but there are always those who aren't prepared to stuff themselves stupid and then exercise it off, and still don't want to get fat. For their sake, I provided tarte Tatin, which I suppose is at least relatively light. Then, for those who simply didn't give a damn, there was a Sussex pond pudding.

By the time they'd finished, and then we'd finished, I was so full my stomach was pressing painfully to the button of my jeans. I was also drunk, having been unable to even begin to get my head around people who could order such delicacies as *Grand Cru* Tokay d'Alsace and fifteen-year-old St Croix-du-Mont and leave the half-finished bottle on the table. Emma was worse, having been drinking tail ends from the bottles. She'd also pinched the rum, claiming it was to keep the cold out as we walked down to the farm.

I should have been exhausted, but after kissing Toby and promising to see him later I found myself full of energy and in seriously high spirits as we set off. It was frosty, every twig and blade of grass outlined in brilliant white ice from the house lights, and pale with the moon in the lane. I knew it was cold, but only in a detached, factual sort of way. I couldn't really feel it at all.

We drank the rum anyway, taking turns to swig it from the bottle as we walked arm in arm talking complete nonsense in very loud voices. There was nobody to hear, fortunately, the night empty and still, with even the motorway close to deserted. By the time we got to my cottage we'd finished the rum, so we stopped to pick up a bottle of champagne, too drunk to know better.

It was well gone midnight, and at Bourne Farm the lights of the main farmhouse were off. In the extension, where Luke and his wife, Milly, were living, they were on, and we could hear music and laughter long before we got there. When we did, Emma hammered on the door with the champagne bottle, until finally Mark let us in, greeting us both with kisses, and ushering us into the main room where everyone else was – and how.

It was quite a sight. Mark was barefoot, but I hadn't thought anything of it. Some of the others were more than barefoot. Luke had nothing on but his pants, with his broad, hairy chest running with sweat and cider as he drank from a bottle. Milly was as far gone, flushed with drink and excitement, wearing nothing but her knickers, with her pregnant belly showing beneath large breasts already swollen with milk. Danny had done better, and his girlfriend Lisa, too, with just her jeans off. Ray hadn't been touched. Their other man, John, had his chest bare. Sally, Mark's girlfriend, was not only stark naked, but showing a suspiciously red bottom as she turned to reach for more beer. At the centre of the circle, among beer cans, bottles and cigarettes, the cards had been spread.

Emma greeted the sight with a peal of giggles, made a taunting remark about what had happened to Sally and demanded that we be dealt in. I was just too drunk to think twice. Five minutes later, I was laughing with the rest of them as Lisa accidentally pulled up her bra along with her jumper. Ten minutes later, I was biting my lip as Luke proudly pushed his pants down to show off his cock and balls. Twenty minutes later, I was topless. Thirty minutes later, I was laughing so hard it hurt as Milly used a wooden spoon on her husband's bare backside. Forty minutes later, I was naked. An hour later, I was sucking on John's cock to the cheers and delighted catcalls of the others.

Two hours later, I was leaning on a gatepost and wishing the world would stay still for even a minute.

Three hours later, I was asleep in bed with Toby.

I did not feel good about what I'd done. There was guilt, but not much, and that was not the real problem. Guilt was pointless. I'd done it, sucked John, who was pretty much a stranger, all the way, even showing off when I'd swallowed at the end. It was a pretty dirty thing to do, and in front of everybody, but that wasn't the problem either.

The problem was that while I felt bad about it in a rational way, I didn't feel bad emotionally. I hadn't felt any loyalty to Toby, any reason I should be faithful, either then, or afterwards. I knew full well that when I'd put down my miserable pair of fours and realised I'd lost I could easily have backed out, or done something that wasn't such a blatant breach of trust. When Emma had lost after Ray had passed out in a drunken stupor she'd been naked too, and had let Milly take the spoon to her bottom in forfeit. I could as easily have accepted the same. No, I'd turned to a big, handsome farm boy and offered to suck him off, and thoroughly enjoyed it.

There was simply no way I was ready for marriage. Maybe I needed to grow up. Maybe it was just me. Maybe I never would be ready, never feel that sense of faithfulness, that sense of belonging, which comes so easily to most women or, at least, is supposed to. So I swallowed what little guilt I had, made it clear to John that it had been nice but wasn't something he could expect on a regular basis, and got on with my life.

I didn't really come to understand the full effect of my Christmas feast until after the New Year. Normally, the first January party was the least well attended, and in some years didn't happen at all. This time it was oversubscribed, and the vast majority of bookings came from the recommendations of the Christmas party.

Suddenly I was in demand, and I made the best of it. The party left impressed, and the next, the last of the season, was more popular still. With most game birds coming to the end on the last day of January, Toby and Donald had organised a spectacular competition shoot, using all three fields, one after the other.

That was followed by a dinner every bit as grand as the Christmas one, although this time I didn't end up at a drunken orgy. I did end up exhausted, though, and, with the season over, I went down to my parents' house to recover. It was an easy two weeks, letting my mum look after me and going on long runs and longer walks to work off the half a stone of spare flesh I'd managed to put on despite every effort. By the end, I felt ready for anything, and returned to Berkshire determined to sort myself out, one way or another.

After unpacking, I walked over to Alderhouse, where I found Toby in the office. After a hug and a kiss, along with the mandatory grope of my bottom, he sat back down, clearly excited over something as well as my return.

'I have some splendid news. You've been such a success we've decided to expand. The idea is to set up what is now the dining area as a proper restaurant, not just for our guests, but for outside customers.'

'Wonderful!'

'It's sure to be a success, if only because so many of our past guests will want to visit to taste your cooking again.'

'I don't know about that! After all, I've only been doing it for a month or so.'

'Anyway, we feel confident, and Daddy and I have already been sounding out a few of the firms who generally have block bookings for shoots. They all sound pretty keen.'

'So they'll come out this far, just for the evening.'

'I would think so. One hour out from London to junction thirteen, and a few minutes to here.'

'Yes, I suppose so. Good . . . great! How do I fit in?'

'You'll run it, of course.'

'Run it!?'

'Yes, why not?'

'To be honest, Toby, I simply don't have the know-how. I can cater, yes, and do a good deal of the cooking, but you'll need somebody with more experience to actually manage the kitchen.'

'Oh . . . well, if you're sure? I mean, we'd anticipated taking on another two or three staff.'

'That's another thing. If you get anybody half-competent, they're going to resent being under me. I was never anything more than a trainee.'

'But you're brilliant!'

'Thanks. Sorry, Toby, I'm just trying to be realistic here.'

'No, you're right. I'm getting carried away and you're being very sensible. So how do you see your role?'

'I'll cater, and play a part in deciding what to serve. I'll stick with the wine as well. We should really have a much broader selection.'

'Hmm, we certainly want to improve our list, but I don't think we should tie up too much money in it.'

'We don't need to. The thing about a restaurant wine list is that to a customer it's just a list of names on a sheet. For the better wines, you so rarely actually sell any that you only need a few bottles, perhaps just two or three. That keeps the costs down while allowing you to have a truly impressive list. Some restaurants in London go one better. They club together to buy just one bottle of some real rarity, say a nineteenth-century Yquem. It's kept at the most convenient premises, but it appears on all the lists as if they have cases of the stuff. Then if somebody does order it, they simply courier it across.'

'Clever, but what if someone orders more than one bottle?'

'At thirty-six thousand pounds? That's what we were offering the eighteen forty-one Latour for at The Seasons. The actual bottle was held in the cellars of one of the Park Lane restaurants.'

'I see. Well, I don't think we can quite run to that, but if you could sort something out, I'll see what we can do in the way of budget.'

'Great. I'll see if any auctions are coming up. There are sometimes mixed cases, and they tend to go for well below the usual rates. The best prices are generally for bankrupt stock when it comes up in the smaller houses.'

That was it. Several thousand pounds to spend on wine and all my personal difficulties went straight out of my head. Toby was also desperately busy, so when we did get together, sex was generally brief and eager and boisterous. I let it go, neither willing nor able to indulge in a possibly disastrous heart to heart when everything was going so well.

I visited London, Bristol, Winchester and Norwich, each time buying as if I was possessed, and coming away with some impressive bargains. By the time I was finished, we had guaranteed regular supply for all the basics, and fine wines ranging from a sixty-four Graacher Himmelreich Finst Auslese, through an assortment of Claret from the fifty-five and fifty-nine vintages, to a single bottle of 1905 Malmsey. I was sure nobody could fail to be impressed.

The wines bought to budget and a little beyond, I suddenly had nothing to do. With no guests and the place still full of builders, my time was my own again. Toby was busier than ever supervising, and had no time to spare during the day, although he did his best to make up for it at night. I still said nothing, content to go with the flow, and despite one or two further hints and some prodding from Donald, he did not ask me to marry him.

So I spent most of my time with Emma, or just wandering in the woods trying to resist the temptation to pinch things or sabotage Ian Marsh's assorted traps. Not that there was all that much to pinch, with winter still locked hard on the land, or as hard as it ever seems to get anyway. I visited the shrine too, and several times waited nearby in the hope of catching Marsh making his pagan offerings. I never did, but I did manage to work out that he came late at night or in the very early morning. I was even tempted to leave a note, or an offering of my own, but it was impossible to predict his response.

Instead, I sat down to work out if there was any pattern to his visits and decided they might be in some way linked to the phases of the moon. I left the warmth of Toby's bed before dawn one freezing February morning when the moon had been full, only to find the altar bare, and walked on to my cottage, to make some extremely strong and hot coffee and chat with Emma.

It was mid-morning before I started back, only to meet Toby before I'd gone a hundred yards. He smiled and waved as he caught sight of me, then sped up to bring himself into talking distance.

'There you are, Juliet. You would not believe the slice

of luck we've had. Guess who we've signed up to run the restaurant?'

'I don't know ... Ralph Brookman?'

'No, Gabriel Blane.'

9

It couldn't have been worse. It couldn't have been worse if Toby had invited some crazed vegan to run the place. At least then I'd have had the customers on my side. Now they'd just think I was some worshipful little acolyte to the great Gabriel Blane.

I could have told Toby what Blane was really like, and he would have believed me, almost for certain. I didn't want to. It made me look like a victim, in the modern sense, and I will not allow that. I couldn't resign either. I couldn't afford to. I didn't want to either. I had been doing well, and I had been setting my own stamp on Alderhouse. I would just have to put up with it and do my best to get on with him.

That proved impossible.

Blane was taking it seriously, as I discovered when I learnt he'd rented one of the flats owned by the Paxham-Jenningses in Ilsenden, for next to nothing. He came up to the house socially, but I'd made my excuses and didn't see him, determined to keep our relationship strictly professional. I was also dreading a visit from him at the cottage, as inevitably he'd found out I was there. I'd had to tell Toby that much anyway, and that I'd been sacked, but not why. That alone hurt.

He didn't come to the cottage, but I had to go to Alderhouse to attend the meeting at which we were to plan our opening night. Just walking there felt as if my precious land was now tainted, especially the house.

I walked around the back, and there he was standing

with Toby in the now enlarged restaurant area looking out at the prospect as if it were his own. He looked as smug and as weasely as ever, more so, because he'd grown a nasty little goatee beard. I didn't acknowledge him, and he didn't respond. Indoors, I spoke briefly to Elizabeth, then went in. Toby looked up, smiled, kissed me and took a step towards the door.

'No need for introductions here, eh, Juliet? Now, I'll leave you two to get on with it then, as I'd only be in the way.'

With that, he left me to face Blane, who didn't waste any time in putting me in my place.

'Juliet, hi. Now look, I know we've had our differences in the past, but here we have to work together, so I'm prepared to forgive and forget.'

It was so outrageous I couldn't find words, at least, not before he had gone on.

'This could work, I can see it, with my touch. Yes, it could really work. Get the opening night right, that's the first thing. We need a centrepiece, something grand . . .'

I rallied myself, determined to be professional.

'I was thinking, maybe carp Chambord?'

'Carp Chambord? Don't be absurd. That takes hours, days if you include the time the carp takes to cleanse. We're not in medieval France, Juliet.'

'Renaissance France.'

'What?'

'Renaissance France. The recipe was invented at the beginning of the sixteenth century. I know it takes a long time, but we should do it. I've done it twice and it's been a great success.'

'Don't be such a pedant, and don't try and tell me what I should do. You are the caterer here. I am the chef. I decide what is to be done. You buy the ingredients. And God help you if they're not up to my standards.'

'It should be a joint decision, and carp Chambord is perfect.'

'No. I decide. That's the only way I work.'

'It may have been the way you worked at The Seasons, Gabriel, but here I have a say. In fact, it would be better if I selected the ingredients and you stuck to the preparation.'

'You, select the ingredients? Now that's funny! You wouldn't know where to start. Sure, you can buy decent stuff. I know that, I taught you. But it takes more than that. You have to judge how much is needed, and what to serve so that there's something suitable for everyone, but the standard doesn't have to be compromised.'

'That's what I've been doing.'

'Badly. I've been looking at the books. Your wastage is totally unacceptable, you're using far too many suppliers, and you're serving dishes nobody's ever heard of, or worse, that you've just made up.'

'You do that all the time!'

'I am Gabriel Blane. You are nobody.'

I sucked my breath in, struggling to control my temper. He went on, not talking to me at all, but just enjoying the sound of his own voice.

'What we need is something spectacular both in appearance and in taste, a true sensation.'

I opened my mouth to suggest the medieval peacock recipe but shut it hastily. He wasn't taking that away from me. He paused, fingering his beard as he stared out over the lake, then went on.

'Yes, my venison dish, but served as a haunch and carved from the bone. Perfect.'

'Which venison dish is that?'

'Magdalen Venison, of course. Since Signor di Gavi tasted it the night you disgraced yourself it had become very popular at The Seasons.'

I could only stare, amazed that he could lie so outrageously, but he went on, oblivious.

'I've had to make a few improvements, of course, a shorter marination for one, and in a good, robust Spanish rather than Burgundy, which is far too delicate for . . .'

I turned my back on him, knowing that if I didn't my temper would snap. He was as bad as before, worse maybe, with his super-inflated ego now bruised and more sensitive than ever. Yet I had to cope with it.

Cope with it, yes, but that didn't mean I had to kowtow to him completely. He was no longer the top of the ladder, and if he hadn't been my boyfriend, Toby would have had to see sense. I could speak to him and his parents and nip Gabriel's megalomania in the bud.

Toby was in the office with his father, and both were bending over the computer. They looked up as I came in. Toby spoke first.

'Is everything all right, Juliet? You look harassed.'

'I am. I know you're busy, and I hate to make life difficult, but Blane seems to think I'm simply his assistant, and we'd agreed –'

'Ah.'

'What do you mean "Ah"?'

'Well, it's just that Gabriel insisted on one or two changes to the contract you saw. Nothing major, and I'm sure he'll be reasonable, but he did insist on having the final say on the menu.'

'He did what!?'

'Don't be angry, Juliet. I'm sure he'll let you have fair say.'

'He will not. He won't even listen to my suggestions!'

Donald answered me, his tone very even, but very firm.

'Be fair, Juliet, as you pointed out yourself, you lack

the experience to run an outfit this size on a day-to-day basis, and Gabriel –'

'– is a genius, I know. Sorry, but at the least I should be allowed to select a proportion of the dishes.'

'We did discuss that, and I'm afraid he insisted on complete control. He felt the balance of what was on offer might not be right otherwise.'

Toby gave me a wistful smile and a shrug.

'It really is the sensible choice otherwise, and we have got him at a very good price ... for a celebrity chef.'

Gabriel Blane was earning nearly four times as much as I was. It was enough to make me feel physically sick.

I felt betrayed as well. Maybe it was ultimately my fault for not making my feelings about Blane clear to Toby in the first place, but that was no reason to set the wretched little man up above me. As it was, not even Toby had made any effort to stick up for me. I was left with only the mundane part of my job, excepting the wine, and even there I'd only got away with it because the list had already been printed.

He'd also cut back on my policy of explaining the dishes to what he'd been used to at The Seasons. His argument was that people only needed to know what would affect the flavour, and not the background. My response was that people could read it or not as they chose, but as usual it cut no ice.

As the final insult I was banned from the restaurant floor, with instructions to remain firmly out of sight. The same went for Emma, the two assistants and the trainee he had hired. Only he and the two waiters could come out, and they were under instruction to be silent and respectful. It was The Seasons all over again, with everything focused on him and everyone else kept well out of sight.

What I couldn't deny was that he'd organised well, with an efficient system set up so that everyone knew what they were doing and food could be served quickly. The key to this was the reception area, where a range of aperitifs could be enjoyed in comfort, and to which diners could retire after the meal for an equivalent range of digestifs or coffee. It made sense, and increased our potential capacity considerably.

For the opening night we invited forty carefully selected guests. Carefully selected by Gabriel Blane, that is, and among the critics and vaguely foodie minor celebrities there were several of his cronies. He had even arranged a seating system, to make sure that each critic was close to a guaranteed sycophant and a pretty girl or a handsome young man, according to taste. It was sure to be a triumph.

It was also a little different from what I'd always thought of as his style. From what he'd ordered me to buy, it seemed he had largely abandoned his focus on English cooking, going for a broader, more continental choice, also a less ambitious one. Possibly The Seasons going down had dented his ambition, possibly it was an attempt to reinvent himself.

The centrepiece, at least, was everything it could possibly have been, even if he had pinched my recipe. An entire haunch of venison had been marinated for three days, with skewers driven deep into the meat to allow the mixture of wine and herbs to penetrate. It was fallow deer, and I was extremely pleased with my choice, although I knew I'd not get an iota of the credit.

It was not the only choice. It was really too late for grouse, but he had included his classic recipe anyway, with frozen birds, perhaps because he felt it was expected of him. The second alternative was turbot in a complicated sauce not dissimilar to a tapanade, with capers, olives, tomatoes, fennel and more; far too strong a taste for the fish in my opinion. The last was Tornedos, which I couldn't fault, but then it was simply to be pan-fried, classic in its simplicity.

There was also a choice of starters, very simple fare when compared to some of the extravagant creations we'd put out at The Seasons. He had langoustine in a piquant sauce, quails' breasts in Sauternes jelly, a selection of pâtés from different game birds, my own included, although he didn't know it, and snails.

It was while I was helping prepare the snails that he came over to us, looking irritable and waving a piece of paper. He spoke to me sharply, not troubling to address me by name.

'Both Lance Bagnall and Amy-Jane Bacau have changed their order. They want snails.'

'Tough. We've only got twenty-four. Tell them to choose something else.'

'Not possible. You do know who they are, don't you?'

'Sure. Critics.'

'Critics? Jesus, Juliet, you really do not have the fucking foggiest, do you? A bad write-up from either of them and we're fucked.'

'I disagree. We've relied on word of –'

'Oh, just shut up, you little airhead! You have no idea. Just do it!'

'I can't, not unless we ask two of those who ordered before –'

'For God's sake! It's simple enough, surely, even for you. Six people now want snails. Half-a-dozen each, that makes thirty-six and we only have two dozen. Now, go and get another dozen ... that's twelve.'

'Where from?'

'Snails, Juliet. They live in the garden, under flowerpots and things.'

'Common garden snails, yes. Not Roman snails. They don't even live in this country, do they?'

'God give me strength! The taste is identical, Juliette, and you do have Roman snail shells, don't you?

'Yes, you know –'

'Good. Now fetch!'

'But –'

'Fetch!'

I went, my teeth gritted in anger and shaking hard, but I went. Outside it was wet and cold and snail free. After ten minutes of damp exploration of flowerbeds I was struck by an inspiration and went into the greenhouse. There I found what I needed, big black and brown garden snails, sleeping out the winter under overturned flowerpots. I took a dozen of the largest and brought them in to Gabriel, who was just about beginning to foam at the mouth.

'Jesus, Juliet, where have you been, France?'

'Outdoors, and it's wet. I'm –'

'You're doing nothing. Sort out the shells and plates while I boil these buggers.'

Things were getting frantic, and I delayed changing to help, sorting out the presentation while he stood over the pan with one eye on his watch. When he had finished my efforts were greeted with a grunt, yet it didn't seem to trouble him that the snails were half the size they should have been, and I watched in disbelief as he pushed the bodies into the shells and carefully capped each off with garlic butter.

They looked right, and it was tempting to taste, but we had not a single second spare, so instead I beat a hasty retreat to get changed. That meant a jumper and jeans, which was all I had in Toby's room, but then I had already been banned from the restaurant floor.

By the time I came down the evening was in full

swing, and I joined Emma at a window from which we could see into the glass section of the main room. It certainly looked as if it would be a success, with the diners in their suits and posh frocks, all apparently having a whale of a time. They had finished the first course, and Blane was there, carving the venison with an air of confident control, every inch the suave patriarch ministering to his flock.

I had to be pleased, for Toby, yet I had never felt so cheated. Blane had done things I could not have, bringing in influential critics and the celebrities of our trade, also arranging the seating so perfectly. Yet without me, he would never have had the setting in which to work his magic and, as I knew from bitter experience, the credit would be his.

Sure enough, the reviews were good, and varied from understated approval in the upmarket magazines to an ebullient 'Blane is Back!' in one of London's trashier events guides. There was no mention of me, or of Toby, never mind my contribution to the food. Lance Bagnall even mentioned the snails, stating that they had been 'raised from the egg in the village of St Romain, quite the prettiest in all Bourgogne, where they were fed on vine leaves and bran soaked in the local wine'. Either he was making it up, or Gabriel had fed him a whopper to end all whoppers. Amy-Jane Bacau declined to mention the snails, but gave a lengthy and unctuous description of the venison, describing it as 'a classic example of Gabriel's brilliant defiance of the conventions'.

That was that. I wasn't out, but I might as well have been. Within a week, I'd been relegated to the status of errand girl, with Blane deliberately stamping on my every attempt at innovation. Toby was no help, enthralled by Blane's charm and well pleased with the instant success of the restaurant. I still didn't feel I could tell him what Blane was really like, and it was soon plain that he felt my resentment was simply rather childish pique.

I stuck to it, swallowing my pride again and again as my position was slowly eroded. I had paid my tax bill, which left my bank balance looking less than healthy, and I knew I couldn't afford to quit. Still less did I want to sell the cottage, or work slinging burgers in a pub, or shovel shit at Bourne Farm, but it was getting close.

He had changed everything. Instead of buying at local markets and farms, we had most of our produce delivered by specialist companies he had used before. That left me to make the orders, check the quality and accuracy of the deliveries, oversee storage, and very little else. Even then, he kept a close eye on what I was doing, and continuously overruled me or changed my decisions.

That did mean I had more spare time. He filled it, pushing the most menial and least skilled tasks onto me, either trying to get me to quit, or simply for the fun of degrading me. I resisted, but he only managed to make me seem petty and arrogant in front of the other staff. Before long, I was taking my share of the washing-up, mopping, even the trash. Had it not been for Emma, I would have given up; she kept me at it, despite growing more resentful herself.

I took to walking up from the cottage with her every morning, a brief stroll that was now a last taste of freedom, at least until Gabriel chose to introduce lower-priced set menus at lunchtime. Inevitably, I hadn't been consulted – even by Toby – which rankled and, as Emma and I left on the first morning, I was steaming. She was trying to be philosophical.

'It's just men.'

'Gabriel, yes, he makes Napoleon look modest, but Toby? He's not like that when we're together.'

'No, 'cause he's on a main chance, isn't he?'

'I'd like to think there was a bit more to it than that.'

'Maybe, but in the end they're after what they want, and that's cool, if it's what you want too.'

'What I don't want is an extra four hours' work a day.'

'It's still not that bad.'

'No, but it's not what I want.'

'How many people get what they want?'

'Not many, I suppose, really, but that's no reason I shouldn't try.'

I knew where the conversation was going, so I shut up. She could never see that life could be more than working and raising a family, just as I could never understand how she could be so content with what she had.

We walked on, making neutral conversation, reaching Alderhouse to find the kitchen already working at full pace. We went to check the stock inventory over, only to have Blane push into the storeroom behind us.

'What are you two doing?'

'Inventory.'

'Well don't. There are more important things to be done and, in future, I want you here on time.'

'We are on time.'

'No, you are not on time. Nine o'clock, sharp, every morning from now on.'

'But there aren't any deliveries.'

'Then do something else! For now, you can clean the Gents, and –'

'Gabriel, I am the catering manageress, not the toilet cleaner! I've told you –'

'For God's sake, Juliet, how about some teamwork here? Everyone else is busy, so get on with it, and take your fat friend with you.'

'No, I . . .'

The door was open. Several of the others were visible, all working. I knew those who couldn't see could hear. They'd all be listening, and thinking what a stuck-up little bitch I was for refusing to take on the unpleasant task. It had been the same every time, more or less, and every time I had given in. I knew what was coming too, the inevitable word.

'Please?'

It was said just so, firmly but reasonably, so that I had a straight choice, comply or look bad in front of everybody. So I had to do it, or tell Emma to and, when I hated being put upon myself, I could hardly do it to her. I put my clipboard down.

'OK, this once, but this is not part of my job.'

'Good. Thank you.'

There was no real gratitude in his voice, only sarcasm and a malign satisfaction at one more petty victory. I went to deal with the lavatory, my throat bursting with bitter hatred. The job didn't even really need doing, but I knew that didn't matter. What mattered, to him and to me, was that he had made me do it.

When I came back, Emma was still doing the inventory. Blane was instructing our trainee with all his normal lack of patience. He stopped as he saw me, and cut me off before I could reach the storeroom.

'No, not that. I need you, you too, Fatty.'

Emma came out of the storeroom, holding the clipboard. She was wearing her normal easy-going expression, save for a touch of annoyance in her eyes. Blane took no notice.

'Miriam's sick, so you're waitressing today, Juliet, and before you start, no bullshit. That's what's happening.'

'But how can I? I haven't a uniform.'

'Wear Miriam's. You'll fit, unlike Chunky here.'

'But...'

Emma passed me the clipboard and reached back to pull her hair free.

'Forget it. Go fuck yourself, Blane.'

'What? Who the hell do you think you're talking to?!'

He'd gone red, instantly, and there was real anger in his face as he turned on her. She took no notice whatever, settling her curls around her face and turning to me.

'Sorry, Juliet, I've had it with this arsehole. See you later, yeah?'

'Sure.'

It was all I could manage, too taken aback by her casual exit to protest. Blane wasn't, he was shouting as she made for the door.

'Where the hell do you think you're going? There's work to be done!'

'Do it yourself, arsehole.'

She left, just stepping through the door and closing it gently behind her. Blane was left standing.

'Jesus! Women!'

'Perhaps if you went and apologised?'

'Apologised? What the hell for?'

'Forget it, Gabriel. Look, I can stand in for Miriam, but we need to talk about job description here.'

'No, Juliet, we do not. You need to learn some loyalty and some respect, that is all. Now go.'

He stormed off, launching into a tirade against the unfortunate trainee, who had managed to commit some unspeakable sin with a bunch of spring onions. I stayed put, shaking my head and suddenly feeling very much alone. Emma had quit, the one person I could really talk to, the one person who always made it seem OK.

Lunch was awful, with six tables to serve and very little idea of what I was doing. It was not my job, and everybody seemed to want everything at the same time, and to treat me as a complete moppet into the bargain. One man, a businessman with a braying laugh and greasy black hair, even pinched my bum, and it took all my will power to hold myself back from slapping his face.

By the end, I had had enough. I had not been hired to be Gabriel Blane's skivvy, and I was not spending my afternoon clearing, washing up and then preparing for dinner. I had a couple of deliveries to take in, and that I would do. Until they arrived, it would take more than Blane to find me. So, once I'd changed, I nipped out of the back door and around to the front, almost colliding with Toby as he came down the steps.

'Whoops, sorry, Toby.'

'Any time, sweetie. Look ... er ... um ... are you working?'

'Not really, no. I was coming to look for you.'

'Good. Would you like to come for a walk?'

'Yes, very much. There are a couple of deliveries due, but Gabriel can handle them. He always double-checks anyway.'

'Very thorough, Gabriel.'

'Yes, I suppose so. What's on your mind?'

'Oh, nothing. I just felt we haven't been spending enough time together.'

Something was on his mind, I could tell, maybe something important, maybe just sex. I wasn't really in the mood, but I could take it or leave it, which was more than I seemed to be able to do with work.

We turned right at the gate, up the lane and towards the motorway, Toby speaking again as soon as we were out of sight of the house.

'So ... er ... do you think the lunches will be a success?'

'Yes, judging by today. But there's a problem. Gabriel managed to insult Emma, and she walked out.'

'Oh ... Not one to suffer fools gladly, is Gabriel.'

'I wouldn't have put it like that, Toby. He repeatedly insulted her.'

'Well, you know how chefs are, ever the temperamental artist, and she hasn't been doing a great deal lately. But never mind that, the last thing I want to do is talk shop.'

He'd started the conversation, but I didn't press the point. He put his arm around me, and I responded, snuggling into his side to enjoy the sense of comfort and security. It was there, but diluted, as it had been since Blane's arrival. I cuddled closer, absolutely determined that I would not allow Gabriel Blane to destroy my relationship. Suddenly, I did want sex, not for the high, so much as for comfort.

'Are we heading towards my cottage by any chance?'

'I was thinking of the woods.'

'A bit chilly, no?'

He chuckled and patted my bottom through my coat. I smiled and looked up to kiss him, allowing my hand to slide down onto his crotch. He felt hot and big, his cock just a little stiff. I squeezed as our tongues met and I was stroking him as we kissed, his cock swelling beneath my hand as he gently kneaded my bottom. In a sudden fit of mischief, I took hold of his zip, easing it slowly down. He broke away.

'You wouldn't dare!'

'Not here, no, but it is tempting. If your parents weren't quite so likely to choose this exact moment to take a walk I think I just might.'

'No, not even you!'

I eased my hand into his fly and down the front of his pants, to squeeze his cock. He felt very hot and very big in my hand, and the temptation to pull it out and pop it into my mouth was very high indeed. Then he would take me back to the cottage, teasing me for my dirtiness as we went. We'd fuck, naked in my bed, work and Blane and everything forgotten as we took pleasure in each other. Afterwards he would hold me, and I could cry out my feelings on his shoulder, even persuade him to do something about Blane, even . . .

It wasn't right to use what we had to manipulate him. If I began, then we could never really be lovers, but only users, each seeking to manipulate the other to his or her ends. I couldn't do it, and least of all with Blane as the cause. I pulled my hand from Toby's trousers, leaving him to hurriedly do up his fly.

We nearly did get caught, the blue nose of Ian Marsh's Land Rover pushing around the corner on the far side of the motorway bridge an instant after Toby had made himself decent. I found myself giggling and, as the car stopped, wondering if Marsh might have glimpsed anything, and what he would think.

The noise of the motorway had drowned out the sound of the approaching Land Rover, and made conversation next to impossible on the bridge. We crossed, Marsh waiting with just a hint of impatience at the mouth of the footpath. He had a bunch of snares in his hand and clearly wanted to speak to Toby, then get on with his work. I found myself envying him, and wishing I could have shown the same complete lack of subservience in front of Gabriel Blane. Toby spoke as we approached.

'Something up, Ian?'

'Just to say I'm putting out traps, so be minding your feet if you've a mind to go in the woods. You too, girl.'

'We'll be careful. Have you checked the enclosures?'

'All done. There'd been a fox, him with the earth over Lord Randal's copse, that's all. Too cold for poachers, I reckon. That or I've scared him off.'

'That's the way. If they're going to do it, make sure they don't choose us.'

'Right enough. Will you be wanting any rabbit?'

He'd turned to me and, as always, my knees turned to jelly at the sound of his voice. When I spoke, my own was unnaturally high.

'No ... thank you. It ... it's not really the sort of thing Ga ... Mr Blane's after just now.'

'Won't take good rabbit? Must be a fool.'

I found myself smiling on the instant, and wishing Blane had been there to hear Ian's words, so full of disdain. Ian, I knew, would not have taken any nonsense from Blane. To him, the idea of a cook being an artistic celebrity was absurd, a risible indictment of all that was artificial in the modern world. Yet, at the same time, I had no doubt that he would appreciate good food as well as any. He turned without another word, taking his handful of snares into the wood. Toby and I walked on as far as the entrance to the old track, where he stopped.

'Shall we?'

'If you like.'

I gave him my most mischievous smile, ignoring both my bad feelings from earlier and that if I was turned on it was as much from merely being near Ian Marsh as anything. There was the pleasure of being naughty in the woods too, always something special to me, and enough to let me set aside all but the most bitter cold or heavy rain.

Toby pushed in and I followed. I expected him to stop just as soon as we were safely out of view of the road, but he didn't, pushing deeper until the bare trunks of the young trees shielded us completely. Only then did he turn, grinning in the boyish embarrassment I had always found so appealing.

'There's something I want to show you.'

'I bet there is.'

I'd come close and I once more cupped his crotch in my hand, to squeeze the soft bulge of his cock and balls. He was still a little stiff, and this time I didn't hesitate, but sunk down, my mouth already open as I fiddled with his fly.

'No, not that.'

'No?'

'Not yet, anyway.'

He finished by blowing his breath out, because I'd put my hand into his fly and was holding his cock, the shaft thick and rubbery in my grip as I began to tug.

'Are you quite sure about that?'

'No. I mean, yes. I just ... Oh, my!'

I'd taken his cock in my mouth, to roll his foreskin back with my lips, one of my favourite tricks. He groaned as I began to nibble on the head of it and I knew he was lost. Whatever he'd wanted, it could wait, and I was guessing he'd simply been keen to take me further in, where he could find a fallen tree to bend me over to indulge his obsession with my bum. I didn't want to go bare, it was too cold, but I did want to suck, and I did want to play with myself.

As I settled down to work on him, I undid my own trousers and slipped a hand down the front of my knickers. I was wet and ready, the first touch of my clitoris sending a delicious shiver through me. Immediately, I began to play with myself and to concentrate my mind on the now fully erect cock in my mouth.

I just adore cock, everything about it: the male taste, the heat, the firm, masculine feel, the very essence of virility. Sucking is the best too – safe, fun and a surefire way of impressing any man. For myself, I like to come under my fingers as I make my man do it in my mouth.

Toby had put his back to one of the bigger trees and was groaning and stroking my hair as I feasted on him, his cock, and his balls too, which I'd pulled out to add to my pleasure. He wasn't going to take long, I knew, and nor was I. As I began to masturbate him into my mouth, so I began to rub harder, and to fantasise.

I was in the woods, my woods, squatted down as I sucked my boyfriend's cock. The lust was completely mutual, a simple act of pleasure, yet it might have been so much more. He might have taken me in to ask me to join with him in some ritual, some piece of sexual devotion to the spirit of the woods. He might have had me sucking, just as I was, but naked, on my knees, his cock deep in me, both down in mutual adoration . . .

Suddenly I had pulled back and I was scrambling over, to turn my bottom up. My fly came open, my jeans and panties down, and I was offering myself, flaunted to the cool woodland air, my hot sex suddenly chill. Toby gave a pleased grunt, no more, and then he was on me, pushing himself into my body to fill me with his big, beautiful dick as I went back to masturbating.

Now I was as I had imagined myself, in a pose of both worship and joyous sexual abandon; worship without fear, without holding back my instincts. Far from it, I was revelling in them, lewd and animal as I rubbed hard at my clit and he pushed into me, faster and faster. I heard my own cry and I started to come, and found an image of myself rising up, as I was, bare and wanton, but before the little shrine, and with not Toby inside me, but the man who worshipped there – Ian Marsh.

I came, and only by a supreme effort of will did I stop myself from calling out Ian's name. Then I was gasping in raw ecstasy, too far gone to speak, my whole being centred on the big cock inside me, on which my pussy was contracting over and over. A second peak hit me, and a third, my muscles jerking in instinctive reaction.

Toby stopped. For one awful, glorious moment I thought he'd come inside me, and then he was out, and groaning in his own orgasm as he emptied himself over my bottom, his semen as hot as the devil's as it spattered down on my bare, cool flesh. I let him do it, holding still to give him the full pleasure of my bare bottom even as a great wave of guilt flooded through me. He'd been in me, and I hadn't orgasmed over him, but over Ian instead.

I didn't let it show. Once I'd got to my feet, I gave him a big hug and a lingering kiss, before even pulling my knickers up. He was pleased with himself, and my warmth was genuine, for all my wayward thoughts. Once he'd released me I tidied up, then helped him as, being a man, he'd neglected to think of bringing tissues when he was after a romp in the wood. Once ready, I had expected him to move on, but he started back the way we had come.

'Did you really want to show me something other than your cock?'

'No. Well, yes –'

'I thought you were going to take me deeper in, to . . . to put me across a tree trunk the way you like.'

He laughed.

'Something like that, yes.'

I tried to give him a playful swat, but he caught my arm, swung me around and gave me a dose of my own medicine. I squeaked and pulled away, but he held onto my hand, drawing me close. We kissed again, then began to walk, slowly, and not speaking, until we reached the lane. He stopped, kissed me again, suddenly nervous, and spoke.

'This has been a wonderful time for me, Juliet. The most wonderful.'

'Thank you.'

'I . . . never thought I would meet a girl like you, so . . . so –'

'Dirty? Easy?'

'Don't muck about, Juliet. I'm serious. What I mean is . . . what I'm trying to say is, that I would like you to . . . to be my wife, if you would accept?'

He had delved into his coat pocket, and was holding out a ring, a band of gold set with a single dark ruby, cut in some complex way to make light strike from every facet. Suddenly I was close to tears, with a huge lump rising in my throat, and quite unable to speak. Finally I found the strength to shake my head. Toby rose, without a word, to walk back towards the house, and I burst into tears.

I stood – I don't know for how long – just staring at the muddy ground with the tears streaming down my face. Inside my head, my thoughts were raging. I was telling myself to run after him, to accept, to tell him I was sorry and that it had just been too much to take in. At the same time, I knew I'd done the right thing, the only thing I could, to turn him down when, even at what should have been a moment of perfect intimacy between us, I had been thinking of another man.

At length, I turned my face back towards the house and began to walk, slowly, dragging my feet, thoroughly miserable as I dabbed at my eyes. The light was beginning to fade, and I knew that there would be a thousand tasks waiting for me at Alderhouse, but I didn't care. It was habit more than anything that made me go there at all. No sooner had I stepped through the door to the kitchen area than I found myself face to face with Gabriel Blane.

He was standing in an open area of the floor. At his feet was a fat puddle of mashed vegetables mixed with and surrounded by shards of broken china. His face was red, his expression of barely controlled anger. He looked around as he realised I was there.

'Juliet? Where in God's name have you been? Never mind. Clean this mess up, now!'

His voice was loud, close to a shout. I shook my head, too numb to react, but with my own anger rising fast inside me. His response was a scream of fury.

'Just fucking do it, you stupid, lazy little bitch. Jesus, why do I have to put up with this shit? I cannot work with this.'

He threw his hands up in the air, then kicked out, sending the base of the broken bowl skidding across the floor with a trail of mess behind it. When he spoke again his voice was a low hiss.

'Clean it now, or get out!'

I got out.

10

I'd thrown it all away – my boyfriend, my job – just for the sake of my own pig-headed nature. All I'd had to do was accept Toby and I'd have been in clover and able to tell Gabriel Blane exactly where he could stick his spilt mash, china shards and all. Either that, or I could have swallowed my pride one more time and cleaned up the mess he'd made. I'd have had Toby, or at least my job. As it was I had nothing.

There wasn't even much I could manage in the way of self-pity. I couldn't tell myself that Gabriel had forced me to quit. He treated all his staff much the same way, more or less. Nor could I really pretend that I'd been under some vast weight of moral responsibility to refuse Toby. There are married women who'll quite happily admit to fantasising over some pop star they've never met, and nobody seems to think the worse of them for it. It was just me, stubborn, oversensitive Juliet, unemployable and unmarriageable.

My first thought was to find Emma and for us to get roaring drunk together, drowning our sorrows in several bottles of wine. Unfortunately she'd had the same idea earlier, as I discovered when I reached Bourne Farm. She was with Ray in the Royal Oak. I couldn't face joining them, and ended up going home to drink myself maudlin on a thousand pounds' worth of Romanée-St Vivant.

All I got was a headache. Emma didn't make it either, so I was woken by the clamour of the animals and ended up feeding them in just my slippers and a coat. Done, I washed, dressed and made coffee, all very mechanically, while I wondered what to do with myself.

Going back was out of the question, either to Toby, or the restaurant. There had been something horribly final about the slow, silent way he had walked off, while I knew that I would sooner starve than work for Gabriel Blane again. I could attempt to soldier on with my business, but there was no reason it was going to be any easier than before. If anything, it would probably be harder as I had given up once and buyers would be reluctant to trust me. I could get another job, maybe locally, or now that I could drive, further afield. That was the sensible option but it wasn't what I wanted to do and, as I sat staring morosely out of the kitchen window, a new idea began to form in my head.

Once my savings were below a certain level, I would be entitled to whatever pitiful sum the government saw fit to dish out as social security. That would keep me in the basics of life: clothes, toiletries, essential foods. The rest I could grow myself, or trade with Emma's family and the other farmers I knew, or poach.

It was a crazy plan and deep down I knew that it would never even have occurred to me to try if I hadn't been in such an emotional state. Yet it appealed, promising me the freedom that had come to mean so much. I'd been good at poaching, daring enough, patient enough and, after the incident with the pike, I knew that I really did have it in me to be bloodthirsty enough. I didn't even have to stick to the Alderhouse Estate, but could go out elsewhere, alone or with Emma and her brothers. I didn't even have to worry about the seasons, for meat. I'd be a thief, after all, and my needs were too small to matter within the great scheme of things. Besides, what was the point in holding back from taking pheasant eggs if the unfortunate creatures were only being reared for a bunch of rich city boys to take out their bloodlust on anyway?

Much of what I grew myself I could preserve, as people had for centuries before the arrival of refrigeration and vacuum packing. I'd have food and comfort, yet not be forced to play my part in the modern world save as I chose. There would be nobody over me, nobody to tell me what to do or where to be.

I knew, in the back of my mind, that it was a pipe dream. As with my business, there were sure to be drawbacks I hadn't foreseen. For one thing, there was the government, with their ghastly Protestant work ethic. There was no way *they'd* be content to leave me in peace.

Pipe dream or not, one thing was certain. I was going out poaching again.

I didn't do it for three days, but sat in the cottage and moped, vaguely hoping for Toby to come around and sort everything out. He didn't, and as I grew more bitter, so I grew more determined.

By dusk on the fourth day, I had decided that I'd waited long enough. I was going to stop sulking and pick my spirits up. Outside, the evening was chill, with the sun sinking slowly down behind the stark black fingers of the woodland trees. I watched, my sense of detachment growing, as orange dulled to red and the light drained slowly from the landscape. At last it sank, with a last red flicker throwing the harsh outline of a bramble into sharp relief before it vanished in shadow.

I was ready, with the thrill of the illicit bubbling up inside me. There was more too: anger, a desire for revenge, vicarious maybe, but still revenge. I had it all worked out in my mind. Marsh had set snares, but he wasn't going to be the one to reap the benefit. I would go out late, in the early hours, and take whatever he had caught. If I was careful, he might not even realise what was going on, but that wasn't what I wanted. What I wanted was to duel with him, to stay one step ahead of him and thus Toby too.

It was two in the morning when the alarm clock woke me after a few hours of fitful sleep. The rush of adrenaline at the memory of what I was about to do had me fully awake in moments, making the traditional splash of water in the face and mug of hot black coffee secondary. As I slipped into my combats, my fingers were shaking with anticipation, as if of sex.

The moon was at half, throwing a dull sheen across the fields and woods like old pewter, with the shadows black caves of nothingness. For a long moment I stood and listened, but even the motorway was quiet. My sack in one hand, the other extended to feel my way, I pushed into the bushes across the lane, to follow the now familiar route down along the old field boundary.

Ian Marsh was not somebody to be underestimated, but I needed light. So I had the torch set on red, to keep the glow to a minimum, and masked behind cloth. I kept it pointed low, my eyes fixed to the shape of dull, orange brown it provided, moving slowly forwards. My choice paid off within minutes. A snare had been set, on the run below the bank, exactly where my feet went. Unseen, I would have put my foot right in it.

It was empty, but the next was not, nor others. By the time I had made a long loop through the woods, I had four rabbits. It was enough and I turned for home, feeling thoroughly pleased with myself. Back at the cottage, I hung my bag in the scullery, showered and went to bed, my head still filled with thoughts of dark trees against the moonlight, the feel of tight wire in my hands and the smell of rabbit.

I had hunted, after my own fashion, and well, providing enough meat to last me several meals. It had been a good poaching high too, perhaps the best, but by the time I'd had my morning coffee I knew I'd need another, and soon.

I'd risen late and Emma had been and gone without waking me. Once washed and dressed, I sat down to skin and joint the rabbits. There was really more than I needed, and I decided to invite Emma up, as we hadn't had a proper chance to talk since we'd both quit. Twice I'd seen her, but both times she'd been with Ray.

She might guess what I'd been up to but I didn't mind. I might even tell her. I wanted to share my triumph and I knew she wouldn't disapprove. So I put a selection of rabbit joints in a marinade, then called her up. She accepted cheerfully and was with me shortly after dark, kissing me as soon as she'd bounced through the door, then sniffing deeply.

'Yum! What are you cooking?'

'A casserole. Rabbit.'

'Double yum. I can't wait.'

'Well you'll have to. Wine?'

'Sure.'

I led her into the kitchen, where I already had a bottle of Jumilla open. She drew in her breath again, her eyes closed and her face set in a smile of pure bliss.

'Hmm ... I love rabbit. How have you done it?'

'In stock, red wine and thyme, plenty of pepper.'

'Triple yum! What have you been doing, putting snares out in the wild patch?'

'Not exactly, no.'

I handed her a glass, trying to look sweet and innocent. She wasn't fooled.

'You've been up to no good, haven't you? I can tell, Juliet.'

'Yes. They're poached.'

'On Alderhouse? Not good. Marsh knows every inch of his land. He'll pinch your snares.'

'No he won't, because I took them from his.'

Her hand went to her mouth, purple Jumilla spurting from her fingers.

'You did what? He'll kill you! He'll wait up every night with a shotgun and give you both barrels in the arse!'

She was shocked, but she was laughing too. So was I.

'No he won't. Even Marsh has to sleep sometimes.'

'Don't count on it. Remember, we're off season now. He can sleep half the day if he wants to, so long as he sees to the pheasants.'

'I know. I don't plan to go out all that often, at least, not here. Do you think your brothers would mind if I came out with you?'

'No problem, seeing as you're well blooded.'

'Great. Be sure to let me know when you're going.'

'Will do. Meanwhile, I just know that casserole is going to be the best.'

'I know, there's no meat like poached meat.'

We chinked glasses, toasting each other and grinning mischievously. Suddenly I felt really good, accepted and wild too. Emma busied herself about laying the table as I checked the casserole. After a slow, even four hours it seemed ready enough, especially with Emma drooling in anticipation.

I'd been into Ilsenden for bread, and served it in doorsteps thickly spread with Jersey butter. It was glorious, with the juices from the casserole soaked into it, and soon we both had faces as greasy as any two urchins and lips stained red with the wine.

The meal finished, we sat up late, drinking and talking, until at last Emma fell asleep in her chair. I put a blanket over her and retired, unsteadily, to bed.

* * *

Poaching made me feel better, and it also made me one of the family at Bourne Farm. Emma's parents turned a blind eye, and I suspected that he, at least, had been as bad as any of his offspring in his day. His own father had been a labourer, for one thing, and worked his way up by renting land. Certainly respect for his 'betters' was not something he was big on.

I went out with them, to a trout farm on the Kennet, where we netted so many fish we had to pass the bags over the fence in relays. Drunk on success, we drove back singing loudly and at the farm I made them trout in cashew-nut butter. For once, the lack of flavour in the meat didn't bother me.

The next day, Danny and Emma went in to Reading, to sell door to door. My share was seventy-two pounds, plus a bag of trout, which I smoked. It was more than I'd have got in Social Security; for one night's work that would, in all probability, go undetected or so the boys assured me. Suddenly, my ideas of supporting myself while indulging my love of excitement and wicked behaviour didn't seem so distant.

I waited until the moon was past full before I went out on Alderhouse again. It was the perfect night, clear and still, but not so cold that there would be a telltale frost to show my footprints. Taking Emma's words to heart, I didn't go in by my usual route, but followed the lane, ready to nip in among the bushes at the first sign of an approaching car. None came, and I ducked into the wood at the old track, moving in stealthily and again and again stopping to listen.

There were no snares, but I thought of the thin path beside the altar tree and went to it, also just to see. Sure enough, as before, a bunch of grapes lay on top of the pedestal and, as before, they had been put there recently. Not one had been touched, each as plump and green and smooth as when it had been picked, so fresh that I found myself sinking back into the complete blackness behind the trunk, thinking that he might still be there.

As I waited, with my heart hammering and my ears strained for the slightest noise, I realised that something else was different. There was a smell, a smell alien to the woodland or, if not alien, then out of place here and now. It was sweet and rich, honeyed like a heavy Malmsey wine. Puzzled, I risked a burst of torchlight, full on the grapes. Some, I saw, at the centre of the bunch, glistened with some sticky, yellow fluid. I sniffed again, and this time I caught the scent, not wine, nor honey, but mead. He had poured a libation, something he had never done before.

I moved back, intrigued, trying to work out if it was a special night. There was a Celtic festival, Imbolc, to celebrate the pregnancy of the Goddess. It was something I would love to have celebrated, with my man, in the right way, taking his seed into me in ritual veneration. It was past, with the Vernal Equinox yet to come.

The experience left me with a haunted feeling and deep need in my belly. I moved on, my sense of detachment from everything mundane stronger than ever before, at one with the land around me as I stole down to the track, as silent as the sprit of the wood ...

Straight into Ian Marsh.

He'd been crouched down, low among the bushes, looking out along the moonlit track. As my knee struck his back he gave a yell of surprise, then a roar of anger as he spun around. I went down, onto my back, and he was clutching at me before I could scramble up. Then his weight was on me, pinning me helpless in the mud and leaf litter, and, as his thick, hard finger groped at my balaclava, he spoke, angry and grating.

'Right, let's be seeing you, you little bastard!'

I snatched at his arm, struggling to stop him exposing me, but I might as well have tried to wrestle a bull. My balaclava came loose, my hair fell free, and I was staring up at him, his bulk silhouetted black against the trees and stars. I was shaking, sick with shock and fear, but that wasn't my only feeling. I could feel his crotch, hot and solid against my belly, and the urge to completely and utterly surrender was burning in my head. I had to speak, to tell him, but he spoke again before I could find my voice.

'You've had it, you little shit! I'll teach you to thieve in my woods, I'll –'

His arm had come back, the fist balled. He was going to hit me. Immediately, I was babbling.

'Stop! No! Don't do that! It's me, Juliet . . . Juliet . . .'

He stopped.

'Eh?'

'Just stop it, you great ox! It's me. I'm not poaching. I . . . I want you . . . I want to suck your cock. I want to fuck you. I want . . .'

I was groping at his body, barely knowing what I was doing, only that I had to make him want me, to turn his aggression to lust. He caught my wrists, one handed, holding both in an iron grip. His other hand reached out to touch my chest, feeling the swell of my bandaged breasts. I lay still, panting in reaction as he felt me, never speaking. My jumper was hauled up, rude and hard, my shirt torn wide with one vicious jerk. His hand settled on my chest, again touching my breasts, feeling the bandage, gripping and yanking hard down. I gasped as my breasts were spilt out into the cold night air. He grunted as he once more began to feel. I gave no resistance, helpless and wanting nothing more. Even when his fingers went to my trousers button, I could only moan in surrender and push up my belly to him. One hard pull and my button was torn off, another and my fly had been ripped wide, a third and my crotch was splitting, exposing my panties.

He dismounted, his grip still fast on my wrists. His hand fastened to my trousers and they were jerked down, to my knees, and off, coming free with my boots to leave me spread bare in the mud beneath him. He caught my ankles, opening me as he groped for his fly.

'Right, you little witch, now you learn what a real fucking feels like.'

'Please, Ian, yes ... now ...'

His dick came free and he was settling onto me, his knuckles smacking on the tuck of my bottom, the fleshy tip of his cock pressing to my sex. I was wet, I knew it, wet enough to take him easily, and I did. He pushed into me before he was even fully erect, stretching me wide as I was filled. Then it began, the fucking I had imagined so often, come over so often.

I took him into my arms as he came fully on top of me, holding him to me, so big, so male. My legs cocked wide around the solid muscle and heavy bone of his hips as he began to work his cock in me faster, and faster still. His grunts grew louder, more animal as his instincts took over, and I was there, on my back on the woodland floor, fucking like a wild animal, my body bucking to his motions, screaming in wanton ecstasy as he drove into my body again and again, harder, faster, crushing me in his arms and pressing me down into the mud.

I just came – screaming as it hit me – from his cock, from the rubbing of his coarse trouser cloth on my clit, from him. It was hard, sudden, and my fingers were digging into his back as it tore through me. Then I was scratching and tearing at him, biting his neck and shoulder, writhing beneath him as wave after wave of ecstasy hit me, until I could bear it no more, at which exact moment he went rigid on top of me and I felt the wet at the mouth of my sex as his come pumped into me.

He didn't kiss me, or speak. There were no insecure questions, no defensive little jokes. Not from Marsh. He simply stood up, put his cock back in his fly and reached down for me. I was limp, exhausted by the sudden, rough fucking. For all of me he could do as he pleased, and the ruder, more male his treatment of me, the better.

I was lifted, effortlessly, and slung across his shoulder, my naked bottom high and vulnerable. He carried me, unhurried and so easily, as if I weighed nothing at all, past the enclosures and up the track, back to his cottage. There, he opened the door with a kick and dumped me in the hall. I went sprawling on my back, legs up, my cunt open to him. I was filthy, my clothes soiled, my hair full of mud and leaves and bits of twig, my bottom caked with the same thick mess. I didn't care, and nor did he.

His hands went straight to his belt and, for one horrible moment, I thought he was going to whip me with it. That was not what he had in mind. The belt came open, then his trousers, to let him pull out his cock. I'd felt it. Now I saw it – a monstrous thing, thick and brown and heavy, veined and gnarled, at once grotesque and magnificent, still glossy with my juices and his own.

I opened my mouth, eager to suck, and just as well, as he gave me little choice. One stride took him to me. He snatched my hair and my mouth was filled with thick, salty penis, tasting of man and of me. I sucked, feeding on him, so high on raw, animal sex that I had immediately cocked my legs wide.

He eased me down, still holding my hair, his huge, rough hand finding my pussy as I was laid out on the floor. One thick, muscular finger entered me, probing deep, then a second, and he was masturbating me as I sucked, readying me for the cock in my mouth.

I needed it, desperately, and I needed it naked. I began to wrench at my clothes, tugging my jumper up once more, pulling my ruined shirt wide, jerking the bandaging away to spill out my breasts. He saw, gave a satisfied grunt and pulled his finger from my sex to grope me, smearing my own juice over my nipples as he tweaked them roughly to erection.

His cock was fully erect once more and jammed deep in, his hand locked tight in my hair to force me to take every inch I could. Still I mouthed on him, even as I took my breasts in hand, to squeeze them together. He took the hint, calling me a witch again as he threw his leg over my prone body and settled his massive cock into the valley of my cleavage. He began to fuck my breasts, the fleshy mass of his dick and balls moving against my skin, his clothes rubbing on my nipples, until I had my teeth gritted in mingled pain and ecstasy.

It was quickly too much. I tried to wriggle away, but he was having too much fun, and just went on rutting happily away. I put my fingers over my nipples to stop the unbearable rubbing, telling myself I should let him have his fun, but hoping he would take me further without wasting his second orgasm between my breasts.

He didn't disappoint, but stopped in his own good time to dismount and help me to my feet. I got up, feeling a little weak, but very horny, and was sent up to the bedroom with a firm slap to my bum. I scampered up the stairs with his eyes glued to my wiggling bottom. He came after, cock in hand.

The bedroom was big, most of the roof space, and spartan – bare boards, old furniture and an iron bed with the sheets in disarray. I caught his scent immediately, strong and male, maybe too much, had I never been so turned on. I'd paused in the doorway and another hard slap to my bum sent me in. He followed, growling at me as I turned to face him.

'Strip off then, girl, all the way. Let's see what young Mr Paxham-Jennings gets a portion of.'

He was revelling in it because I'd been Toby's girl-friend, grinning and stroking the massive erection sticking out from his fly as he watched me. I was in disarray, and there wasn't much to strip off, with my shirt ripped open and my trousers and knickers lying on the mud of the track. I did what I could, peeling my jumper high and shrugging the remains of my shirt off my shoulders. He stared, his eyes flicking over my body in blatant lust. I turned for him as I pulled the bandages free, to show my bottom, and bent down.

With one truly bestial snort he came forwards, grabbed me by the hips and pushed his cock hard up inside me, calling me a little tart even as my cunt filled with him. I couldn't have answered if I'd wanted too, my breath pushed out by the sheer force of his entry. Then I was gasping and clutching for support as I was lifted bodily onto his cock to be fucked like a doll, completely clear of the ground as I was worked up and down on him.

He took pity, walking me forwards to the bed so that I could kneel as I took him, but never once leaving my body. Still I could barely breathe, only gasp and grunt out my ecstasy as he slammed into my body as before, harder, and harder still, to finish with a furious crescendo of shoves that made me scream. Then he stopped, and was draining himself into my body, groaning deeply, his fingers locked deep in the flesh of my hips. He let go, and I collapsed face down on his bed, panting.

I was bruised, sore and sweaty, but my head was spinning with lust and need and dirty thoughts. My hand went back, straight between my legs, as I lifted my bottom to him, to show him what he'd done to me, to show him what I was doing, to show everything. I heard him grunt as I began to masturbate. I pushed my bum up higher, my orgasm already rising in my head, utterly wanton as I showed off to him, my fingers rubbing frantically on my sex – my clit burning, my pussy starting to pulse – and my bottom hole.

I came, right there, in front of him, nude on his bed, everything showing to him, nothing hidden, screaming out my pleasure and his name, again and again, as my body jerked in orgasm. Only when I finally stopped and sank down limp on the bed did he speak, a single word.

'Dirty.'

When I awoke, Ian was already out of bed, shaving in the little adjoining bathroom with the door open. Bright winter sunlight was streaming in through his window but the bedroom was still dim behind the curtains, and warm.

I was in a state of bliss, just lying there with the scent of him all around me, watching the muscles move in his back and arms as he scraped the stubble from his face. I was bruised where he'd held me, even where he'd slapped my bottom and on my shoulders where he'd crushed me into the ground. I didn't care. The dull ache merely reminded me of what I'd done, of what we'd done together. He had given me such a wonderful experience, something to be remembered and treasured, something with a magic that far transcended the ordinary sexual experience, yet a magic which still needed one crucial ingredient.

He had been to the shrine perhaps moments before we'd met in the woods, yet he still had no idea I knew. I needed him to, and to accept that knowledge in me, and share it with me. To him it was private, and he had no reason to speak. I had to, but it was hard to know what to say, how to broach something so personal, perhaps not so personal as what we had already done together, but very different.

I struggled for the right words as he went on shaving, but when he had finished and turned back to me, with his hard face set in a pleased smile, it came simply.

'I was at the shrine, Ian, just before –'

His expression barely changed, but he spoke, cutting off my words.

'What's that?'

'Your shrine, Ian.'

'Shrine? Like an altar, you mean?'

'Yes.'

'In my woods?'

'Yes. Just beyond where the caravan is beside the big enclosure, a few yards off the old track.'

'No, don't know anything about no shrine.'

He had to know.

'You can tell me, Ian. I want to know, I want to share.'

'Sorry, girl, I don't know what you're about.'

He was relaxed, friendly, even amused – a good act if it was an act, and it had to be.

'Please, Ian! I know! There were grapes there, yesterday, just before . . . before we met.'

'No grapes. Not in my woods.'

'Ian, please? You know the big beech just off the old track. There are initials carved in it and a small pillar in front. You left fresh grapes on it, last night. Please tell me you did!'

'Sorry, girl. I know the place, yes. Out of the way it is. Why would I go wasting good grapes anyhow? Kids, most likely, the same as carved their names there, I dare say.'

'No, that was my cousins, years ago. The grapes were fresh.'

He shrugged and shook his head, then spoke again.

'Now don't you mind that nonsense. How about a kiss before I go to work?'

He didn't mean on the lips. He had pulled out his cock and was holding it up to my face. I took him into my mouth but, as I began to suck, my main feeling was of resentment.

He had to be lying. He knew about the altar by his own admission and the only other people who could possibly have been using it were the Paxham-Jenningses. I couldn't see it, not Toby for certain or Donald. Both were very much the country squire, well in tune with the land, maybe, but educated, occasional churchgoers. Nothing Toby had ever said or done indicated that he was superstitious or held any particular beliefs. With Donald it was yet harder to accept. Elizabeth was different, always quiet and reserved, yet certainly intelligent, and perhaps a little fey. I could imagine her doing it, at a pinch, but while she rode and I had seen her in the lane often enough, she never went into the woods. It had to be Ian.

I didn't expect Emma to know, but I did feel she might be able to shed some light on it and, in any case, I wanted to talk and she was the only person I could tell about Marsh. By good luck she was still there when I got back, sitting soaking up the weak sun in the open doorway of her caravan. She looked up as I came in at the gate and put on her best expression of mock disapproval.

'Dirty stop out. Back with Toby, are ... Hang on, what's with the gear? You might have told me if you were out on an all-nighter.'

'I wasn't ... well, not that way. Look, Emma, do you remember when I first moved in, how you poured a libation on the doorstep?'

'For luck, sure.'

'Well . . . I don't know . . . is it . . . something meaning-ful, or something you just do?'

She made a face.

'Just do, I suppose. But, yeah, I believe it. Can't hurt anyhow.'

'You don't go to church, do you?'

'I can't be bothered. Granny used to make us all go when we were little, but it's so boring.'

'It's not because you're a pagan then?'

'Pagan? What, all that witchy stuff and wanting to do weird dances at Stonehenge? No.'

There was a giggle in her voice, something close to mockery.

'Yes. I think Ian Marsh is into all that.'

'Ian Marsh? No way!'

'Not in a modern sense, not Wiccan, or anything like it. I think it's more abstract, less conscious, probably something dating right back, like your libation.'

'Marsh? I wouldn't think so. He's not really the type, is he?'

'No, not on the surface.'

'Not at all. He's just a lump. So, why the questions? Something's happened, hasn't it? Tell.'

'I was with him, last night.'

'With Marsh? Fuck me! What –'

'I was out poaching.'

'He caught you? He had you?'

'We had each other. Yes, he caught me, sort of. He was hiding in the bushes and I tripped over him.'

'You didn't! Oh my God! And he took you back to his cottage for a shag? You are one smooth talker.'

'It wasn't like that. If I hadn't been a girl I think it would have got nasty, but once he knew what I wanted he was OK. He's such an animal, Emma. I have never had

217

it so hard or know a man get ready so quick, and again, back at the cottage.'

'You sure play hard, Juliet! You are fucking lucky he didn't beat the shit out of you!'

'No, he wouldn't, not to a woman.'

'No, he just fucks you senseless instead!'

'That's what I wanted.'

'And you got it. So what's with the pagan stuff? Did he get weird on you or something? Not Marsh, surely?'

'No, not at all. He was as straight as they come, all cock. But there's a little altar up in the woods, where he leaves grapes as some sort of offering. He'd poured mead too, last night.'

'Nah, doesn't sound like Marsh. Kids?'

'That's what he said. But in his woods, with his reputation?'

She shrugged and made a face.

'Maybe they don't know, or don't care? You know what we were like.'

I didn't answer. The thought that all my elaborate and lewd pagan fantasies might have been an illusion based on nothing more than a children's game was not only a let-down, but embarrassing. I didn't want to accept that Emma was right, anyway. That meant that Marsh was no more than a coarse, selfish brute, with no depth, no hidden sensibilities.

Unfortunately, the way he'd behaved suggested exactly that.

There was only one way to be sure. If I could actually be there, to see him, then I'd know. Then there would be no denial. He might be angry, but it would be a chance I had to take. If I was to let the love I felt for him grow, I needed us to share everything, and most especially that. Otherwise, there would be nothing.

* * *

It was not to be so easy. The next day I was ready to go by mid-afternoon, hoping that having spoken to me about the altar would draw him up there. It was still clear, but colder than before, with ice on the puddles where the sun hadn't struck. I walked quickly up the lane and struck into the woods before the track, concerned that he might have an eye out for any disturbance near the tree. With the trees bare, I could make out the big beech from a fair way off and I took cover behind a bank of brambles, squatting low.

I gave up three hours later, cramped, cold and thoroughly fed up. Sneaking about the woods was one thing, but staying still for hours on end on a chilly winter afternoon was quite another. So I went home, sure that there had to be a better way to find out what I needed to know.

My first thought was to pinch one of Ian's poacher traps and relay it close to the altar tree, carefully concealed. Unfortunately, he wasn't likely to be in a very devotional mood after having one of his own shotgun cartridges go off unexpectedly just a few feet away. It was tempting anyway, just so he'd know how it felt, but I had to abandon the idea.

A microphone was a much better bet and satisfyingly sneaky. I went into Reading and managed to get one sufficiently sensitive and sufficiently powerful to pick up any noise near the tree and relay it to me in the warmth and comfort of my cottage. After an enjoyable afternoon's expedition to lay it, I spent the night listening to woodland noises, close up, which was more than a little eerie.

So it went, night after night, until I'd grown used to the odd snuffling noises, yammering barks and sudden calls. It still came as a hell of a shock when I heard my name spoken right in my ear just as I was drifting towards sleep. I sat bolt upright, my hand on my chest.

There was utter silence and, after a moment, I began to think my mind was playing tricks on me. Then it came again.

'Juliet, my love.'

It was unmistakable and so was the voice. An instant later, I had tumbled out of bed and was snatching at my clothes. By the time I'd put my knickers on backwards and had the sense to turn the light on, I was already sure I would miss him. Catching him on the track or in the lane was pointless. It had to be at the altar.

I threw myself into my clothes, jeans over back-to-front knickers, a thick jumper over nothing, bare feet in boots. As I left I grabbed my darkest coat and was struggling into it as I padded down the lane as fast as I dared. I reached the track, unable to see more than shades of shadow and sure I was making more noise than a herd of bulls in a glassware department. Then the great beech was looming above me against the stars and, as I caught a glimpse of light, I froze.

There was a lantern, hung from the branch of a hazel, throwing light the colour of the richest butter out among the trees. Toby stood at the centre of the pool of light; his head was bowed, as if in prayer, his eyes closed. Before him, on the altar, lay a bunch of fat golden grapes, mead glistening on their skins as it ran down.

I stepped close, my heart in my mouth, with emotion welling up so strong I knew that in moments I would be in tears. Toby never heard me, never saw me, until I gently took hold of his hand. He jumped, stammering something unintelligible as he turned sharply towards me, then speaking again in a rush of words.

'Juliet! I didn't see you. I . . . I was just . . .'

He had gone red, his whole face suffused in a hot blush. I stepped close, put my finger to my lips and he went quiet. I kissed him, on his lips, then lower, on his chin, on his neck. Already my hand was on his crotch, squeezing at the full, soft bulge of his cock and balls. He didn't resist, or speak, until I had eased his cock free and was holding it in my hand.

'Oh yes, here . . . that is so right!'

I sank down to take him into the warmth of my mouth and suck, my eyes closed in bliss as I took in his taste. His hand found my hair, but not to clutch and force me to suck deeper, as Ian had done, but to stroke, to soothe me as his cock grew to erection in my mouth. I held on, my feelings rising, both lust and a need to cry. When he was ready I let him free and sank back, kneeling, to quickly expose myself, my jumper lifted over bra-less breasts, my trousers and panties pushed quickly down.

He swallowed, his eyes feasting on my body as he took hold of his erection. I met his gaze for one moment, looking deep into his eyes, and turned, to take hold of the pillar, bracing myself as I pushed my bottom out to invite entry. I closed my eyes as he sank down behind me, so close to tears as he took hold, cupping my breasts gently from behind, as his rigid cock settled into the crease of my bottom. For a moment, he rubbed, enjoying me, and stroked my nipples, which were already taut and sensitive from the cold air. Then I felt his knuckles, and the head of his cock, pushing down between my bottom cheeks, brushing the soft bud of my anus, and pushing to my sex.

I cried out as he entered me, gripping the pillar tight. He began to fuck, pushing into me as I squatted in his lap, also stroking me with his hands, cajoling me to lose every last inhibition as I began to rub my bottom in his lap in wanton pleasure. For a long, long time we fucked, him easing his cock in and out and teasing my breasts, me wriggling myself against him and shaking my head at the sheer joy of being taken the way I had imagined so often, wanted so desperately.

At last his hand moved down, sliding over my belly to find my sex and to rub me, even as his cock moved inside me. I was lost on the instant, all my feelings coming together, the tears welling in my eyes as he brought me up towards orgasm, and bursting free as I came, to run freely down my face as I broke into gasping, choking sobs of pure, raw ecstasy.

It seemed to last forever, with great fierce spasms running through my whole body as my pussy contracted over and over on his cock. He held me all the while, tight to his body, still rubbing and pushing gently into me until my climax at last began to subside. Only then did he take me by my hips, pushing deeper and firmer, moaning and then crying out in his own moment of rapture, pushing himself hard in one last time, to come, deep, deep in my body, and hold himself there as I sobbed out my emotion to his altar.

He never let go, even as he eased himself gently from my body. Instead, he turned me gently around to take me into his arms and lay me down, cuddled close, heedless of the cold, damp leaf mould against the bare flesh of my hip, lost in the warmth and comfort of his arms and in the satisfaction of what we had done together.

For a long while neither of us spoke, Toby just stroking my hair and occasionally kissing me as we clung together. Part of me wanted to lie there forever, just close to him, but at last the effect of the cold on my bare bottom and back became too much. I pulled away and knelt up to adjust my clothes. Toby watched, his face set in a gentle smile and, as I fastened my trousers, he spoke.

'How did you know to find me?'

'I ... call it women's intuition. But I have been here

before, and seen grapes. I was fascinated. I wanted to know who could do something so wonderfully pagan. I thought it was Ian Marsh.'

'Ian Marsh? He knows, yes, but he just thinks I'm eccentric. Do ... I mean to say, don't you?'

'No, Toby. I think you're ... I think it's special. I think it shows you're not like ... like them, like the shooting party guests, and ... and just people, all those horrible, boring people who live their lives out of the pages of a magazine, people who worry about what make-up some film star wears, and use margarine, and ... and do everything in moderation, and ... I'm not making much sense, am I?'

'Maybe not, but I think I understand.'

'That's more than I do! But I want to know more, everything. Do you follow rituals, like the Celtic cycle, or is it more abstract, just a private way of worship?'

'Neither ... well, in-between really. The altar is dedicated to Pan, the Greek god of woods and pastures.'

'That's wonderful! And what we did! Where does it come from, in you?'

'From school. I used to love the Greek gods. They seemed human, with human faults and human ambitions, so much more real than what we were supposed to believe in. Christianity to me is a big cold hall, full of disapproval and fear. Pan would have approved of what we just did, seen it as an act of joy and honour, not something improper.'

'I agree, exactly, absolutely.'

'I always resented the idea that sex was wrong, that any physical pleasure was wrong really.'

'Yeah, like it being holy not to eat. Bullshit!'

'Exactly. After Sunday service I used to go out into the woods and say my own prayers, to Pan, and to Dionysus, because he was the god of wine, and just being caught with a can of beer was a caning offence. I hated school, and church, and all the hypocrisy and repression. It was only in the fields and woods that I felt free, and I suppose I fell in love with them . . . like, like I have with you.'

It took me a moment to answer and I had to choke back tears.

'I feel the same way . . . that is, about that, all that . . . and I love you too.'

I was crying and, as he took me into his arms, there was one perfect moment of togetherness before it broke and I was giggling as I pulled back.

'And anyway, I suppose I'll just have to marry you now. I'm not protected, you know.'

'Good.'

Toby and I married in May, rather hastily, as my belly was beginning to swell. Emma was a bridesmaid and looked every inch the rustic hearty lass, while Ray and all their mates put on a fine show of drunken dancing and singing at the reception, that will surely go down in Berkshire history as one of the most raucous the Paxham-Jenningses had ever seen. The atmosphere was superb, with rustic locals and young society ladies all mixing happily after the two-hundred-and-fiftieth bottle of champagne had been emptied. We honeymooned in Greece, touring the islands and searching out remote temples dedicated to Dionysus, Pan or Artemis, where we would make love on the ancient stones with the scents of wild thyme and sage strong in our heads.

When I finally plucked up the courage to tell Toby about my poaching escapades, he simply laughed and started calling me Artemis, which was a better nickname than Snooty. Once we were back in England we even had a shrine built in the grounds at Alderhouse, on a little island in the lake to guarantee our privacy. What I didn't tell him was what had happened with Marsh, but as Emma had so rightly predicted, the secret was safe. Nor was there any desire in me to do it again. Toby was better, deeper, dirtier, more intelligent; more me.

My wedding present from Donald and Elizabeth came in the form of shares in the Alderhouse Estate company. That gave me a say in how everything was run, but while I made a point of continuing to work in the kitchens, I made no real use of it until the late summer. We'd had a bad review, for the first time, no less a critic than Amy-Jane Bacau casting doubt on the quality of a sirloin Blane had offered done as a variation on Beef Wellington. At the monthly meeting, he was doing his best to dismiss it as unimportant.

'The woman's growing senile. She lives in the past or some imaginary past.'

It was true, but it wasn't necessarily a bad thing. I put my ha'p'orth in.

'A past when English food was something to be proud of?'

It was a near quote from him. He looked around, with more than a touch of anger.

'No. I simply mean that she's beginning to think everything's going to pot. A lot of people start to do that as they get older. Their senses get duller and they won't accept that the problem lies in themselves.'

'Maybe, although I don't suppose she's past sixty, and she has a lot of experience. How was the meat sourced?'

'Our usual suppliers.'

'From what herd? How long was it hung?'

'I . . . I'm not certain. They've expanded, and Dereck Jackson's no longer –'

'There's the problem then. They've got bigger and they've been forced to drop their commitment to quality in order to keep up with demand. No supplier of any natural product can maintain any real quality in bulk production.'

'I am aware of that, Juliet, but –'

'No, no buts. We have to maintain our integrity. What we should do is source locally, from Bourne Farm, for instance. They have Red Herefords, which produce excellent beef and which we can monitor, to ensure that we only get the best. That's the only way we're going to maintain our reputation.'

'We can't work like that! It's wasteful, expensive, time consuming –'

'I'm happy to do it.'

'I hardly think that's necessary.'

'Very well, Mr Blane, we've heard your opinion, but as you're not a shareholder you will please simply do as you are told . . .'

LOOK OUT FOR THE ALL-NEW BLACK LACE BOOKS – AVAILABLE NOW!

All books priced £6.99 in the UK. Please note publication dates apply to the UK only. For other territories, please contact your retailer.

THE TUTOR
Portia Da Costa
ISBN 0 352 32946 7

When Rosalind Howard becomes Julian Hadey's private librarian, she soon finds herself attracted by his persuasive charms and distinguished appearance. He is an unashamed sensualist who, together with his wife, Celeste, has hatched an intriguing challenge for their new employee. As well as cataloguing their collection of erotica, Rosie is expected to educate Celeste's young and beautiful cousin David in the arts of erotic love. **A long-overdue reprint of this arousing tale of erotic initiation written by a pioneer of women's sex fiction.**

Coming in September

SEXUAL STRATEGY
Felice de Vere
ISBN 0 352 33843 1

Heleyna is incredibly successful. She has everything a girl could possibly want – a career, independence, and a very sexy partner who keeps her well and truly occupied. Accepting an invitation from her very naughty ex-boss to a frustratingly secretive club, she begins a journey of discovery that both teases and taunts her. Before too long she realises she is not the only person in the world feigning a respectable existence. **Sexual experimentation at its naughtiest!**

ARTISTIC LICENCE
Vivienne La Fay
ISBN O 352 33210 7

In Renaissance Italy, Carla is determined to find a new life for herself
where she can put her artistic talents to good use. Dressed as boy –
albeit a very pretty one – she travels to Florence and finds work as an
apprentice to a master craftsman. All goes well until she is expected to
perform licentious favours for her employer. In an atmosphere of
repressed passion, it is only a matter of time before her secret is
revealed. **Historical, gender-bending fun in this delightful romp.**

Coming in October

SOMETHING ABOUT WORKMEN
Alison Tyler
ISBN O 352 33847 4

Cat Harrington works in script development at a large Hollywood studio.
She and her engineer boyfriend enjoy glittering parties, film screenings
and international travel. But Cat leads a double life that would shock her
friends and her beau: she engages in rough and ready sex with the head
of a road crew, who knows how hard and dirty Cat likes her loving. What
begins as a raucous fling turns far more complicated when Cat's
boyfriend is put in charge of her lover and they begin to run into each
other in the workplace. **Explores the appeal of hot and horny blue-collar
guys!**

PALAZZO
Jan Smith
ISBN O 352 33156 9

When Claire and Cherry take a vacation in Venice they both succumb to the seductive charms of the city and the men who inhabit it. In the famous Harry's Bar, Claire meets a half-Italian, half-Scottish art dealer who introduces her to new facets of life, both cultural and sexual. Torn between the mysterious Stuart and her estranged husband Claire is faced with an impossible dilemma while Cherry is learning all about sexual indulgence. **Sophisticated and sexy.**

Black Lace Booklist

Information is correct at time of printing. To avoid disappointment check availability before ordering. Go to www.blacklace-books.co.uk. All books are priced £6.99 unless another price is given.

BLACK LACE BOOKS WITH A CONTEMPORARY SETTING

☐ IN THE FLESH Emma Holly	ISBN 0 352 33498 3	£5.99
☐ SHAMELESS Stella Black	ISBN 0 352 33485 1	£5.99
☐ INTENSE BLUE Lyn Wood	ISBN 0 352 33496 7	£5.99
☐ THE NAKED TRUTH Natasha Rostova	ISBN 0 352 33497 5	£5.99
☐ A SPORTING CHANCE Susie Raymond	ISBN 0 352 33501 7	£5.99
☐ TAKING LIBERTIES Susie Raymond	ISBN 0 352 33357 X	£5.99
☐ A SCANDALOUS AFFAIR Holly Graham	ISBN 0 352 33523 8	£5.99
☐ THE NAKED FLAME Crystalle Valentino	ISBN 0 352 33528 9	£5.99
☐ ON THE EDGE Laura Hamilton	ISBN 0 352 33534 3	£5.99
☐ LURED BY LUST Tania Picarda	ISBN 0 352 33533 5	£5.99
☐ THE HOTTEST PLACE Tabitha Flyte	ISBN 0 352 33536 X	£5.99
☐ THE NINETY DAYS OF GENEVIEVE Lucinda Carrington	ISBN 0 352 33070 8	£5.99
☐ DREAMING SPIRES Juliet Hastings	ISBN 0 352 33584 X	
☐ THE TRANSFORMATION Natasha Rostova	ISBN 0 352 33311 1	
☐ SIN.NET Helena Ravenscroft	ISBN 0 352 33598 X	
☐ TWO WEEKS IN TANGIER Annabel Lee	ISBN 0 352 33599 8	
☐ HIGHLAND FLING Jane Justine	ISBN 0 352 33616 1	
☐ PLAYING HARD Tina Troy	ISBN 0 352 33617 X	
☐ SYMPHONY X Jasmine Stone	ISBN 0 352 33629 3	
☐ SUMMER FEVER Anna Ricci	ISBN 0 352 33625 0	
☐ CONTINUUM Portia Da Costa	ISBN 0 352 33120 8	
☐ OPENING ACTS Suki Cunningham	ISBN 0 352 33630 7	
☐ FULL STEAM AHEAD Tabitha Flyte	ISBN 0 352 33637 4	
☐ A SECRET PLACE Ella Broussard	ISBN 0 352 33307 3	
☐ GAME FOR ANYTHING Lyn Wood	ISBN 0 352 33639 0	
☐ FORBIDDEN FRUIT Susie Raymond	ISBN 0 352 33306 5	
☐ CHEAP TRICK Astrid Fox	ISBN 0 352 33640 4	

To find out the latest information about Black Lace titles, check out the website: www.blacklace-books.co.uk or send for a booklist with complete synopses by writing to:

Black Lace Booklist, Virgin Books Ltd
Thames Wharf Studios
Rainville Road
London W6 9HA

Please include an SAE of decent size. Please note only British stamps are valid.

Our privacy policy
We will not disclose information you supply us to any other parties. We will not disclose any information which identifies you personally to any person without your express consent.

From time to time we may send out information about Black Lace books and special offers. Please tick here if you do <u>not</u> wish to receive Black Lace information. ❏

Please send me the books I have ticked above.

Name ....

Address ....

....

....

....

Post Code ....

Send to: Cash Sales, Black Lace Books, Thames Wharf Studios, Rainville Road, London W6 9HA.

US customers: for prices and details of how to order books for delivery by mail, call 1-800-343-4499.

Please enclose a cheque or postal order, made payable to Virgin Books Ltd, to the value of the books you have ordered plus postage and packing costs as follows:

UK and BFPO – £1.00 for the first book, 50p for each subsequent book.

Overseas (including Republic of Ireland) – £2.00 for the first book, £1.00 for each subsequent book.

If you would prefer to pay by VISA, ACCESS/MASTERCARD, DINERS CLUB, AMEX or SWITCH, please write your card number and expiry date here:

....

Signature ....

Please allow up to 28 days for delivery.